The Dark Horse

The Dark Horse

JACK CHATELAIN
with SCOTT T. E. JACKSON

SWEETWATER BOOKS
An imprint of Cedar Fort, Inc.
Springville, Utah

© 2022 Scott Jackson
All rights reserved.

No part of this book may be reproduced in any form whatsoever, whether by graphic, visual, electronic, film, microfilm, tape recording, or any other means, without prior written permission of the publisher, except in the case of brief passages embodied in critical reviews and articles.

This is a work of fiction. The characters, names, incidents, places, and dialogue are products of the author's imagination and are not to be construed as real. The opinions and views expressed herein belong solely to the author and do not necessarily represent the opinions or views of Cedar Fort, Inc. Permission for the use of sources, graphics, and photos is also solely the responsibility of the author.

ISBN 13: 978-1-4621-4224-8

Published by Sweetwater Books, an imprint of Cedar Fort, Inc.
2373 W. 700 S., Springville, UT 84663
Distributed by Cedar Fort, Inc., www.cedarfort.com

Library of Congress Control Number: 2022930430

Cover design by Courtney Proby
Cover design © 2022 Cedar Fort, Inc.
Substantive by Rachel Hathcock
Edited and typeset by Valene Wood
Editor-in-chief, Heather Holm

Printed in the United States of America

10 9 8 7 6 5 4 3 2 1

Printed on acid-free paper

For Diana, always.

—Jack

For Aubrey, Eden, and Landon.

—Scott

This is both Jack's and Scott's debut novel.

Other books by Scott T. E. Jackson

Looking for Luck: Four-Leaf Finding Field Guide

The Park-eontologist

1816 would become known as the year without a summer.

The creeping darkness from an immense volcanic eruption in 1815 cooled the earth and marred the sun with dark spots. These "signs and wonders" left many in England believing that the sun would die on the summer solstice— July 18th—ending the world in apocalyptic destruction.

It was a dark and fearful time as crops failed and many wondered if they would survive the year, but Miss Katherine le Chevalier did not join in the rampant concern.

For her world had already ended on February 10th.

Chapter 1

February 14th

His eyes were the key to places in my heart I had never known. A single look, a minute rise of his dark brow, could send my heart into loops. A touch erased every fear and pain.

But now he is gone, and I shall never love again.

—Katherine, Huxley House

Miss Katherine le Chevalier stood alone, watching an ornate casket lower slowly into the ground, her tears like ice on her cheeks in the early morning wind. It should have been her wedding day, but the guests witnessed a far different sacrament—ribbons exchanged for shrouds, dancing for dirges. A black bonnet and veil hid her tightly pinned onyx hair.

When the men lowered the remains of Katherine's love and her hopes for a happy life those final few feet, her stomach roiled in on itself. Her lungs screamed to release the sobs that her ribs could barely contain. The pain inside her surged like the hungry tendrils of an August wildfire six months early, doubling her over around it. Each staggering step leading her farther from the truth, the endless cavern beneath her feet: *he is gone, forever.*

Katherine braced herself against another wave of pain, the sobs finally escaping her ragged throat. This was supposed to be the beginning of her life.

Not the end.

❧

After the services ended, Katherine's sister Elizabeth found her shivering on a bench in the garden—the place Katherine and her William had often sat and listened for the calls of songbirds, challenging each other to name them first. This should have been her garden, her garden to share with her husband, but now William's distant cousin, Sir Stephens, had moved in. He and his two daughters, with rumors of a new bride, would be the happy recipients of this beautiful home; Katherine had no hold on it.

What a change four days had wrought.

"Come now, Kit, you're freezing," Elizabeth said, throwing her own shawl over Katherine's shoulders with concerned eyes. Elizabeth's shawl, made for her taller frame, dropped low over Katherine's knees. "We need to get to the coach." When Katherine didn't rise, Elizabeth sat down beside her, enfolding her in her arms.

"He was everything to me," Katherine whispered, her voice raw from her quieted sobs. "But now, he's gone . . . and everything is gone with him." Katherine's pain tightened around the void inside her as Elizabeth helped her to her feet. Then numbness drowned her thoughts as she turned for the awaiting carriage. *Let it take me away . . . just away.*

Elizabeth walked next to Katherine with their arms linked, Elizabeth sharing a little of Katherine's load and lending warmth. For the last time, they passed the greens, gardens, and topiaries that she had so loved to walk through. Then they turned past the parish where Katherine's betrothed was buried. Elizabeth, sensing the rising storm, held Katherine's arm tighter as they passed. Katherine's steps faltered, renewed suffering crushing the numbness within her. Slowly, leaning on her sister, she passed the small hill of dark earth without opening her streaming eyes.

Their father, Lord Blakesly, had stayed behind to notify their kindred of the wedding's untimely cancelation. So only Lady Blakesly,

Katherine's mother, was waiting beside the carriage to journey with them. It would be night before they arrived at Applehill Cottage, their small estate.

The footman handed each lady up into the carriage before returning to his place. Sir Stephens had graciously offered the use of his new carriage to his predecessor's betrothed. Lady Blakesly would be sure to send a note of the warmest gratitude once she could find the time amidst the chaos that an engagement, wedding plans, subsequent cancelation, and hurried funeral caused. Katherine would have owned the carriage if events had transpired differently, *but it is best to be grateful for what is given*, Lady Blakesly thought.

Elizabeth and her mother watched the receding estate's aspect through the windows as the carriage pulled away. The pain of losing association with such a wondrous place pricked their minds even as their hearts ached for their Kit who sat between them, her face in her black-gloved hands. Elizabeth turned from the window and wrapped her arms around her elder sister as Lady Blakesly placed her hand on Katherine's head.

Katherine felt none of it.

Despite four consecutive nights without any rest from her anguish, Katherine's mind still fought the rhythmic rocking of the carriage, refusing to sleep. For when she awoke, there would be no note from William, there would be no call at breakfast—far earlier than was completely proper, after a night of laughing and dancing—no William to speak of at all.

Throbbing anger surged in Katherine's chest as she sat up, dislodging Elizabeth's arms and her mother's hands. "He told me that he didn't want to go!" Katherine shouted into the silence. "He wanted to stay—I *made* him go!" Katherine's eyes burned with her aching rage and exhausted tear ducts.

Lady Blakesly grasped Katherine's shoulders and looked into her eyes with conviction. "You are not responsible for this tragedy! Do you hear? You did not send him to die. One so young and strong as he to be gone in an instant speaks to the will of Providence." Lady Blakesly's eyes softened with her own unshed tears as she placed her gloved hand onto Katherine's cheek.

3

Katherine shook her head, pulling away from her mother's hand, her rage fracturing and falling into sorrow. "Providence did not kill William, Mother. It was that horse," she said, squeezing one final tear from her tired eyes. She lowered her face into her upturned palms.

The carriage traveled the rest of that day into the night, exhaustion ultimately subduing Katherine's pain. Finally freed from the weight of that agonizing day, Katherine dreamed of happier times for the briefest of moments.

The dappled mare's back rolled beneath Katherine as the animal huffed its final steps up the long hill. The golden rays of the setting sun warmed the cold evening and set a timeless magic over the wintry climb. Elizabeth, acting as their chaperone, sat on her horse at the bottom of the hill, holding back a little more than she probably should, to allow them the semblance of privacy.

William cocked his head, his handsome curls falling to the side of his face. "That old mare is certainly struggling." A light kindled in his eyes. "You know, I think I may have just decided what to give you as an engagement present."

Katherine felt the new and exciting flutters in her chest that he could summon with an errant glance or simple word. "Oh, you needn't get me anything—your heart is all I could ever ask for." In only a week his heart will finally be all mine, Katherine thought.

William shrugged, his mind already made up. Then he leaned over the side of his stallion to pick a green sprig from a bush. He righted himself and clicked his tongue, the stallion turning at his master's insistence. Then William rocked slowly toward Katherine. The distance between them shrinking until he was within arms reach. He held out the sprig and Katherine took it in her hands.

"You know that my heart is yours . . . so take this little branch as a promise of an evergreen love." He smiled, his joy radiating brighter than the sun.

Katherine held the token to her breast. "Oh, William, my William. I will love you forever!"

The light changed and Katherine's essence knew that the dream had shifted.

It was morning in the wood bordering Applehill's orchard.

A flurry of flapping wings was cut short by a shot from a rifle. The boom spooked the beautiful black mare who rode beside William's proud stallion. William had made good on his promised gift for their impending wedding.

The young mare's eyes rolled in fear with each echoing blast from the hunters' rifles and she wrenched the reins from William's hands. She ran, her midnight mane streaming through the winter cold and looking all the more like Katherine's obsidian hair. That resemblance was why William had chosen this gift; he had seen Katherine's strength, poise, and beauty reflected in the mare's own.

"There she goes, old boy! I told you not to bring a new horse on a hunt!" The best man called. "Especially not one as fast at that!"

William laughed and kicked his stallion's sides, taking off after the fleeing beast. He called back over his shoulder as his curly hair bounced around his smiling eyes. "But then I wouldn't be having all this fun!"

Katherine's disembodied mind followed as he pursued the mare through the snowy meadow. *Please William . . . just let her go. Don't chase her.* But the dream continued.

The mare was fast, but confidence and determination were on his side, and he gained ground each time the mare reared and balked at shadows. Drawing beside her and matching pace, William caught the lashing reins with a triumphant shout and a laugh.

Katherine's thoughts screamed.

Right when he pulled the reins to slow her, the mare's front hoof sank into a hole. The mare pitched forward, ripping William off his horse. He flew headlong, still smiling, into a gnarled apple tree at the edge of the wood.

Her horror unveiling before her eyes she whispered, *Please no . . . my heart can't bear it. Please don't let me see his—*

Beautiful blue eyes, now dull and lifeless, stared unblinking upward to their mother sky—their color in stark contrast to the single drop of blood on his cheek.

A jolt awakened Katherine from her dream as the carriage left the road onto the cobbled drive to Katherine's home. The end of her night visions granted no comfort. *That is the last I shall see of my William: memories of his battered smile.* Katherine squeezed her burning eyes closed, unprepared for her mother's and sister's solicitous questions.

After traversing the winding way through the mature trees, the carriage stopped before the stone and ivy manor of Applehill Cottage. Applehill was the remains of a once great duchy, granted by the Conqueror himself. The only remaining buildings built by the great duke were the formidable wooden stables where he had maintained his knights' horses. Katherine's grandfather had always said that the cottage's stones were from the original manor that had burned down. He would continue that each block held a memory of greatness and honor that they bestowed on each descending Lord and Lady Blakesly in turn. *One day that will be your blessing . . .* he would say, *If the blasted orchards will produce their apples again.*

Though the cottage was not as grand as most lords' homes, it held a special grace, nobility, and goodness. Seeing the cottage after a long journey had always warmed Katherine's heart, but this time, her home gave no respite.

The carriage door opened, and Katherine stood quickly. She took the footman's hand before Elizabeth could and rushed out across the courtyard. She ran right through the front doors as the servants opened them and fell into her father's waiting arms. She stifled her renewed sobs in his shoulder as he held her close.

Lord Blakesly looked down on his daughter, his sadness creasing his brow. "I am so very sorry, my dearest Kit. So awfully sorry," he whispered, as the footmen carried in the luggage.

Katherine cried all the harder, her muted sobs further muffled by the discreet stamping of the footmen's traffic.

Lord Blakesly squeezed her one last time, then Katherine pulled back, her tears falling freely. "No Father, *I* should be sorry. If it weren't for me, William would be alive, and I would not be causing you pain." She wiped the tears from her cheeks with the palms of her hands and she rushed down the corridor to the stairs. Her father stepped after her with a pained expression. Lady Blakesly, still with her travel furs, caught his arm and stopped his caring pursuit.

She looked into her husband's eyes with her own sadness mirroring his. "She needs time to be alone. Nothing we can say will stop this pain. Only time."

"Can time even heal this?" he asked, catching a lump in his throat as the sound of Katherine's door closing above them echoed mournfully in the gallery.

Lady Blakesly took her husband's hand with tears in her eyes. "We can only pray that it will."

Chapter 2

So alone.

⟨⟩

Katherine pretended to sleep, slowing her breathing as Elizabeth slid into their shared bed. They had kept the same room since their youth, resisting their mother's injunction that they take their own quarters when Katherine turned eighteen two years previous. The warmth and comfort of sharing their bedding had been too much for them to give up, but now it reminded Katherine of what she had lost.

Elizabeth settled down quietly, trying not to disturb her apparently peaceful sister, though, in reality, the fitful rest in the carriage and the still-burning discomfort of Katherine's eyes had driven sleep far from her. Her thoughts circled like cackling crows.

He would have stayed if I had asked him!

I could have made him leave the horse!

Oh, why did he gift me that cursed mare?

She lay there in quiet agony, covering her head with her blankets to stifle the sounds of her pain as Elizabeth and the rest of the house settled down to sleep. Then one last thought drove away all the others:

This should have been the happiest night of my life.

Katherine couldn't breathe under the weight of her covers—couldn't breathe for the weight of her grief. She clawed her blankets

8

off and rose, her tears scalding her pale cheeks. Visions buffeted her mind, flickering between William's smiling face and the cold emptiness of his grey countenance lying in a coffin. Teetering across the floor in her bare feet, she lurched out of her rooms in nothing but her bed clothes.

She walked blindly, bruising her hip on the balcony's rail overlooking the corridor below, feeling her dark braid swing out over the twenty-foot drop. Clasping the banister, she stumbled down the stairs, her thoughts raging out of control.

In the hallway, she threw open the door to her father's study, finding it empty with no fire to warm the winter night. Katherine fell into the reading chair, her back arching and her lungs heaving as her cries finally escaped her constricted throat. Her heart hammered erratically against her ribs as the room swirled around her. Then, with the walls still spinning, she lurched to her feet, knocking her father's spectacles to the floor.

Her legs shaking beneath her, she clutched the edge of the great oak desk, the sharp edge digging into her palm. She dragged her wracked frame hand over hand, shaking leg over shaking leg, to the other side, pulling open the drawers as a new thought rose through the raving tempest.

Where is it!? Where does he keep it!?

She wrenched another drawer open, shifting something heavy in the back with the movement. *There.* In the deepest corner of the center drawer, she felt it: her father's pistol. She grabbed the cold steel, the unfamiliar weight nearly pulling the weapon from her hand as she drew it from the drawer. Its dark metal glinted dully in the moonlight like the peeling eyes of a sleeping wolf. She fell back into the desk chair and lowered the pistol onto her shaking knees. It rested on the white fabric of her bed clothes, its cold seeping through to her skin.

Katherine stood slowly, cradling the pistol with one arm against her breast. Then she slowly closed the drawer, turned, and left the study. Shadowy impressions led her away, down the corridor. Before she knew it, she was out the entrance way into the cold courtyard. No one was awake to stop her from treading into the deep freeze outside the swinging door.

The icy stones stung like militant blades, gripping her bare soles—tearing at her skin whenever she paused between her halting steps. The stinging soon had her running. Her braid flew wildly behind her, slapping her back and snagging in errant branches on her way to she-knew-not where—just, away.

She pressed on harder despite the fire in her lungs. It felt good to gasp for something other than her sobs, to hurt somewhere other than her heart. Even so, her tears still fell, blurring her vision and turning the night shadows into a black and navy watercolor.

An ancient wooden structure loomed blearily before her, and Katherine found where her feet had led her. Cold fury exploded within her as she pushed against the great doors. They resisted her shoving, locked from inside. Her fury curled tighter as her pain roiled on the edges—unable to scream through the stinging lump in her throat. She trailed her left hand along the wall, feeling splinters sink into her pale and fevered flesh, the gun dangling in her limp right arm beside her. Around the corner, she came upon a servants' entrance that creaked at her touch, and she pushed her way inside.

The familiar scent of well-kept horses and the quiet whickering of the dozing inhabitants fell on her deadened senses. She walked down the aisle, seeing a dozen unfamiliar beasts in the light of the few burning lanterns before she finally saw the black shape in the darkness. Its eyes were wide, the whites reflecting the lantern's sputtering flames that blew in the wind from the open door.

Katherine raised the pistol straight out before her, pointing it at the horse's chest. She stood before the inscrutable blackness of her broken wedding gift, shivering in the cold whiteness of her night clothes, her black braid coiling down her back. Black and white—sharp and stark like her thoughts.

It's your *fault! It wasn't mine! I didn't—I couldn't . . .*

Katherine pulled the hammer back with her left hand, the cold metal pressing a splinter deeper into her palm. The gun wobbled, her exhausted arms struggling to keep the gun trained. Then a voice spoke from the darkness.

"Pardon me . . . Madame," a young man rose slowly out of the shadows beside the horse, raising his hands before him.

Katherine jumped in shock. The pistol bobbing wildly caused the man to duck back down. The weapon wavered, pointing vaguely toward the man intruding on this mortal appointment, but then returned to the horse. Her arms trembled even more from the newly remembered cold and an unknown man crouching before her in what should be the empty stables. The tempest of words and thoughts returned, swirling through the torrent of her pain.

Pull the trigger!

Cold. So cold.

Who is he?

Peace, please, *peace*

What is he *doing here!?*

Do it now!

The man rose slowly again and spoke in slow and soothing tones, covering the nervousness in his chestnut eyes with pretended confidence. "I am under the impression that this horse is your property . . . and if so, you have every right to dispatch it." He squeezed himself closer to the wooden boards, his tall frame shrinking the little it could. "But might you let me get out of the way first?" He paused for a moment, to see how Katherine reacted to his words. Then, discerning no objections, he stepped out of the stall, and off to her right, his cloak whispering against the wooden gate. He slowed his retreat one pace from the stall and turned to face her.

In the dim lantern light, the man's sandy hair glowed like a weathered halo; his once-nervous brown eyes warmed to concern. Katherine stepped backwards, the fire of her furious madness snuffed, leaving a single curl of disoriented smoke. She shook her head, trying to pull the threads of her thoughts together. The question *Who is he?* spun round and round, threatening to sever the tenuous connection to her remaining resolve. Her arms remained frozen out in front of her, her mind losing its grip and unable to loosen her hands. Her body tensed as her eyes squinted, her finger preparing to fire.

The horse is responsible . . . it deserves this . . .

The man cleared his throat quietly, not wanting to endanger himself but needing to help. "I beg your pardon, my lady . . . I mean no disrespect, but if you aim to finish this animal, you will need to shoot it in the head." He pointed at the horse's skull with his other hand out in front of him in a disarming manner. "It is likely that it won't perish if you shoot it in the chest and you will only add to its agony."

Katherine's eyes flicked to the young man standing near her, and back to the horse, desperation weakening under the weight of her despair. "It killed him," she whispered, even as she saw her pain reflected in the horse's eyes, its right ankle bandaged and lifted slightly off the ground. "It deserves . . . "

The young man took a slow step forward, then another as Katherine remained frozen. He reached a calming hand around her shoulders and placed his other hand lightly over hers and the hammer. "It may be your right . . . but you might regret it, if you go through with this." Then he slowly lowered the hammer back down, and without any resistance from the slight and shivering woman, he removed the pistol and stuck it in his belt behind him. The fire gone from inside her, Katherine's body crumpled, the man catching and supporting her sinking frame before she could hit the hard dirt floor.

The night's cold and the effect of her actions crashed in like grey Atlantic waves, drowning her in momentary oblivion. Her head lolled onto the man's awaiting shoulder as his arms reflexively enclosed her. Her sensations overwhelmed the numbness inside her—the cold on her feet, the bitter taste of tears in her throat, the scent of simple but clean wool, and the firm brace of the arms supporting her. She heard muffled words from the man, but all fell as unintelligible noise through the fog in her mind. All the same, the man kept talking, reassuring her subconscious that everything would be okay.

In her immediate need, their stations were forgotten and a woman rested in the arms of a man, her unknown benefactor. His broad chest warmed her shivering skin, perhaps even touching the black cavern of her loss for a moment. She hung there in his encircling support like a dove in a cote. Then the man carefully removed his cloak and placed it over her. She felt his strong hands form to the shape of her shoulders and a feeling somewhere between terror and yearning stole through her, awakening her mind to her surroundings.

"Get away from me!" she shrieked, her face blooming crimson as she broke out of his embrace.

He stepped back quickly, his own cheeks coloring as he turned around. He studied the ceiling as if the joists had some important message etched into them. She pulled off the cloak in distress, but looking down at her ragged bed clothes she grew redder and threw the cloak back over her cooling shoulders. She arranged it as best she could, the over-large garment folding over itself in the front but reaching no lower than her thighs. Then she straightened the skirts of her bed clothes with the practiced poise of a lady about to enter the theatre and she turned on her bare heel to walk back the way she had entered.

Katherine stopped in front of the door at the edge of the night, a plea for secrecy forming in her throat as she turned her head back to the young man. The words died with a puff of cloudy breath in the cold air. He did not turn around as she rushed out into the gloom, her red cheeks cooling to white. *Who are you?* She thought as she stumbled through her exhaustion toward her home.

Miles away, the town clock tolled twelve times.

Katherine did not rise from bed for a week, her body fighting a sickness from the exposure. The rest of Applehill's estate, thinking she was laid up due to her sadness alone, passed their days in woe. When the week passed, Katherine showed signs of improvement, responding to the maids who attended her and even taking sips of broth and crumbs of bread. Her body was healing, but her heart was unaffected—still raw with the spurting frenzies of sudden memories of moments with her William. The only thoughts that ever pierced her melancholy were the discomfiting memories of standing shivering in her night clothes in front of a man she had never before seen.

But what has he done with Father's pistol? Surely Father must have noticed it missing?

The cloak, the proof that it was not all a horrible dream, now lay hidden in the back corner of her summer-things chest, a constant reminder of her shame.

Every common stable hand, shepherd, and farm boy must know the color of my ankles and the shape of my shoulders by now. That man will have told everyone who would listen. Oh, what would William have thought!

Katherine spent another week in her quarters, living a bitter shadow of a lonely honeymoon. Still, her peaceful mourning could not be respected by the invading memories of the man in a stable, the trunk with his cloak finding itself open far more often than a summer chest should.

I must do something about this, or I will go mad.

⌒⌒

Two weeks and one day after the funeral, Katherine descended the stairs in full mourning, a black gown and veil, a little before tea. The rest of the family and the servants had moved to half mourning now that over a month had passed since William's death. They all felt the loss of the wonderful William, but they had to continue on with their responsibilities. Katherine understood their decision. *But I will wear my widow's black until my dying day.* Under her arm, she carried a small package neatly wrapped in brown paper.

"Katherine, dear . . . how are we feeling today?" Lady Blakesly rose in her charcoal gown and walked her eldest daughter to a place at the table where bread from luncheon had sat waiting for Katherine's hoped-for appearance for hours. Similar spreads had waited every day, after every meal, for over a week.

Katherine curtsied to her mother, giving her a quick peck on each cheek before they both sat down. Katherine placed the paper package on her lap without commenting about it, hoping her mother wouldn't notice the odd occurrence.

Lady Blakesly opened her mouth to ask but decided against it, switching to a more comfortable subject. "You seem to have some color back in your cheeks." Lady Blakesly loved her daughter immensely and didn't want to cause her any unneeded pain.

"Thank you, Mother. I feel better. Well enough to be out of bed for a spell." Katherine didn't really feel that much better; the color in her cheeks was the residue from her most recent dream. She had seen the image of a groom pointing and laughing at her as her clothes slowly tore at the seams. That had been the final nudge Katherine needed to motivate her.

It cannot wait another hour! she had thought. *I must be rid of this devilish cloak so I may mourn in peace!* And now there she sat with a package obscuring an incriminating cloak *and speaking with my mother! Surely she will suspect me of something.* Katherine had thought of burning the cloak, erasing any evidence of ever having possessed it. But it had been given as an act of service, of apparent kindness . . . *and it would be wrong to repay that with destruction. After all, most common men would not have offered their cloak, would they?* Truthfully, someplace deep within her housed a well full of horrified curiosity that *needed* to look into the man's eyes and know if he had told anyone. A piece of her could hardly believe it had happened at all, but her flushing cheeks and shivering shoulders remembered the way it had felt to have his arms around her.

But what if he has told everyone about what he saw? Me returning the cloak will only prove it! Katherine exhaled slowly, steeling her will. *These endless circles will not close until I know.* And she returned her attention to her mother. Katherine put on her best ballroom manners and tried to secret her shaking hands beneath the table. "Are Father and Eliza near?"

Lady Blakesly cringed. "No, Kit. They went to the village to see about the dress we had ordered for Elizabeth's . . . " She hesitated.

Sensing her mother's discomfort and not wanting to be a greater burden, Katherine spoke into the space with more assurance than she felt. "It's all right, Mother. Is it for the ball at Milford Manor?" Katherine asked the question lightly, but the tone sounded feigned even to herself. "It will be good for Elizabeth to finally be out in society." Katherine exhaled again, this time for a different reason. *That should have been William's and my first ball together as husband and wife . . . the first time we wouldn't have to spend any of our dances with anyone else.* She couldn't think of that right now. *I shall do nothing but dwell on my love for William the rest of my life the instant after I am certain that everything at the stables has been cleared up properly.* The package crinkled on her lap as she shifted in her seat.

"Yes, it is. Elizabeth was adamant that she should not go after . . . well, after everything. But your father prevailed upon her, saying that you would not want her to do that." Lady Blakesly looked a little guilty, but seeing Katherine maintain her calm expression and collected deportment, the lady continued. "I don't believe he had to insist too hard, but it was sweet of her." She searched Katherine's face to see if he had been right.

Katherine's lips pulled into what must have once felt like a smile. "I am glad that he did. I would not want her to be denied any happiness on my account." She really did want to be happy for her sister, but happiness was elusive at best. *But at least she can be happy. Maybe she can be happy for the both of us.*

Lady Blakesly nodded and cupped her daughter's cheek with her hand. "We all feel your sadness, my love, but I am glad you do not lose sight of those around you in your grief." The lady rose, her daughter following out of respect. Katherine allowed the package to dangle carelessly to her side, hoping to mask it with brazen nonchalance. Then Lady Blakesly gave her daughter a somewhat stiff, but genuine embrace. Everyone was so careful around Katherine now. None of her family knew how to truly ease her pain, so they did the best they could to be near and to listen, hoping that would be enough.

With her mother's touch, Katherine felt the familiar ache and tightness in her chest. *If only you could hold me in your arms again, William . . . How I miss the smell of the rain on your jacket when you couldn't wait through the storm before you'd see me. And the sound of your boots on the cobbles. You filled my life with joy and hope for a beautiful future . . . How can I ever go on without you?* Katherine would be in piteous sobs if she didn't act quickly, so she shook William's tender memory from her mind and spoke.

"Thank you, Mother. I do appreciate your kindness." She stepped back from Lady Blakesly with a slight curtsey. Then they sat back down, her thoughts returning to the package in her lap and a memory of cold steel in her shaking hands one February night. *Would William even want me now, after I've brought such shame upon myself?* Her voice cracked as she asked, "Father didn't mention anything . . ." she cleared the crackling from her throat, took a calming breath, and continued ". . . about receiving anything from the stables in the past few weeks, did he?"

Lady Blakesly tilted her head slightly, like when she had been suspicious of something Katherine and Elizabeth had been doing in their youth. "No, dear. Are you waiting for a delivery . . . or something?"

Katherine paled, wringing her hands where she hoped her mother couldn't see. *She is only concerned for me, she doesn't know about what happened . . .* "No, Mother. I was just curious," Katherine rose once again. "But I had thought that I might stroll down to the orchard to clear my mind before tea," she curtsied. "So, I should like to be going."

Lady Blakesly's eyebrows rose nearly to her immaculate hairline. "Before you've breakfasted? How can you have the strength to take such a turn?"

I have a different kind of motivation.

"I shall be all right, Mother." The paper crinkled again. "I shall be back for tea," she said quickly as she glided toward the door. Mother was always more likely to acquiesce if one acted with high bearing.

"Oh, all right. But I will be requesting double portions of the sweetmeats and a hearty soup for your tea. I won't hear of you fainting from exertion after all you've been through."

Katherine closed her eyes in relief, her back to the lady. "I wouldn't dream of it, Mother," and she was in the corridor and out the front doors. Katherine hurried as quickly as she could over the uneven cobbles with the package under her arm and a veil obstructing her view. In full mourning she should not *really* be leaving the house, but as she was on her own estate, the little impropriety could be overlooked . . . and the idea of wearing anything less, *especially* to meet the unknown man, had felt wrong.

She passed the regular foot traffic between the cottage and the carriage house with many a polite salute and bow from the men and deep curtsies from the women. The servants were nearly as heartbroken for their young mistress as her family was, having seen her grow up from childhood. Most were not on close enough terms to say so, but they had all wished her every happiness on her betrothal and now shared her pain in their caring hearts.

Still, ignorant of their intentions, Katherine thought to herself, *How many of them have heard by now? How many are imagining me in my bed clothes?* Her cheeks heated as she folded her arms across herself, trying to look smaller and still maintain her balance. Continuing her way down the thin cobbled avenue to the stables, she tried not to look anyone in the eyes.

Seeing the stables' imposing structures come into view, a cold fear iced its way down Katherine's back. *He could be in there, right now.* Only one of these stables, the last remaining monuments to the old great duke, was ever in use at a time due to their immense size and the relatively few horses the family kept. Despite their names, the le Chevaliers had little to do with the dealings of the stables these days.

William would have had all three filled if he could help it . . . he loved horses so.

Katherine walked up to the bustling building and saw several unfamiliar horses exchanged for others as they took their turns working in the paddocks further down the lane. A particularly tall roan stallion reared on its hind legs as his boy handler lost his grip on the reins.

The stable master rushed in to calm the beast. "WHOA!! Whoa there. No need to crush any skulls today—no matter how much it's deserved." The confidence of his leathery and gnarled hands calmed the horse, and he continued with a harsher voice. "Now see to it, *properly* boy. If you fancy keepin' your position!" The youth blanched and nodded quickly, leading the roan away. The stable master shook his head after the youth, muttering to himself.

Katherine waited a moment, but seeing that the man either had not, or would not address her himself, she cleared her throat politely and spoke: "Excuse me . . . ?"

The rough-looking man turned to her, taking in who she was *and perhaps a little more* with a glance from toe to bonnet. "Is there something I can do for ye . . . m'lady?"

The look unnerved Katherine's already fragile confidence. "Yes, thank you," she fought the urge to hide the package behind herself. *He doesn't even know what it is.* "I was wondering," *how to word this . . .* "If any one in particular had been tending my mare."

He scratched his head, squinting at a surprisingly opulent pocket watch. Despite its costliness, it bore the marks of the same disinterest with which he treated the rest of his person and was currently treating Katherine with now. He sighed, but spoke. "I'm seeing to the beast m'self. Though with respect, m'lady, if I had my way, the beast'd be put out of its misery."

He whistled at a handler leading a white gelding out of the stable and motioned for him to go back, then continued: "It won't be worth much to you or anyone if the tear even heals. It'll favor that leg forever . . . " He paused when the same handler brought out a dusty colored gelding and the stable master waved him on, shaking his head. "That intolerable doctor trainee thinks otherwise, like *he* has worked with horses for thirty-six years like I have. I told him he's up a tree, but he insists anyway."

Katherine breathed through her nostrils, only just controlling her frustrations with this disrespectful man. *If William were your lord, he would have seen you dismissed!* she thought. But with the memory of William, her frustrations deflated with a small sigh: " . . . did you say doctor?" Katherine's eyes drifted back into the stables where she thought the man might have stood that night. A flash of laying her head on his shoulder jolted her from her reverie with a shiver.

"'Doctor *trainee*,' I said. From the town next. Says he can heal that horse, but I says—"

"I am sorry to interrupt, but is the 'doctor trainee' here now?" *I must get rid of this shameful cloak!* Katherine wasn't really sorry to interrupt such a rude man, but as it would be rude not to excuse herself, she apologized notwithstanding.

The stable master scowled at her interjection but answered anyway. "No, he isn't. He said he'd be back in a day or so to 'look in' on it. I told him it's a waste of his time, but he's making me change that ruddy bandage twice a day and feed it regular rations. That beast'll eat me out of the stable's allotment if I let that *doctor* get his way." The man grumbled as he turned and left without being dismissed.

"I suppose I will be back then," she called after him with her arms stiffly at her sides.

I should tell Father on him. I wonder if he would walk away from him *without being dismissed?* Katherine turned to leave, the disrespect nearly sending her marching right back to the cottage. But after one step in the cold air, the irritation decayed to nothing. *Did this "doctor trainee" tell him about what he saw? Is that why he is so short?* Katherine imagined bringing her father down to scold the man and, in so doing, inviting the man to divulge a far grosser crime. *I suppose I should wait until I've returned the cloak, at least.*

Katherine's desires to be up and moving were gone, but her mother would be expecting her to be out for some time. So she decided to walk the quarter hour to the orchard. Katherine's stomach gurgled at the thought of the apples still hanging on the trees. She and William had taken that walk a dozen times together, eating the shriveled but sweet fruit each time. *If only he were here now.* Katherine closed her eyes against the renewed stinging and began to walk.

Reaching where the cobbles turned toward the village, Katherine continued straight, plodding down the packed dirt path that had once been one of the most frequented of all the roads on the estate. The orchards had been her grandfather's pride and had brought in nearly 1,100 pounds annually on their own before blight spoiled their fruit forever.

What we could do with 1,100 pounds . . .

She arrived at the edge of what looked more like a graveyard than an orchard, with scraggly apple trees. She picked one of the sad fruits and holding up her veil, she bit into it with abandon like she had as a child. The juices spilled from the corners of her mouth, sliding down her chin and for a moment there was nothing but the fond flavors of youthful memories. She felt the juice drip from her chin, a drop landing on her bodice. She paused, slowly wiping the darkened spot on the fabric then wiped her mouth with the back of her gloved hand.

I am in mourning! This does not become me. Katherine took a smaller bite, turning toward the southeast corner of the orchard where the badger hole had taken her William. It was not an hour's walk from where she stood, barely fifteen minutes on horseback.

I will grieve for him forever.

She dropped her half-eaten apple and began the long slow walk back.

Katherine spent the rest of that day struggling to ignore the tightly wrapped package secreted once again in the chest upstairs. In her apprehensions, she sat at the pianoforte staring through the music sheets on the stand. She used to play and sing for everyone who cared to listen, and *William would always sing along with the refrain. How did such joy turn to such sadness?* She touched the ivory with her fingers, but the cold cleanness of them seemed too like the skin of his brow, the dark keys like the locks of his hair covering his unseeing eyes—the open lid like his coffin.

Later her father and sister returned just in time for the evening meal with Elizabeth wearing her new gown. Lady Blakesly and Katherine rose as they entered, and Elizabeth rushed to hug them both.

Katherine's eyes burned as she tried to hold her tears in. *Elizabeth will find her "William" now . . . and I have lost mine.* Still, she pulled her face into a smile and embraced her sister as hard as she could. "You look divine, Eliza. Like a distinguished lady of twenty." Katherine smiled again when Elizabeth let her go, and she sat down.

Elizabeth twirled. "Do you really think so?"

Lady Blakesly responded. "Yes, Elizabeth, you look positively radiant . . . but for all the looking like twenty you are not yet eighteen. Is not your dress a bit mature?" Lady Blakesly eyed the neckline and the boning down the bodice with a raised eyebrow.

"I'm *almost* eighteen," Elizabeth stated, "and I must do everything I can to stand out at my debut."

Lord Blakesly smiled even as he furrowed his brows at her. "Oh, I do miss when you were obsessed with books on trade and the languages of the continent . . . this recent obsession with men will make people think that you are silly." He chuckled as Elizabeth tilted her head in a near-perfect impression of Lady Blakesly.

Elizabeth raised a finger like her mother had done when scolding them as children. "Well, we would not want to look interested in men, at our debut into society, now would we?" Elizabeth laughed with Lord Blakesly. Even Katherine found the corners of her mouth lifting of their own accord. The only person *not* enjoying the caricature was Lady Blakesly herself.

"I should think that you might study my words as aptly as you consider my manner!"

After dinner and an evening of reading—and *still* ignoring that plaguing cloak in the crinkling paper—Katherine retired early to bed as much from a desire to be alone as to actually rest her overworked eyes. *How can I go on this way?* she thought as she climbed the impossibly daunting stairs. *Why do I leave my bed if I am only to return to it each night? What is the purpose in anything?* She hadn't even been able to return that cursed cloak.

It wasn't long before Elizabeth retired to their room as well, carrying a pensive look on her face. Elizabeth walked to the vanity and reviewed her dress in its reflection, admiring her profile in the look-ing glass like she had many times before, but the thoughtful look remained. Katherine laid on the bed, fully dressed in her mourning clothes. They would wrinkle, but she couldn't care enough to call the maids to help her change.

Elizabeth turned to Katherine as her thoughts exchanged for worry. "Kitty . . . is it wrong of me to come out so quickly after—" Her throat caught, stopping before she said his name or what had hap-pened to him. "It is selfish of me. I shouldn't go." Elizabeth reached behind her to undo her dress with a determined expression. Besides Katherine, Elizabeth had spent more time with William than anyone else, often acting as their chaperone. Elizabeth had loved William like the older brother she had never had.

She must be hurting too. Katherine lifted herself out of bed and crossed to her sister, calming Elizabeth's searching fingers. She turned her sister around, cupping the sides of Elizabeth's face and looking into her eyes with kindness. "No, Liza. Please don't feel that way." Katherine stepped back and looked at the beautiful gown, feeling the fabric in the shoulders as Elizabeth continued to listen. "We planned your debut long before any of this had happened—lords and ladies are riding in from all around for the ball. It would not be right to cancel something planned for over a year."

"I know, but . . . " Elizabeth covered her quivering lips with the back of her hand. "But William won't be there." Tears filled her eyes as quiet sobs lifted her shoulders up and down over her robin-egg blue dress.

Katherine felt her own eyes well up with love for her sister and her lost beloved. "Oh Elizabeth, don't cry." Katherine pulled her sister in and embraced her.

Elizabeth laid her head on Katherine's shoulder, whispering her next words to mask her whimpers from the servants quietly snuffing the lanterns in the hall. "I've been *trying* to keep it in—trying to be strong for you, but I *am* selfish, and I miss him too." She swallowed and continued. "He was to be my brother, I was going to share all my favorite books with him and—and," she clenched her teeth to stifle a stronger sob, "and he promised to introduce me to everyone he knew, all of his handsome friends . . . who will do that now? Father? I shouldn't be crying about something this silly and childish—I should be strong for you."

Katherine imagined what the ball would have been like as the new Mrs. William Huxley, seeing old acquaintances and greeting them together as a couple. *William and I would have introduced Elizabeth to every eligible bachelor at the ball and made sure her dance card was full. Then William and I would have danced the rest of the night together, holding each other close and whispering about who we thought had caught Elizabeth's fancy . . . What happiness we should have shared together.*

Katherine's own sobs threatened to grab hold of her, as she said, "Oh, Liza, cry if you want to. I can't stop you. I can't even stop myself." And so they cried, holding each other close in front of the looking glass, their reflections mirroring their matching tears.

In bed, after helping each other undress from their layers of formal wear, they stared up at the ceiling, each in her own thoughts.

Elizabeth broke the silence. "Do you think things will ever be as they used to be?"

Katherine squeezed her eyes closed against the pain. " . . . No, not like they were with William."

Elizabeth sighed, her ragged voice a hold-over from her sobs. "Do you think we'll ever laugh again . . . not like with William, but maybe as we did before?"

Katherine opened her eyes to the ceiling above them again, trying to remember what joy felt like. "Maybe . . . but I cannot see how." Katherine was so tired of crying, her body ached with the aggression of her sadness, but the tears still fell as she continued "I feel like Echo from the myths—that I will slowly waste away saying nothing but William's name over and over until there is nothing left . . . " She continued in a whisper, "I almost wish there was nothing left now."

"Oh, Kitty." Elizabeth's voice whispered in commiseration. "Would it help to talk about it?"

No. Nothing will.

Katherine turned away from her sister and closed her eyes. "Good night, Elizabeth."

Chapter 3

March 1st

Gone are the days of light and fire when my William would hold my hand. Gone are the flutterings of my new heart and the whispers of my enlivened soul. Gone with a handful of earth. Gone with a storm of rushing tears. Gone like my love.

—Katherine, Applehill Cottage

Katherine awoke reluctantly with her sister and breakfasted with her family. She wore her usual black. Elizabeth elected to wear her own full mourning gown in solidarity. For all her self-accusations of selfishness, Elizabeth was a caring sister.

Katherine saw the sad way her father looked at her as she entered the room and sought to cheer him up a little. "Father . . . Did you hear any news from Town when you were in the village?" Current events had always been her father's favorite subject.

A light briefly flashed in his eyes, but then was gone. "No, nothing but the same talk of the sun snuffing out come July, and news of the Napoleonists continued unrest in France—you would think they would be over him, having lost twice. No, no, nothing new, nothing of consequence, nothing worthy of note." Before William's passing, Father would describe the goings and comings of the high lords, discuss his views on the doomsayers and why it was all nonsense, but this halfhearted attempt carried none of the energy of previous tirades. Each member of her family carried William's loss in their own way.

After breakfast, Elizabeth went to practice her song at the pianoforte. She was to perform her song at Milford the night before the ball. The entire le Chevalier family had been invited to stay the week as guests of honor, but Katherine would not be going. That was not what one did in full mourning.

When Elizabeth began to play, the deliberate notes of her learning hands transported Katherine back to the last day she had spent with William. They had sat together at the pianoforte as he turned pages for her, laughing and singing without a care. *Only love, and hope for a perfect future. All gone now.* Elizabeth continued to play. Katherine tried to listen, even thinking of notes for Elizabeth's improvement, but the vivid memories drawn out by the melody eventually drove Katherine out of the cottage. *I would rather face the "doctor trainee" again than relive this anguish.* She collected the package and a basket to make it look less suspicious and escaped the echoing corridor into the soothing silence.

Katherine walked down the cobbles, not allowing herself to rethink her decision. *Perhaps after this business is done, I can bring a few choice apples from the orchard and have Mrs. Goffin put them into a tart for Father.* Normally, the sight of his shriveled inheritance put Lord Blakesly in a sour mood, but if the apples were hidden within Mrs. Goffin's exceptional tart or baked into a pie, he overcame his usual aversion.

Imaging her father's smile at receiving the pastry was still not enough to distract her from what she expected at the end of her journey. Katherine kept her face lowered to avoid making eye contact with any of the servants. *Surely, the man must have told everyone by now.* She remembered her dream from two nights before and she wanted to run back to the house to hide. Somehow, she maintained her steady pace toward the stables.

She walked past the carriage house and through the other buildings, down the brief cobbled road once again. This time, she strode right into the stables and directed herself to the black mare's stall.

It was empty.

She felt panic gnaw at her chest, thinking that the horse might have been killed. *He was right. I would have regretted killing her . . .* She saw the same young handler from the previous day and asked, "Pardon me, but what has happened to the black mare who was here before?"

The youth glanced at her black clothes and then down at his feet. "Uh, g'day, ma'am."

He wonders why I am out like this. Please *don't ask why—I'm not sure I could give a convincing answer.*

The boy continued, "The doctor took Stormy out on a walk."

They named her Stormy? Katherine refocused on the youth. "The black mare is on a walk already? So soon?"

"Well, it's more of a hobble, really. She probably shouldn't be out yet, but the doctor said the fresh air clears her head." He looked over his shoulder then craned over some of the stalls before turning back to her. "Is there anything else I can help with, ma'am? Or can I go now? Stable master has some chores I need to do before I can eat lunch." The boy's fervency brought a smile to her face.

"Of course. I have just two questions: Which way did the man take the horse? And what is your name?"

"The name's Thom, and he took her over toward the paddocks." And with that he was off at a run, presumably to make up for the few moments he had lost in speaking with her. Katherine shook her head and walked out of the stables. She headed to the paddocks, her apprehension growing with the prospect of finally meeting the man once again.

Katherine looked out over the green and small pastures on either side of the cobbles. Lord Blakesly had sold the sheep fields to a neighboring lord a few years back. He had said that he couldn't be bothered with the shearing, but Katherine had wondered if they hadn't needed the money. She had asked her mother if they were poor, but Lady Blakesly had only laughed and told her not to worry. Katherine still worried sometimes.

What will happen now that I must stay on at the cottage? Am I too much of a burden?

Katherine happened upon the paddocks deep in thought and was only prevented from missing them entirely by the loud whinnying of a gorgeous dun stallion striving to buck a terrified rider from its back.

"No, no, no! I told you to stand your ground! You can't let him walk all over you like that," the stable master called as he crossed the paddock.

Katherine looked away from the stable master before her dislike for the man could distract her from the task at hand. Over to the side of the first paddock, her black mare was being led slowly, one halting step at a time, around the inside ring of the piled-stone wall. She watched for a minute as the sandy-haired young man, the very one she hoped and feared to see, led the mare patiently along, never rushing her.

My heart will beat out of my chest if I don't do something soon. This man holds the le Chevalier name in the palm of his hand. Certainly that was the only reason she felt the way she did. Katherine shook her head then took a steadying breath, exhaling slowly before leaving the packed earth for the spongy verdure of the green. Despite her small strides, she quickly overtook the ponderous creature and its mysterious handler. *He's taller than I remember.*

Katherine paused behind the man and the horse, her stomach dropping into a pit within her. *What am I supposed to say to him!?*

'Hello sir, have you, perchance, told anyone about the night a few weeks ago when you saw me in my night clothes? I dreamed that you did, and honestly, I can't imagine a man of your station doing anything differ-ent . . . oh, and here is your cloak.' Luckily the man spoke first:

"Good morrow, Miss le Chevalier." His strong and cheerful voice broke her cycling thoughts, smoothing the frown that had wrinkled her brow.

"Oh, yes. Hello, Mr. . . ." Katherine felt her cheeks heating and found looking into his dark brown eyes uncomfortable and, somehow, inescapable.

The man bowed with practiced ease and a disarming smile. "Charles Patrick Francis. I am sorry that I have yet to make your acquaintance. I am from the university in the town next and I have been tending your horse for the past several days." He spoke louder than one normally should in speaking to a lady in a public place, but his apparent indelicacy spoke to his hidden propriety.

Katherine took a moment to catch onto what he was doing, but was immediately grateful for the farce once she had. "Right, yes. It is a pleasure to be meeting you . . . for the first time," *and fully clothed.* "I am happy to see my horse in such great repair." *And not with a bullet in her head.* "So, I suppose that . . . well," *there is no way to do this naturally . . .* "Well, here is this package that will help with the horse . . . somehow." She blushed even deeper as she pulled the crumpled paper package out of the basket and presented it to the young man. Her chest constricted, remembering the feeling of the pistol in her hands and the shameful warmth of his arms. *I just need to be sure that he tells no one else . . . then I can mourn in peace.*

Mr. Francis inclined his head in a short bow then he reached for the package. Their fingers barely grazed as he accepted the crinkling paper, but the touch sent tingling memories shooting down her arm and straight to her brain: a warm embrace on a cold night. Her heart thumped furiously as she took a slight step back. *There! I gave him the cloak. Now I should run back to the house and forget that anything ever happened!*

But she didn't.

She just stood there with a half blush on her face in the cold morning wind, grimacing at the kind cordiality in the man's eyes. *Running would look suspicious, anyway.*

The horse huffed beside them in restless pain, and Katherine found herself speaking again. "Is the treatment going well, then?" she cringed as she asked. *How could treatment of a lame horse be anything but dismal?* Katherine looked around at the other grooms' faces for any questioning looks, but no one paid her any heed. *Could he really have not told any of them?* The lens through which she had been viewing the servant's behavior over the past two weeks shifted. *Maybe I could have burned the cloak and avoided looking into his too-knowing face again.*

"It goes well enough. She had a serious accident, I understand."

Oh, William. Why did you take her?

Mr. Francis continued, "But she is young and with the right care I believe she can be better than ever." The horse faltered as he spoke this, snorting in pain. "But this has been quite enough for today, I think." He slowly turned the horse around, directing her toward the gate at the road. The doctor's face turned thoughtful for a moment, and then he spoke. "We are headed back to the stables . . . unless you are in any need of assistance?"

Katherine shook her head, looking down, embarrassed, feeling again the cold night air on her naked ankles and open neckline. "No, that will be all . . . " *How do I know if he told anyone? Just wait and listen for rumors?* She hesitated, then the moment passed as he turned to go, leaving her standing in the grass. She followed Mr. Francis's slow progress with her eyes for a moment before walking to catch up with him. "Thank you again . . . for being so respectful of the *horse's* needs." When he bowed his acceptance with an earnest look on his face, she turned and headed to the road as quickly as she could without actually running, to hide the renewed blush on her flaming cheeks.

Perhaps, I should always wear a veil . . . She turned toward the orchard.

With the scandal apparently undisclosed and a vague assurance that it would remain undiscovered, Katherine could return to her mourning in peace. *At least as much peace as hearing the music of the pianoforte day in and day out affords.* Katherine carried the small basket, now full of apples, to the servant's door and knocked twice with the knocker. The door opened almost immediately showing the flushed face of an undercook. *We really must employ a few more servants . . . They always seem overworked.*

Katherine smiled at the young woman, attempting to calm her. "Hello Amelia, would you give these to Mrs. Goffin? She will know what to do with them."

Amelia's face lit up at seeing her young mistress's smile. "Yes, m'lady. Is there anything else I can fetch for you? Some tea, or something sweet? Oh, we all feel deep for you, miss." She looked at Katherine with such worried kindness that one might have thought that Miss le Chevalier was the overworked one.

Katherine shook her head. "No, thank you, Amelia. That will be all," she said, and headed round to the main entrance. She opened the oak door and stepped inside the quaint country manor. The pianoforte was, gratefully, silent and the normal bustle of the house was a dull buzz drifting in from the servant's corridors. Elizabeth was likely in the parlor, so Katherine made her way there, stopping at the cracked study door upon hearing her father's elevated voice.

"—more time! After all the money the bank has gleaned from my coffers, that should at least be my due!"

I have never heard Father that angry . . . She leaned a little closer.

"I know John—Lord Blakesly, I know. I am doing all I can, but the loans were extended on the supposition that your credit . . . *concerns* would be resolved promptly." *That's Mr. Stewart . . .* The banker cleared his throat before continuing. "It's not *us*, my lord, but the London branch that is calling the loan. We have to pull from there whenever there are large requests—"

Lord Blakesly sighed. "Thank you, Thomas, I know you are doing everything you can . . . Reginald, is there nothing we can do?"

Katherine covered her mouth to silence her intake of breath. *We are worse off than I ever imagined!*

The steward paused a moment before responding. "Not that I can see, your lordship. I have reviewed the entailment time and time again, but there is no way out of it . . . besides selling the property *and* the title together, the only way to have it fall to someone in your line would be to name the eldest son your heir as stipulated. It was a stroke of good fortune that the magistrate ruled in your favor to accept the husband of the eldest daughter when the entailment is so specific."

Lord Blakesly's voice drew out with a wry tone, "Indeed . . . the 'twain shall be one flesh' argument was brilliant, Reginald. If only fate had not intervened."

Mr. Stewart spoke with fervency, "What of the dowry, my lord? I do not mean to be callous, but if Miss le Chevalier is . . . not in need of it for the time being, could it not be used to stave off the London branch a little longer?" He sounded triumphant, but Lord Blakesly responded with pain in his voice.

"Already spent. It was all I could do to send the man away with only that before my wife and daughters returned. William was hardly in the grave, and they descended upon Applehill like jackals.

"The indecency!" Reginald exclaimed.

Katherine found herself biting the skin on the side of her hand, breathing too fast—seeing the edge of her vision begin to blur.

"Without young William's—or some other rich suitor's—credit and the promised wedding gift to pay the bill, I cannot find a way to appease the banks but to . . . " Reginald, trailed off.

Lord Blakesly finished the sentence for him, "Sell the title and end the le Chevalier legacy forever." Silence met the lord's statement, but Katherine imagined the grave nods from each of the loyal men. "Then, Reginald, review the deeds. I should like to fetch the best price I can if I am to give up the title. If there is anything left after the bank takes its share, it will be all we have to live on."

An audible gasp finally escaped Katherine's mouth and so she stumbled away before they could find her listening. She clutched at the lace around her throat and staggered up the stairs to her rooms. Passing into her chamber, she tore the ties of her dress open then fell onto the bed gasping.

"How are we to go on!?"

Chapter 4

March 2nd

My heart shrinks from what I must do. I long to be true to you, my William. But the bond formed in the blood of my family calls through even to my broken heart.

If I hold to you and all that we were—my new heart, I would betray the heart that carried me until the moment I laid eyes on you—the heart that struggles on after losing you.

In keeping my promise to the grave, I would bury them with you.

Please forgive me, for I shall never forgive myself.

—Katherine, Applehill Cottage

The evening passed as a mirage in the Serengeti, dazed and with no real hope of succor. William was her heart and her life, but little had she known that he was also her family's savior. And he was gone. Katherine slept with fitful dreams of burning keeps and rotting apples, her family pulling carts of horse manure with the stable master glaring at them. *"Now see to it . . . . if you fancy keeping your position!"* The morning came with no relief, for the nightmare was real; the world had ended now twice, before the apocalypse foretold that coming summer solstice. *Can my heart bear any more sorrow?*

Lord Blakesly had no remaining family and Mother was the best off of all her siblings . . . *maybe Aunt Mary will have a place for us to stay.*

Katherine sat at breakfast, trembling. *Does Mother know? Elizabeth? How can Father remain so calm?* Katherine's mourning masked her fear like her veil blurred her countenance. Lady Blakesly lightly placed her hand on Katherine's shoulder, but no one asked why she was shaken. *Is there no other way?*

Katherine steeled herself and looked up from her plate. "I have something to say . . . " She placed her fork down with the uneaten bite of ham she had been holding for a quarter hour and stood. Her family looked up at her. "I . . . I feel that it is time that I end my mourning."

Lady Blakesly gasped, and Lord Blakesly furrowed his greying brows. Elizabeth froze with a spoonful of egg hovering before her mouth.

"But darling, surely it is too soon?" Lady Blakesly stated, concern lining her face.

"He was not—" Katherine swallowed the lump in her throat, though that did nothing to stem the flow of tears down her cheeks. "He was not my husband. I am no widow. And as the eldest, I cannot—" She swallowed once more. "I cannot allow my misfortune to detain me from my familial responsibilities. I will be 'out' for the ball with Elizabeth." *And on the hunt for a rich husband.* Katherine looked them each in the eye, seeing a pained hope grow in her father's.

Lady Blakesly did not look convinced. "But surely—"

Lord Blakesly touched his wife's arm. "It will be all right, my lady . . . she knows what she is doing," the lord said.

But will it be too late? Katherine thought as she curtsied with a painful solemnity. Then she turned to leave. Katherine glided like a ghost from the dining room through the hall, up the stairs, and into her rooms. She allowed herself one last daydream of wasting away as an old maid, forever remaining true to her one true love . . . but that was not to be.

I shall never be happy again . . . but perhaps I can be of some use.

The thought gave her no comfort. Instead, she imagined the hand of another man holding hers before the altar, an unfamiliar voice wishing her good day every morning, children that looked like him. Her lungs constricted within her chest, robbing the air from her lungs.

She lay trapped in the agonizing waste between a gasp and a sob for what seemed an eternity before her breath finally caught. She fell back onto her bed, and all went dark.

***

It wasn't until the evening meal that Katherine descended in a dark gown, barely on the violet edge of black. It reflected darkly the glowing lanterns like her midnight hair. The air felt strange around her bare neck that had worn a shawl nearly every minute since that fateful morning. *Except for that one night weeks ago . . .* Katherine's cheeks warmed less ferociously with each memory. *Still, I must forget about that, even if I am not able to continue in full mourning.* She had contented herself with half mourning for as long as possible. She would present her sister at the ball and then she would begin the heart-wrenching farce of courting in the shadow of her grief. If she failed in finding a suitable match to save the estate . . . *I cannot think of that, the future cannot be so dark as that.* Katherine almost wished that the world *would* end to escape the feelings of hopelessness swirling around her mind.

Katherine entered the dining room where she was met with a veritable feast. Lady Blakesly must have notified the kitchen of Miss le Chevalier's decision. *But what a strange celebration.* Not a servant, nor a family member wore a smile. All looked on her with concern. Lord Blakesly rose as she approached the table, and sat again as she did.

Like a sluggish bubble rising from a dark swamp, a memory of propriety expanded within her mind. "Thank you for this beautiful meal . . . " Her stomach curled in revulsion as bile rose in her throat. "I am not sure I will be able to eat much of it."

Lady Blakesly had little on her own plate. "Of course, my dear . . . but you do look stunning." Her mother said as a single tear rolled down her cheek. *How much does she guess? Has Father told her everything?* Katherine wasn't sure.

Elizabeth whispered across the table, with a guilty expression, her hoarse voice still filling the entire room. "You are not doing this for me are you? Father *could* present me."

Katherine smiled, *if only it were that.* "No . . . for my own reasons." *For all of us.*

Lady Blakesly wiped the tear, and her face resumed its usual regal expression. "Will you . . . be courting again?"

Katherine looked away from her mother's searching eyes. "Yes, I believe I shall." She turned to her sister. "I hope not to overshadow you, Liza, is it all right?"

Elizabeth laughed, for the first time in a week. "We shall see, big sister. As Mother said, *I* look the eldest."

Katherine smiled, though her heart wasn't in it.

"All right, all right, let's eat this meal before it grows cold," Lord Blakesly said, giving a proud nod to Katherine.

<hr />

The night passed uneventfully, but Elizabeth exhibited a marked change once they returned to their room.

"Do you think there will be very many eligible men there? I don't think I want to be married *right* away, but it would be nice to be married say, by Michaelmas."

Katherine's jaw dropped even as her heart sank. "Michaelmas, but you'll be barely eighteen by the time of the ball." *You would not have a dowry . . . and Father might not even have a title by then.*

Elizabeth smiled then tapped her chin with a thoughtful expression. "Perhaps by Christmas then. I shouldn't mind Christmas either."

She can't be serious? "My word, Elizabeth! Do you have a particular young man in mind? That might improve your chances with such an audacious goal."

"Well, I don't see any sense in *dragging* it out. There is so much I would like to do in my life, and I need a husband for most of it." Elizabeth's verbal pace accelerated with each passing word as if she had been holding in her thoughts for so long that they could no longer be contained. "You and William met at a ball only six months before *your* engagement, so I thought—" Elizabeth covered her mouth, only her horrified eyes showing over her interlocked finger.

How could I forget . . . I met William at a ball.

Elizabeth's face shone pale in their candle's light with vivid red splotches on her cheeks, "I *didn't* think. I am *so* sorry, Kitty." Elizabeth took Katherine's errant hand and lowered them both onto the edge of the bed.

Katherine steadied her breath, a little amazed that no tears fell. "No, it is all right."

Elizabeth shook her head. "No, it is *not* all right. I should be more thoughtful. Oh, how will I *ever* be a lady like you or Mother? William was so noble and so handsome—but well," Elizabeth slapped her forehead with her palm. "There I go *again!*"

Katherine felt a strange bubbling warmth rising in her abdomen. It took a moment to recognize the once familiar sensation. *Is this what it feels like to laugh?*

Elizabeth sat back on the bed, still a little pink and with a slightly irritated expression. "Why are you laughing at me?"

Katherine found the laughter as difficult to control as her sobs had been removing her mourning clothes for the last time. "It's just . . . he passed away . . . and I've been *devastated* . . . and you keep . . . keep on . . . bringing him up!" Katherine knew that her explanation was horrid, but it was the best she could do amidst the painful, side-splitting laughter.

Elizabeth's lips twitched and before long, she was dragged into the chorus, the two of them feeding off each other's hysterics. As laughter begets laughter, they shared silly memories of moments before their time with William and the many happy ones after he came into their life: the time they set the goose upon that annoying shepherd as children, and the time that William fell into a puddle when they were playing lawn bowls in the green. Laughter echoed loudly through the sleepy house, but no one minded being disturbed.

The clouds of sadness were not driven away from Applehill cottage, but they were held at bay for a time. A little laughter goes a long way.

Chapter 5

March 6th

I dreamt my first happy dream, my dearest William. You held my hand as we ran under ephemeral arches of airborne rice and ribbon. I was finally yours and our happy life was beginning.

I awoke with my hand empty beneath my pillow, but for a moment you were here again.

—Katherine, Applehill Cottage

Like a stone arch cut to rest against itself, stone by stone, the crushing weight of worry and heartbreak closed in from both directions within Katherine's breast. She could not announce her status until the ball in a week, there was nothing to do to solve the one pain or heal the other. All she could do was appreciate the quiet warmth of familial pastimes and discuss with Elizabeth how to best enjoy her first experience "out" in society, and sadly, that did little to alleviate her anxieties.

After breakfast, Elizabeth wanted to practice her song once again, and for all the times Katherine's had sat turning pages at the pianoforte in the preceding days, Katherine's heart still ached when she listened. "Mother, I think I will take a stroll in the garden. Would you care to join me?" Katherine asked.

"Oh dear, it is much too cold for my old bones. I never take a stroll before May Day. Do go on without me." Lady Blakesly acted like some ancient dowager whenever she had a new Austen novel to read.

Katherine's lips lifted in a small smile. "That is quite all right, Mother . . . enjoy *Emma*." She winked, but her mother was already looking back through her small golden spectacles with a concentrated expression. Katherine walked out into the side garden.

The weather was the nicest it had been in weeks, despite her mother's protestations. The clouds were thin, revealing the yellowed sky and occasional beams of sickly light in places. Katherine walked for a quarter hour, admiring the work the arborist had done to prepare for the still-delaying spring. Then, not having done with her energy, she decided to stroll down the green. Katherine walked the length of the green and found herself at the thin cobbled road. *Should I return to the cottage or . . .* Katherine saw horses plodding down the lane, following their handlers going in both directions. *Perhaps a little farther would do me good . . .* and so perchance, she passed by the paddocks on the way toward the orchard.

There, coincidentally, she saw her black mare walking slowly but confidently under the watchful care of the doctor trainee, Mr. Francis. With a little shake of her head expelling the dreadful memory of cold steel, frigid ankles, and an icy heart on that bitter night, she crossed the green to the cobbled road.

"Hello, Mr. Francis. How is the mare?" Other horses pranced in the wintry air. "She seems to be doing better?" She noticed that he was wearing the cloak that she had recently returned and, without reason, her heart skipped a beat.

Charles smiled and waved kindly, and Katherine couldn't help but notice how pleasant his countenance was. The cloak covered what Katherine *shouldn't* know was a tall and brawny frame. "Good morrow, Miss le Chevalier! It is a pleasure. And yes, she is doing quite well. I think she could do with a longer walk today." The cheerful confidence in his voice bordered on familiarity, like they were long-time acquaintances, or even good friends. Somehow, he managed to leave that impression without feeling too forward. *I suppose he is more familiar with me than anyone else save Elizabeth . . . or my dressers.* She shook her head again as the horse and Mr. Francis passed and began another loop.

Katherine cleared her throat and spoke again. "Do you plan on only taking laps of the paddock? Is that what is safest?"

Charles paused, the horse stopping obediently beside him, then he turned and led the horse back to the paddock gate. "I did start that way, but a little more diverse terrain would do her good now." He walked over to Katherine, stopping a respectful distance back, but still feeling closer as he leaned in a little to speak. "Honestly, I felt it an imposition to walk anywhere else." He raised his eyebrows, implying a request without stating it, but managing to show more of his deep brown eyes as he smiled. *So different from William's . . .*

Katherine looked at the beautiful black creature, its flicking tail and mane rippling in the wind. *She is the last I have of him . . .* "Well, as a representative of Lord Blakesly, I hereby permit you to walk my horse wherever you please . . . on the grounds, of course."

Charles smiled and bowed. "Thank you, my lady. That will make these rehabilitation treatments much more enjoyable for the both of us, I should think. But while you are here . . . would you like to lead your horse for a part of the turn?"

It was one thing not to shoot the animal, *but to hold its reins?* "I am not sure I can . . . " But Katherine looked into the horse's dark eyes and saw herself reflected. Katherine swallowed down her fear. "Well . . . I suppose . . . "

Mr. Francis clapped his hands in delight, startling both Katherine and the mare. Mr. Francis spoke, "Excellent, she will do better knowing that you're caring for her. Here—" Charles lifted the reins until Katherine could grasp them in her gloved hands. She may have been imagining it, but it seemed that his hand slid slightly closer to hers when her fingers closed around the well-tended leather. Once he was sure that she had the reins firmly, he turned toward the stables. The image of William holding those very reins in his last moments froze her in place. Then she spoke out of the depth of her apprehension, "You would be willing to accompany me. Wouldn't you?"

Charles turned back around slowly, a thoughtful look on his face. "But of course . . . if that is your request?"

Katherine looked again at the mare's dark eyes, the ones that had witnessed her betrothed's last breath escape into the crystalline air. "I—I do not feel confident that I will be able to control the animal," she continued in a whisper "and your presence would be a great comfort."

"Then lead the way, my lady." He smiled, pointing down the lane.

"Yes . . . right. Come now, girl." Katherine started walking and the horse remained standing where it was. Katherine attempted another step, her arm held back behind her with the taut reins. Then she stopped, turned on her heel, and tugged. "Come along." The horse whickered, looking at Mr. Francis.

Mr. Francis chuckled and addressed the mare. "Do as your lady says. I'm coming too." The horse started to limp slowly after Katherine.

The two of them walked slowly down the lane with the horse between them, avoiding the holes and the most uneven of the cobbles. They walked in silence, the cloud shadows drifting lazily across the green to their right and crossing over to the sheep fields on their left. If Katherine were honest with herself, it was rather nice to be walking with someone, even if it was a man she barely knew.

Still, each moment that passed in silence drove Katherine's peace a little further over the cliffs of anxiety. *What is he about . . . what is he remembering?* She clutched the reins tightly with both hands to hide their shaking and glanced over at Mr. Francis to see if she could discern his thoughts. He walked with a confident gait, occasionally clicking to the horse, widening his smile. *He looks pleasant enough . . . in demeanor of course. Though I suppose that he is not unhandsome, either.* She shook her head, instilling the memory of her William's laughing face over the current view of Mr. Francis. She looked at him again, seeing all the differences between them: here was straight hair in a glowing gold, there was dark curls; here was brown eyes when there had been blue; and here was a certain rugged strength, not to diminish apparent intelligence and—*well, really there is no comparison and I had best think of something else.* She nodded resolutely, content to continue the walk in silence

But then . . . what depraved or scandalous thoughts could be lurking in his undistracted mind!? Oh William, how did I bring myself into such shameful circumstances!?

Katherine could stand it no longer. She cleared her throat and spoke over her shoulder to Mr. Francis. "So . . . is Stormy her name then?" Katherine winced at such a foolish question, but nothing else had come to mind.

Mr. Francis patted the mare's neck and rubbed her muzzle as she turned to him. "Well, that is entirely up to you. I didn't think she had one, so I've been using that in the interim. I hope that I haven't overstepped by doing so? The name needn't be final." He looked at Katherine with a look of pure kindness, such that if he had truly done something wrong in naming the mare, she likely would have forgiven him anyway. *Yet somehow, I feel that he would never take advantage of my grace either . . .* though that would be a foolish thought indeed, about a common man she barely knew.

Katherine pulled her eyes away from his expression, looking down at the road beneath her. "No need to feel concerned—I don't think William had a name in mind when he gifted her to me." Katherine winced. The pain of saying William's name to a man who could never meet him, never *know* him, was eclipsed by her fear of what would happen if she were to say any more than that. *Oh, please don't ask—* she held her breath.

Mr. Francis looked out over the fields for a moment, a thoughtful look on his face. Just as Katherine exhaled in relief, he spoke. "You know, I had wondered at her story . . . you say that she was a gift?" he asked politely, prying without pressing—interested, with a disinterested air.

Katherine bit her lip, glancing over the horse's mane at the doctor's brown eyes. *I couldn't share something as intimate as my broken heart.* She kept her face forward as she responded. "I do not wish to say any more on the matter." She swallowed and glanced back again. *Will he take that as a response?*

Mr. Francis nodded, perhaps a little pinker in the cheeks, but looking calm and, otherwise, even comfortable. "Of course, I apologize for having asked." He patted the horse twice then looked back out onto the green.

Katherine's relief remained elusive as her throat tightened around the words that wanted to emerge, seemingly of their own accord. "It was a gift from William—my William," she said, sucking in a breath.

41

I should not be sharing anything with this man! But she couldn't stop the flow once it began. "He is gone now, and the mare is all I have left of him." She looked over and saw him nodding slowly as he absently fixed tangles in the mare's mane.

He is thinking about it now—thinking about seeing my hair plaited and how foolish I was—and holding me—shielding me from the cold with nothing between us but some paltry night clothes!

Katherine's powerless attempts to forget their nighttime interaction crushed down beneath the raging memories of his breath on her neck and his hands on her shoulders. Her cheeks flamed as frustrated tears streamed out.

"*All right* then." She rounded the horse and stood before him, crossing her arms in front of herself. "You *must* want to know *whatever* I could have been thinking running through the winter's night to the stable in nothing but my—well, in my," Katherine looked around then leaned in to whisper, "*in my night clothes.*" She rose, quickly wiping the cold tears from her cheeks before rapidly covering herself with her arms again.

Mr. Francis said nothing, looking like *he* was standing before her in *his* night clothes for the discomfort evident on his face.

"Well, don't you?" Katherine's hands went to her hips for a moment but then folded back across her bodice. "You cannot say that you haven't been at least a *smidgen* curious?" Katherine felt guilty putting this near stranger in such an awkward position, *but I need to know!*

Mr. Francis swallowed a lump in his throat, his handsome face pale and his strong voice quavering slightly. "I . . . well, I suppose, you might say that I may have been . . . a *bit* curious."

Katherine's eyes went wide. *I knew he was thinking about it!* She shook her head in disbelief, turning and tugging lightly on the reins to get the mare walking again and to not have to look at her importunate attendant. Still, the words coursed out of her.

"My William was the love of my life. Everything was perfect." Katherine slowed her walk as the familiar lump formed in her throat. "Then he gifted me this horse as an early wedding present." Katherine wrung her hands over the reins. *Surely that is enough! I needn't share it all—*

The rest of the words escaped her lips like a drawn-out groan, her heart vocalizing the pain she could not name before. "I didn't want him to miss the hunt with his friends." Katherine looked at Mr. Francis now, his eyes attentive to her sadness.

"He didn't have to bring the mare! I don't know why I allowed it!" Katherine closed her eyes against the burning tears. She didn't see Mr. Francis take an involuntary step toward her, or the force of will it took him to restrain himself. She only continued with her eyes closed, her voice barely above a whisper. "William was laughing even as the horse's foot fell into a hole, right up to when he died."

Mr. Francis took another small step forward, pain written deeply on his caring face. "I am so very sorry . . . "

Katherine's eyes broke open, anguish pulling her brows together. "With his casket, my heart and my hopes for a happy future were buried . . . on what should have been our wedding day." She looked back at Charles to be sure he was following. "That night I couldn't sleep. The thoughts of how it was *my* fault screamed over and over through my mind—But it wasn't! I can't think it was my fault any-more—I *don't* think it was my fault anymore. But whose fault was it, if not mine?" Katherine threw her hands up to her forehead, the reins cold against her fevered skin.

Mr. Francis slid his hand down the horse's muzzle until he could lightly pull the reins out of Katherine's hand. Then standing barely a span away, he spoke, feeling coloring his voice. "It was *not* your fault." He spoke with such surety that Katherine's eyes found his, pleading for him to be speaking the truth despite the disbelief deep inside of her aching chest.

Spurred on by Charles's affirmation, she continued, "In a fog—a daze of distress, I retrieved my father's pistol . . . to end the thing that had taken my William . . . but then *you* were there, where you never should have been!" Katherine's pain surged into a flame of anger feeding on the kindling of her doubt, setting alight the fuel of her shame.

He saw more of me than my betrothed ever did.

"Why were you there!?" Katherine covered her eyes and shook her head, feeling her cheeks warm her frigid hands. Her eyes peeked out through her fingers. "Have you really told no one? Of *course* you've told, how could you not!? 'Say lads, you'll never believe what *I* saw last night at the Applehill stables—what an eyeful *that* was.' Oh, I am *ruined*." Katherine dropped her hands and turned to run in whatever direction took her away the fastest.

Mr. Francis, *Charles*, lightly caught her wrist, slowing her steps and pulling her back from a bramble she had nearly thrown herself into. Her feet stopped, but his hand around her wrist did nothing for the racing of her heart or the color of her cheeks. She turned slowly around and he spoke, her wrist still encircled by his soft, yet stalwart hand.

Mr. Francis looked hard into her eyes. "Miss le Chevalier, I have not told one single soul." Katherine could see the honesty in his eyes, and something more. She could *feel* his pure heart with her own, even with it being broken. Mr. Francis's hand rose as if to wipe Katherine's tears away, but he let it fall as he said, "I swear it, on my honor as a doctor."

A doctor?

Katherine stood before the unfaltering form of Mr. Francis's strapping shoulders, his hand almost holding hers. The deep chestnut pools of his eyes enraptured hers for a moment, feeling something tug inside her chest—like gravity pulling in the wrong direction, forward instead of down. After some unknown passage of time, the young doctor broke eye contact and Katherine slowly extracted her wrist from his loose grip.

Katherine looked at the barren ground, then the dull sky, anything to avoid looking into his eyes again. *I don't know what's come over me . . .* Regardless, she felt better for having shared her pain with him. "Thank you . . . for your discretion. A lesser man would not have thought twice before sharing." Katherine rubbed her wrist absently where she could still feel the heat from his touch. "You must think me insane, for all you've experienced in these past few weeks." As she spoke, something inside her balked at the thought of him thinking poorly of her.

Mr. Francis shook his head with a disarming expression. "No, not at all. You've been passing through trying times." He smiled then scratched the mare between the ears. "Besides, if you only ever judge a person by their first impression, you will miss the chance for them to surprise you . . . and isn't it delightful when they can?" Mr. Francis said, his expression soft and thoughtful. Katherine found her cheeks warming again inexplicably.

"Y-yes, I feel it is . . . " She looked down the lane. "The orchard is less than a quarter-hour from here at Stormy's pace . . . I suppose I should still show you where it is before I return to the house?"

Mr. Francis's smile widened. "I would be delighted." In the glow of his regard, Katherine found herself lifting her head a little higher and straightening her back a little further. As she turned to lead the horse once again, the warmth of his glance tingled at the base of her neck.

Why should I feel as exposed now as I did that night? Katherine fought the urge to look back at the handsome young man to see what he was thinking. *I cannot show my discomfort. I must hold my peace until he says the next word.* The silence continued as Katherine cleared her throat of its tightness. Still, he looked out over the landscape without a sign of speaking again.

But what could he be thinking of!?

She cleared her throat again and spoke. "I had heard that you are a doctor's trainee . . . but you seem more confident in your abilities than a student would be, is that not so?"

Mr. Francis nodded, still looking out at the grass. "Yes, I am a medical doctor, most recently specializing in horses and other livestock. I have opened a practice of sorts supporting the surrounding towns. I suppose the stable master does not consider a doctor who chooses to treat 'worthless beasts' as worthy of the title, but I graduated first in human medicine."

The real question Katherine needed to ask spilled out of her. "So why *were* you where you were when . . . you were?" *All those lessons in rhetoric and that is all you can say?*

He responded without commenting on the awkward question. "I was held up with a sick cow in the village, so I was late in visiting the lord's horse that is letting one of your father's stalls. I came here after that, and while I was assessing the stallion, your Stormy was making such a noise about her ankle that I thought I might offer my services to her. At least for the night."

It appears that he helps anyone he bumps into. The feeling of his arms around her flared through her mind for a moment, and her shame rose to meet it. Then a thought blossomed between the two. *It is not so wrong for a doctor to see what he saw* . . . Still, the remembered warmth pulsed through her shoulders and arms as she wrapped them around herself ostensibly because of the current cold. She responded, "Oh . . . yes, I suppose that makes sense." *But how does Father pay for a doctor for a damaged horse?*

They walked again in silence, Katherine's anxieties calming with the rhythmic pounding of the horse's hooves on the road's packed dirt. They came to the edge of the orchard and Katherine picked a small, gnarled apple to give to the horse. Mr. Francis picked his own, its flesh only slightly rounder than the one Stormy ate.

He tossed the fruit into the air and caught it, raising it to the weak beams of light falling through the clouds. "Why are there still apples on the trees? I would have thought that they would all have been picked already."

Katherine looked over the trees which should have been covered in new growth by now, but looked as if they were still in the midst of winter, laden with last season's forgotten fruit. "The parishioners and servants took what they could before the cold set in and these are what remained. They are too deformed to be saleable, so they've been mostly left to rot. Usually, they are not so well preserved."

Taking a bite, the surprisingly delicious flavor flooded Mr. Francis's senses. Enraptured, he stared with surprise at the little fruit. Katherine's lips twitched, remembering sadly the happiness of William's first visit to Applehill, the first taste of their future together. *The last thing he touched in this life was one of these trees.*

Mr. Francis swallowed another bite and spoke. "I suppose fruit preservation is one benefit of this winter to end all winters. Would you mind if I take a few back for some of my patients? The horses aren't nearly as particular about what shape their sweets come in as we humans are."

Katherine shook William's grey memories from her mind, smiling kindly. "Take as many as you like. They are wasted otherwise."

Mr. Francis picked another while Katherine looked at him. . . . *so different.* It wasn't until his eyes met hers once again that she looked off toward the distant clouds. She nodded like she had seen what she expected and spoke. "Well, I have shown you the way. You are welcome to walk around a bit before you return if you would like, but I must be off." *Mother is like to be wondering where I am by now.*

"I think we shall stay a moment longer. Thank you for expanding our horizons. I hope we did not *overly* distract from your solitude?"

More than you know.

She shook her head, hoping it looked like she was responding to his question. "It was a pleasure. Thank you for your accompaniment—both of you, that is." Katherine curtsied to Charles in parting. Then she turned and left as quickly as propriety and tight shoes would allow.

As she crossed over the line between orchard and lane, Mr. Francis called after her, "If you would ever like to assist in Stormy's treatment again, I will be making my calls here around 10:30 every morning for the next few weeks." His voice was confident and unconcerned—*mild as a mouse in the cheese*—every word devoid of any condemning subtext.

Katherine hesitated, feeling balanced on the rim of a cracked glass, one glance in the wrong direction potentially fatal. "Then . . . perhaps you might see me again." She swallowed.

Mr. Francis waved. "I am forever in your service." He bowed again, turning to take one of the dirt paths between the scraggly trees. Katherine watched him go, then turned back to the lane.

Does he see me as another patient? As a doctor, surely, he has seen loads *of women undressed.* Somehow that did not make her feel better. Her cheeks flamed one last time.

"Oh, why do I think of such things?" And she continued her walk toward home.

Chapter 6

March 7th

I became better acquainted with your gift yesterday. I feel foolish about something that happened a few weeks ago, but I think it is all settled now.

You would have laughed at me, I think. Or have been unbelievably embarrassed, as I was. But I guess we will never know.

There is a young doctor who is helping the mare to heal. I wish you'd had that chance too. Honestly, Mr. Francis may have been able to treat you both.

I miss you and I hope that there are fox hunts in the hereafter where, using your wings, you will never have to fall again.

—Katherine, Applehill Cottage

Katherine ate her breakfast with dignity and precision, the very form of the perfect, proper lady. Then she invited her mother to walk with her once again. *It would be splendid if Mother took a turn leading Stormy around,* she thought as something inside wished silently for her to refuse.

"Thank you, dear, but your walks are *far* too long for my aching bones."

Emma again, it seems. Katherine smiled, curtsied, and walked leisurely and easily down the lane to the stables a little before 10:30. She noticed a black stallion similar in color to her own mare, though with some white markings on two of his ankles.

"Miss le Chevalier!" Mr. Francis called, smiling as he led Stormy out of the stable. Her ankle was wrapped in fresh bandages, but there was already blood seeping through.

"Hello, Mr. Francis . . . what is the matter with the horse's ankle? Is it getting worse?" Her concern surprised her. *When did I start caring for the mare so?*

He patted the horse's head. "No, no, she's all right. We went a little far yesterday, is all. The bandages had healed into the wound, so the surface opened some when I changed them."

Katherine's heart twinged within her chest. "Does the stable master not handle those sorts of things?" *Does he do* anything *save disrespect those around him? I must remember to speak to Father about him.*

Three horses were led out of the stables toward the paddocks as he responded. "Well, he seems rather busy, so I understand a little why this dear mare hasn't gotten all the attention she needs. We'll see to that though, won't we?" He said this last sentence to Stormy herself and she nudged him with her muzzle. "I think she wants more apples, but I fear that may be a little far for today."

Katherine's involuntary smile slowly fell into a neutral gaze as she saw the several grooms running back and forth, looking at her and Mr. Francis. *I am here to treat the mare, nothing else . . . but can they see that?* "Perhaps . . . you could take Stormy onto the green and I could retrieve a few apples, then I can deliver them to you on my return to the cottage?" She could just as easily have sent a servant to fetch them, but she *was* out for the exercise, after all.

Mr. Francis shook his head, his expression a little scandalized. "That won't be necessary. A lady walking all that way to carry some apples for a horse is too much."

A woman walking and carrying a burden is what he finds improper?

"I walked there yesterday, what would make it so difficult for me today?"

He opened his mouth then closed it thoughtfully "Well, I suppose I don't know. It seems farther to walk alone," he said as he tapped the reins against his gloved hand.

"Well, it isn't any farther, and I've been taking the same stroll almost since I could walk. Therefore, I will retrieve the apples and shall deliver them to the *patient* on the green." The powerful, yet polite effect of a well-bred lady left no room for denial.

Mr. Francis chuckled. "I suppose you would not accept my request that *I* go and retrieve the apples?" He looked at Katherine, but saw only the statue of regal certitude that her mother had taught her. He bowed and answered with a practiced soberness in his voice that sounded, perhaps, a little exaggerated. "Then we shall see you on the green, my lady." He turned to the horse. "Come now, Stormy, your mistress will see you get your sweets." He winked at Katherine, and he led the mare at a slower pace than the day before.

Was he mocking me? It seems that none *of the horse men show as much respect as they should . . . but why does it not bother me so much when he does it?* She blew the hair from her face and noticed the young stable boy watching from the servant's door. She tucked the hair behind her ear and hurried toward the orchard.

⁂

Katherine huffed, her legs striding quickly while her lungs strained against the cold air by the orchard. "At this rate there will only be apples an hour from the cottage." She really should have measured the distance from the stables since that was where her walks truly began each day. *The few minutes' walk before that barely counted anyway.*

At the stables, Katherine would check if Mr. Francis had done with seeing any of the other horses before she would set out to the orchard to fill a small basket with apples. They would all meet again on the green for a short stroll where Katherine could lead her horse about, practicing stops, starts and turns. Inadvertently, Katherine's own pace was strengthening due to her brisk walking speed and constantly carrying a pound or more of apples. She wouldn't admit, or perhaps wasn't even aware, that her pace was always quicker on her way to the green than it was on the way home.

Katherine pulled in a few strong breaths as she neared the green, then she slowed her feet and slowed her breathing as much as she could. *It would not be fitting to storm in like a blustering squall.* Then she walked onto the grass, keeping an even pace as she crossed to Mr. Francis and the mare.

"You know, Mr. Francis—" She handed him the basket of apples and took another deep breath as he turned to give an apple to the mare. "I think I may have chosen a name for Miss Stormy."

"And what might that name be, Miss Kath—le Chevalier?"

Katherine's spine stiffened. *He nearly used my name!* She looked across Stormy's back at the doctor who acted as if the misstep hadn't happened. He perchance looked a little pale, but that could have just been the pallid light from the distant sun.

. . . but I suppose that a doctor using my name would not be wrong. She shunned the thought of how kindly his saying her name fell on her ear.

Katherine continued as though nothing had occurred. "I am afraid that you will find it quite stupid . . . "

"Never—not so long as I may be called a man." He bowed low with the same noble flourish she had noticed in their walks together.

Katherine licked her lips—a bad habit she had thought she was done with. "Mr. Francis . . . I cannot help but notice your aptitude for noble pursuits. You are not in fact a nobleman, are you?" Katherine looked away as if she wasn't especially interested in the answer. *Only curious, of course.*

Charles's face went impassive. "No, my lady. No, I am not." He patted the horse's velvety nose. "No, my mother was a lady-in-waiting in London before she met my father, and she always felt it important for me to have a good bearing if I were ever to be a solicitor like him. I became a doctor which, for all the education, is a rather mucky job . . . but I still find ways to use her tutoring on occasion." He smiled then. "But you still haven't shared your horse's new name."

"You do not miss a trick, do you, Mr. Francis?" she asked. He shook his head, but lifted his eyebrows expectantly and she continued. "Oh, all right . . . I was thinking 'Ebony,' like the keys on the pianoforte . . . but you hate it don't you?" *Not that it would matter, either way.*

"How could one hate such a fine name? I think that it is lovely, and what's more, it doesn't much matter what I think because she is *your* horse, after all."

I still like that he likes it. Katherine smiled back. "Then it is settled. *Ebony,* how do you like your new name?" Katherine patted the horse as she asked. "I hope that you do." The horse whickered and bumped Katherine's hand for the final apple. "I shall take that for a yes."

⌒⌒⌒

The next day Katherine stopped by the stables to let Charles know that she would be gone for the better part of a week. It was the day that the entire le Chevalier retinue was to travel to Milford Manor.

"Enjoy yourself . . . and know that *Ebony* will miss you immensely." Mr. Francis tugged once on the reins and Ebony lowered her head as if dejected.

"There's no need for the sadness, dear!" Katherine scratched the mare's ears, though her eyes kept darting to Mr. Francis's face. "I will be back quickly." *Would that I could hide from my responsibilities a little longer, but it is not to be.* Katherine's smile turned sad as she waved goodbye and headed back to the cottage. Mr. Francis stood watching her go, an unreadable expression creasing his brow. *I should have remembered to tell him yesterday . . .* but then she wouldn't have seen him today.

These daily walks had been the only thing that dissolved a little of her nightly anxieties about the advancing ball. Their words and their silences, their shared vision of the dreary earth and sky around them, had protected her from her own horrible heartbreak a little. The impossible thoughts never formed—of finding a man she could feel that safe with, one who was capable, kind, and if she would admit it to herself, immensely appealing in almost every other way. No, she ignored the lightness in her head when she heard his voice, and the warmth she felt when he was near.

After all, she had to find a rich husband.

How will I do it? Katherine bit her lip again, apprehension mounting with each step she took up to Applehill Cottage. *Six days at Milford to find a man to marry.* She would be like Daniel in the lions' den, only, she had to hope that they would bite, and not only toy with her.

Elizabeth, at least, was excited to be passing her eighteenth birthday in such a notable place as that.

The grey clouds closed in, choking out the sun as Katherine walked up the stair and into the dimness of the Cottage. *No way out.* Katherine would be appearing at Milford not as a wife, or as a bereaved lover, but "out" once again in society.

But who will even want me now?

<hr />

Katherine finished her preparations before everyone else and descended the stairs to pass the remaining time sitting at the pianoforte. She looked at the beautiful instrument, running her fingers over the keys silently. *They will ask me to play.* Katherine imagined the laughing *ton* dandies *imploring* her to do so, the sycophants leaning on their shoulders like so many silly birds on a scarecrow, twittering. Katherine folded her arms around the cramping tightness in her stomach and closed her eyes against the images.

What will I say? "No, I cannot share what I shared with William, with you. Though, are you currently looking for a bride? You needn't plan the ceremony." A single tear escaped her clenched eyelids. *"I completed the preparations months ago."*

No, that won't do. *They will tear me to shreds.* Elizabeth would play, though she only had the one song prepared. Katherine unclasped her sleeves and let her hands feel the cool comfort of the keys once more. *Maybe . . . perhaps I could play for you, William, and let them think it is for them.*

And Katherine started to play.

Memories of William's dark curls falling back behind his head as he sang to the ceiling at the top of his voice flowed through her mind like the music now in her ears. Her hands were awkward at first, having passed their time for months wiping tears instead of practicing her scales, but after a few stiff chords her fingers melted into their familiar work.

She played Mozart's *Alla Turca.* Slower than her old habit by almost a half, but the flowing notes soothed her in a way she had forgotten they could. *As long as I do not sing . . . I will be all right.*

She ended the movement with an early resolution and stretched her fingers.

I should play something less technical if asked. My hands could not do that again so soon, and definitely not with an audience. Katherine rose from the chair and, turning round, she saw Elizabeth standing at the door with a panicked expression.

"How shall I ever compete with *that*?" And she ran off.

Katherine called after her sister. "Eliza! Wait! I didn't mean to . . . oh, bother."

Thirty minutes later, the parcels and packages were stowed, the footmen boarded, and Katherine and her family were safely tucked snugly within the carriage. The ride to Milford would take the majority of the day, but the views would be pleasant if the weather would hold. Katherine had searched practically the entire house for her runaway sister, finally locating Elizabeth trembling in an upstairs closet, with her favorite book held tightly under her chin.

Katherine smiled at her sister, and sat down next to her. "It's time to go, Elizabeth." Katherine looked into her younger sister's eyes, but Elizabeth didn't respond. "Eliza . . . the moment you see Milford Manor sitting atop its green fields, commanding the surrounding grounds like a monarch on his throne, you will forget all of your concerns." *If not then, by the time the first handsome man catches your eye, all nerves will be forgotten.*

Elizabeth looked up. "I've only practiced one song, Kitty! I'll have to avoid the pianoforte for days and suddenly pull one little song out of thin air—oh why do you have to be so *good*?" Elizabeth looked back down at her slippered toes.

Katherine couldn't help but notice that Elizabeth had changed into her travelling clothes and, besides her obscure location, looked all but ready to step into the carriage. Katherine smiled to herself and patted Elizabeth's arm. "We *must* go. How better could we celebrate your eighteenth birthday?"

Elizabeth nodded and opened her arms for an embrace. Katherine accepted her into her arms and rested her head on Elizabeth's. After a moment, Elizabeth stirred, and Katherine released her. Then the two walked into the hallway, down the stairs and out into the awaiting carriage, arm in arm.

⌒

The weather did not hold. A cold drizzle and cutting wind left the family huddled inside of the drawn curtains, bumping and rocking past the dreary landscape. Before long, Lady Blakesly and Elizabeth were asleep, resting upon each other's shoulders like a hen with her fluffy chick. Katherine could not sleep. The idea of awakening and immediately being thrown into the games and flirtations that she would need to in order to find a husband overwhelmed the rhythm of the carriage and the stinging in her eyes.

Will Lord Alcott simply turn me out? She would have to convince his sense of propriety that a lady being out of mourning so soon was acceptable. *He did fancy me before William—* Katherine cut off her own thinking with a quick intake of breath, and a controlled exhale. *Everything will be all right.*

Katherine looked at her father, sitting with his paper opened before him. Lord Blakesly had read the paper once and was now beginning his second perusal, as he was wont to do. *How does he look so* comfortable *when the straits are so dire?* Katherine bit her lip, then stopped herself. Then, against the trembling in her heart, Katherine whispered, "Father . . . I have something to tell you that I fear might make you displeased with me."

Lord Blakesly looked over his paper, his eyebrows raising in interest. "And what is that?"

Katherine swallowed, looking to be sure her mother and sister were still asleep. "I may have overheard a conversation you had with . . . "

The lord cleared his throat, taking a turn to glance over at his wife and youngest as he folded his paper. "With Reginald and Thomas, perchance?" Katherine only nodded in reply, her eyes glistening a little in the dim light diffusing between the curtains. Her father continued, "Ah. I thought I had heard something . . . "

Katherine leaned across the small space, looking with dark fervent eyes into her father's light ones. "How bad is it, Father? How quickly must I marry?"

Lord Blakesly shook his head slowly, smiling a sad smile. "How very backward . . . a daughter providing for her father." He leaned forward, lightly wiping a tear from her cheek. "You have cried so many tears . . . and now I am adding to them."

Katherine took her father's hand, the tears falling anew. "Father, *please* tell me." *If I can know how bad it is, maybe I can forget my apprehensions . . . and my broken heart.*

He sighed, letting go of Katherine's hand and rubbing it on his thigh absently. Then he looked at her, seeming to weigh how she would react. Finally, he opened his mouth. "It is bordering on catastrophic . . . " He gave a mirthless chuckle. "I would say apocalyptic, but thought to differentiate from society's current sentiments." He tapped the paper on his thigh. Seeing that Katherine did not rise to his dark humor, he sighed again and continued. "If I am to retain my title, and Applehill, I would need to have proof of continued payments before summer's end . . . how much have you surmised on your own?" His eyes met Katherine's again.

"I knew that we were poor. Grandfather always complained about the orchards, but how did we come to be . . . "

"Bankrupt?"

Katherine looked with fear at her mother and sister, but they dreamed on. Katherine nodded, her tears dried by anxiety.

"Things have been bad for some time. No matter what we have tried, the apples fail. I sold the fields slowly, one at a time, but those were gone after a few years . . . and the loans grew larger and larger."

Katherine barely dared to breathe, the answers to her worried questions as a youth opening before her eyes.

Lord Blakesly hesitated, a pained expression growing on his face. "Then you met your William . . . you courted so quickly—but you were in love, there was no harm in that." He drew in a breath as Katherine's own stopped in her lungs. "You couldn't be wed without a dowry—and he was sure to give a wedding present, so the banks would be satisfied . . . with him married to you and named as my heir, every term of the entailment would have been met, and the banks appeased, but . . . "

Katherine whispered through the constriction in her chest, "But then he died . . . and the gift never came."

Lord Blakesly nodded, reaching for the hand that lay limp in her lap. "I have burdened you with this knowledge, hoping that it might free you." He reached across with his other hand to cup her cheek, his forgotten paper falling to the floor. "It would be near impossible to find a man rich enough to save us in so short a time . . . you can return to your mourning, and I will see to the details of what happens next for us." Lord Blakesly smiled, his eyes glistening with unshed tears.

Katherine closed her eyes, leaning into her father's hand on her cheek and pulling his other up under her chin. She sat there for a moment like she had as a child, when only his arms could heal the deepest pains and solve the greatest wrongs. *Would that life were so simple now.* She opened her eyes and looked at Lord Blakesly's face. "But what will become of us?

The lord drew his hands away, sitting up with his usual proud bearing. "Reginald is doing what he can to understand where we will be when we sell the title. I feel that it will be like we were suddenly the descendants of third sons."

"As if our birth order—birthright—was suddenly changed?"

He nodded, a serious look pressing down on his brow. "It is better than being considered common men, as it is we might still be able to manage a match for Elizabeth and . . . " He looked down. "You could do whatever you felt in your heart."

Katherine nodded, her melancholy disoriented like she was falling upward into suffocating sadness. *I could be true to my William. Father said that I could.* Katherine closed her eyes and leaned on Elizabeth as her father returned half-heartedly to his paper. *Elizabeth is beautiful. Men wouldn't even mind that she was poor.* Katherine squeezed her eyes tighter.

But how could I live with myself, knowing I hadn't tried to save them?

<hr />

The wheels stilled as the carriage rolled onto the fine stone pavers of Milford Manor's drive. Katherine stirred, then sat bolt upright and pulled the curtains open. She looked out over the rolling greens and commanding aspect of the castle on the hill. At Milford, even the air seemed to blow with a nobility that fluttered the aged oaks' leaves like proud banners. Katherine's perennial awe at seeing Milford was darkened by the icy apprehension crystallizing in her core.

Such a beautiful place for a heart's betrayal.

Katherine looked over at her mother and sister and saw Elizabeth gazing out the window over their mother's shoulder. "Here, Liza, take my place. You will get a much-improved view from here." Katherine moved across to be next to her father and Elizabeth pounced on the vacant window like a lioness from the tall grass.

Elizabeth's jaw dropped. "Oh my . . . "

Katherine watched her sister experience the wonders for the first time, a part of her heart warming. But with each passing green, garden, or gable, Katherine drew closer to the eyes and interests of men who would steal her heart from William's. *But what of the alternative? What horror would it be if none of them express interest and my family is left to wallow in poverty and shame the rest of their days?* The shame of financial ruin was far more condemning than even a scandal. Katherine shook her head once, to clear the memory of a man's arms on a cold night. Still, somehow, the thought comforted her a little.

She looked out the window that Elizabeth had been using and knew that there were fewer than three minutes until they arrived at the great doors. *How did I do this the first time? How do I walk into a room where everyone watches everyone, sizing up the conquests and the competition?*

When they had first met, William had been so unbelievably charming, and so inexplicably interested in anything and everything that Katherine had said that after spending one short evening with him, there had been no other man who could catch her fancy. Every other party thereafter, Katherine had bided her time through the other necessary dances, always waiting for when she could hold William's hands again.

Perhaps it will be easier if I am only looking for money . . . love cannot find me anyway.

In time, the carriage halted at the entryway where a veritable host of servants awaited them. A footman handed the ladies down, then the le Chevalier family walked up into the awaiting antechamber, passing low-bowing servants on all sides. In the drawing room, Lord Alcott, the Lord of Milford—and one of Katherine's old pursuers, his steward, and two other well-dressed men bowed at the le Chevaliers' appearance. Lord Blakesly bowed, presenting Elizabeth to the room. She curtsied with practiced elegance, with a demure look at each of the young men in turn.

She, at least, will have no trouble finding men to be interested in her, Katherine thought as she too stepped forward and curtsied.

Lord Alcott, with his typical good grooming, stepped forward and bowed again. "I am pleased to host you at this most exciting time, Miss Elizabeth le Chevalier." He looked to Lord Blakesly from his bow, as he was *really* pleased to be hosting the lord. As he did so, his eye caught hold of Katherine with surprise and he stood up abruptly. "Oh, Miss *Katherine* le Chevalier. It is a pleasure to see you . . . so soon." His brows furrowed in thought. Though Lord Alcott was no more than five and twenty, he had inherited the austerity and staunch propriety of a man easily twice that. He had been born to an aged lord from the wife the lord took in his old age. His drooping mustaches and hound-dog eyes were strangely accented by the rich auburn color of his hair.

Katherine swallowed. *Here goes . . .* "Y-yes, I am here to present my sister, Miss Elizabeth le Chevalier, in her debut." Katherine pointed weakly to her side, wishing that she had sent a card to announce her intentions of accompanying the party. *But then he might have turned me away . . . he still might.*

Elizabeth looked at the strained smile on her sister's face and stepped forward, her own smile beaming like the forgotten sun. "I am *delighted* to be welcomed into such a fine and long-standing estate." Elizabeth stated the words with a practiced formality, somehow managing to include hints of familiarity, as though this was not the very first time that she was seeing this wealthy bachelor. "I would be delighted to see more of it if . . . ?" She hovered on the edge of formality and forwardness, her arm extended and ready to be taken by any of the awaiting men. Her spell was struck. The men behind Lord Alcott looked at each other and stepped forward quickly, one arriving at her extended arm first. Before the second could look *too* disappointed, Elizabeth smiled and raised her other arm.

Lord Alcott looked on the display with a tired annoyance. "I supposed we should commence with the tour . . ." and he drifted off, allowing Katherine to take her first true breath in what felt like min-utes. The issue of Katherine's appearance out of mourning was paused for now, the duty of hosting outweighing the impropriety of *whom* he was hosting in Lord Alcott's hound dog mind. The race was not yet over, but she had made it past the first hurdle.

This will be a long evening.

Chapter 7

March 11th

It has been days since I last wrote. I have been hiding from what I must do, but I fear that my duty has still found me. I wish that William could be here with me . . . but then, I would not have to face these fears at all.

How will I convince a man to love me when I will never love him in return?

—Katherine, Milford Manor

T he party's arrival forced the new acquaintances to share a brief, informal dinner, and then end the night relatively quickly after a few hands of cards. Katherine dragged Elizabeth off to bed. Elizabeth's memory of her earlier apprehensions was completely forgotten, and she chittered about the funny stories that Sir Rodney and Sir Galloway had shared with her. Katherine had been engaged less than a year and already all the players had changed in the social circles. She felt like a spinster swooping in to steal another young bride's match, though she had not yet turned one and twenty. Elizabeth's exuberance at the handful of available men was sure to magnify exponentially with the dozens that would arrive in a matter of days. As it was, she was sure that one of the three currently attending would be her husband before the summer was through.

I hope there will be one that will have me. Katherine disrobed and crawled into her empty bed, Elizabeth in an adjoining room.

Katherine's fitful night passed, but she rose the next morning without the benefit of feeling refreshed. The party was to have an early breakfast then take a stroll through the sprawling lawns and gardens to complete the tour of the grand estate. Outside her window, the weather stared down drearily, reflecting Katherine's melancholy mood—cold, distant, and too tired to shed tears.

Over and over through the night, Katherine had rehearsed to herself how she would broach her current status to Lord Alcott. He was a man who viewed propriety as the pinnacle of English society, and he was wealthy enough that all around him shared his beliefs—at least as long as they were near. *He will think that I should still be in mourning . . . how could he not? I wish I could be.*

Her grim face looked back at her in the glass as her maid brushed her hair. Katherine chose one of her more somber colored gowns hoping that at least *hinting* at a late stage of mourning would assuage Lord Alcott's piercing eye. If she could win Lord Alcott's approval before the other lords and ladies arrived, they would take her status as a matter of course.

Elizabeth walked out of her rooms at the same time as Katherine, her light brown hair pinned back behind her head, curls spilling over her emerald gown. "Kitty, you look like you haven't slept a wink. Are you well?"

"Thank you for your concern, Eliza. I am simply pensive." *Apprehensive, is more like it.*

Her stomach roiled at the prospect of not only permitting but *seeking* the attention of the men who would attend. *I could stay up here in this bedroom—feign a weakness of constitution and spend the better part of the day alone . . .* She just shook her head. The longer she took to face the crowd, the larger and more intimidating it would become. Besides, any rumors that might be circulating were best faced head-on before they could ruin any of her meager prospects. *I wish I were as brave as you William . . . or that you had been less so.*

Elizabeth's face lit up. "Wonderful—I have been thinking, should I ask Lord Alcott to be my first dance? Or should I wait for someone to ask me? I suppose it might be proper to have Papa be my first dance, but it seems such a tragedy to miss a chance to dance with a potential suitor when I could dance with Father any old time at home."

Katherine smiled through her tired eyes. "I think it would be best to let the men ask you, as is customary . . . though if a man tries to monopolize your time, you simply misplace your card whenever he is near."

Elizabeth cocked her head to the side, a scandalized look on her face. "Why sister . . . you've never employed such *dastardly* tactics before, have you?"

Only once . . . .and perhaps that was why Lord Alcott is so quick to judge me, she thought. Then she spoke aloud, "Certainly not. Let us to breakfast." And that was enough to distract the happy little sparrow that was Elizabeth.

∽⟡∽

Already at breakfast, the men had stationed themselves with seats between them, leaving spaces for the ladies to weave themselves wherever they saw fit. Lord Alcott was at the head with Sir Rodney to his left and Sir Galloway two seats down on the same side. Though somewhat dry, they each commanded a fine stipend and in the case of Lord Alcott, a great annuity. Their physiques were not those of the romantic heroes ladies most often fantasized about, but that was not what Katherine was currently seeking, anyway.

Katherine pointedly chose the seat between Sir Galloway and Lord Alcott, knowing that Sir Rodney's marginally improved appearance over his fellows would make him the most appealing to Elizabeth. "Good morning, Lord Alcott, Sir Rodney, Sir Galloway." Each of the men rose and gave their bows before retaking their seats, though Galloway seemed to roll his eyes at the tradition. Lord Alcott returned to eating when Elizabeth had sat between the other gentlemen.

Katherine remained where she was, folding her hands meekly before her. "Lord Alcott, I would like to give an explanation for my unexpected appearance at your home."

Lord Alcott's basset-like eyes left his plate and peered solemnly at Katherine. "It is rather irregular. I should not have expected to see you out until at least the 11th of February next."

She swallowed her nerves. *He was counting?* She shook her head. *I need to focus. How did I put it last night . . . ?* "Though my pain was deep . . . he was not yet my husband—not even a cousin. Thus, I felt that my sister's need stood taller than my grief." *Oh William, if only our circumstances were not so dire . . .*

Sir Alcott's eyes returned to his plate and took a bite of ham that munched and rolled with his thoughts. "Hmmm, well I do say that he *wasn't* your cousin, was he? Then I suppose that is settled." A warm smile brightened his basset-like complexion to one more like a retriever. "It shall be a pleasure to dance with you once again."

Katherine nodded sweetly as she sat.

Oh, bother.

⌒~⌒

Breakfast passed cordially, if not with much excitement. Even in a good mood, Lord Alcott was far from exuberant. Elizabeth managed to keep each of the three men's attention for most of the conversation, only occasionally pulling Katherine from her meal with "oh what was it he said" and "where were we that one time?" Even still, Katherine was relieved when Rodney asked the party if everyone was ready to see the grounds.

The three men and the two women walked out the front doors, waving to Lord and Lady Blakesly heading to their own breakfast. Mother and Father mostly kept to themselves during visits like these. *Fewer opportunities to be asked about how "things" are back at the cottage,* Katherine thought somberly. The party paused at the front door where each was handed a large fur coat to protect against the deep cold that still refused to relinquish its hold over the land.

Lord Alcott looked at Katherine. "May I take your arm as we descend the steps?" He presented his arm.

"Yes. Thank you, my lord," said Katherine, placing her arm atop his. She took the opportunity to look more closely at the young lord. In terms of annuity, Alcott was the most eligible candidate within three days carriage ride, with the greatest potential to solve her family's needs. So, despite his aged manner and dry sense of propriety, his dog-like charm might make for a pleasant companion for a young woman who was committed to never love again. Katherine coughed politely and spoke. "May I ask what a day in your life looks like?"

The two of them descended the old stone steps leisurely, one at a time, leading the other three. Katherine admired the sloping greens before them leading down to a large pond that reflected the steely clouds above. A small river bordered by an ancient mill fed the pond, for which the estate had gained its name.

Lord Alcott raised his bushy eyebrows in surprise "What a question. You shall experience my habits in these next few days . . . but I suppose I see no trouble in giving you a description now." Lord Alcott was not accustomed to young women, especially those as handsome as Miss le Chevalier, asking about anything other than his rents. "Each day, I breakfast; I walk; I luncheon; I hunt; I sup; I recreate, and I rest. Occasionally I am called to Town on some business or other, but I am most often about the grounds here or visiting the dowager at the North Manor. Infrequently I visit Sir Rodney's or Sir Galloway's estates, but they are so dreadfully small as to make them nearly unbearable for a party of more than three."

I wonder what he would think of Applehill cottage . . .

The five took a turn around the southern corner of the estate heading to the topiaries and the labyrinth. The stonework was the most interesting, harkening back to an age when monoliths and arches were hewn, placed, and worked to appear even older than they really were. Katherine imagined a long line of past Alcotts walking their betrothed through the gardens and then envisioned a long line of future Alcotts rolling forward from where she now stood. If he were to marry her, she would be a link in this ancient chain, tasked with caring for and teaching the next generation. *Could I measure up?* The retinue continued onto the browning green.

Elizabeth's voice floated up from behind. "I should think that the honor guard would muster here, don't you?" Elizabeth asked Galloway on her right arm, Rodney had her left.

Katherine looked over her shoulder. "What honor guard, sister?"

"Why, the honor guard that precedes the Prince Regent, of course." Elizabeth giggled while Rodney looked up at the steely clouds with interest and Galloway's ears turned pink.

"What's this? The Prince Regent? Coming here?" Lord Alcott asked in disbelief.

"No . . . " Galloway spoke. "We were only imagining where the parade would start . . . should his majesty grace Milford with his presence, my lord."

"How odd." Lord Alcott lowered his voice and spoke only to Katherine who still had her arm on his. "I suppose the young things need their games, while dignified folk are left to the rationality of our stations."

I should have thought the honor guard would muster on the drive . . . "Uh, yes, quite."

The green was open to the bitter wind and so the young noblemen and ladies made their way to the wood where the time would pass more pleasantly. As they neared the trees, Katherine could not help remembering other such walks on a smaller green with a black horse nibbling an apple and a handsome doctor listening to Katherine inadvertently bare her soul once again. She paused as the other three hastened into the shadowy boughs. "Lord Alcott, do you keep many horses?"

He nodded. "Several more than we need. Did you want to go horse riding?"

Katherine shook her head. "If the weather improved, perhaps . . . I was simply thinking about my horse back at Applehill. Her ankle was injured, but an accomplished horse doctor has been giving her treatments and she seems to be improving." Katherine smiled at the image of Mr. Francis walking Ebony around a green as expansive as this one. "If you should ever be in need of a horse doctor, I would highly recommend his services."

Alcott's brows furrowed. "Hmm. If it were my horse, I would not waste the money. A damaged animal will never improve to what it was." He spoke with the gravity of a puritan pastor on Mardi Gras. "If the weather does improve, perhaps I might show you a little of the southwestern corner of the estate. Milford is *well* endowed with pheasant, boar, deer, and several varieties of fowl." Lord Alcott's face cringed into the rough shape of a forced smile.

Is he trying to impress me? Katherine looked down but responded, "That sounds . . . interesting. Do you suppose we will see any beasts on our walk today?"

Lord Alcott then walked taller, a satisfied air about him, like an old hunting dog after a pat from the hunter. "Perhaps I can scare a few out of the bush for you."

Ever the noble hound, indeed.

And the two followed the others into the wood.

The rest of the morning and each of the subsequent mornings was spent the same way—walking on the green or investigating the ancient wood and the mysteries therein. Thursday came—Elizabeth's eighteenth birthday, as she mentioned to each guest or staff she passed, usually with a flick of her curls and a giggle. Still the day took the same form as the others. The party breakfasted, walked, and then received the usual summons to luncheon as they wandered the wood. Having worked up a significant appetite from the cold and the exertion, the retinue returned promptly to the manor.

Upon arriving at the house, the party was met by the steward with an announcement. "May I present to you, Sir Braxton and the Misses Braxton." Sir Braxton was tall, impeccably stylish, and painfully handsome. He so fit the bill of the romantic hero that Katherine had to stare Elizabeth down to prevent her from throwing herself at him. His golden hair was lustrous and made even more fetching above the vibrant blue of his jacket. All in all, he bore the marks of a regular rakish heir.

"*Un Plaisir, Seigneurs et Mademoiselles,*" Sir Braxton bowed low as his two sisters curtsied behind him. "Lord Alcott, who do you have on your arm there?"

Lord Alcott squinted, very nearly scowled, but responded anyway. "This is Miss le Chevalier, and that is her sister, Miss Elizabeth le Chevalier—it is her birthday, as I am sure she would have told you soon." Galloway chuckled as Rodney looked mournfully at the new challenger. Still, they both looked interested in the new sisters' presence, something that pulled Elizabeth's focus back to them a little.

Braxton stepped forward and gave an extra bow for Elizabeth who blushed as she nodded. Then he spoke to Lord Alcott and his four original guests. "Why, it seems we finish your set! Four couples already and the festivities are not till tomorrow. Perhaps we should take a few turns about the ballroom to warm up the floorboards, eh?" Braxton smiled as he lightly took Katherine's hand and kissed it. He had barely glanced at Elizabeth when Alcott mentioned her, only giving the proper attention for a young lady's birthday.

Oh, you will be troublesome, won't you? Katherine thought, not gracing the newcomer with any of the signs of interest she surmised that a man of his looks and station would likely expect.

Lord Alcott handed his fur to the footman. "Let us luncheon. Perhaps that will be entertainment enough for now?" Alcott proceeded down the hall without waiting for a response from Braxton. Katherine deposited her fur on top of Alcott's and made to follow him, but Braxton extended his arm with another rakish smile. Elizabeth gave a little pout as she passed but winked as she held each of the Misses Braxton's arms. *She is going to interrogate them.* Katherine had little choice but to accept the proffered elbow and the two of them followed the train after Sir Rodney and Sir Galloway who scratched their heads at the women's behavior.

Braxton waited until the party was a little ahead before speaking to his lovely detainee. "Well Miss le Chevalier, I am sure I speak for *everyone* when I say that I am pleasantly surprised to see you out so soon." Braxton glanced at Katherine's face, seeming to weigh the effect of his comment on her. Katherine couldn't help but notice how he looked somehow *smoother* up close, his strong jaw polished like Roman marble or Greek bronze. His eyes shone blue to match his jacket and his teeth practically glowed between his ruddy lips.

Katherine blinked and looked away. "Y-yes, I . . . felt it was my responsibility to see to my sister's—"

"Ah, yes. Say no more." He winked, flashing his practiced grin. "One must do many things out of obligation, mustn't they?" Braxton looked forward, a shadow darkening his brow. If Katherine wasn't focused so closely on the man's face, she would certainly have missed it. All the same, it was gone so quickly that she almost disbelieved her own sight.

Braxton continued unperturbed. "Do you mind if we admire a few of these paintings *en route*? I would not want to delay your luncheon too long, but there are truly some marvelous pieces."

Katherine craned her neck to see how far the others had walked. "We were shown them on our tour . . . and I'm not sure it would be polite to make everyone wait for us."

"Oh, but I'm sure they would start without us. And I mean to discuss the *meaning* of the paintings, not the history of when it was acquired and how many pounds it cost." Braxton paused his step and gracefully turned Katherine on her heel to face a portrait of a well-dressed young woman. "So, what do you think?" Braxton put his free fist to his chin and pouted his lower lip in an exaggeratedly pensive pose.

Katherine restrained her desire to roll her eyes, *I am far too tired for games.* Aloud she spoke with her customary courtesy. "If I recall correctly, this is a twice great aunt who married a duke in the North, or something like that."

Braxton waggled his finger. "Not what do you *recall*—though an impressive memory, I must say—but what do you *think*? Why did the painter give her that expression? She cannot have been holding it the *whole* time he painted."

Katherine suppressed her impulse to sigh. She had not much enjoyed flirtations before meeting William, and having lost him had not added to their estimation. "I suppose she may have liked the way it softened her jawline."

Braxton turned his head, taking a step closer to the frame. "Was that why you did it?" He put his hand to his ear as if to listen to the painting whisper.

I should have preferred these theatrics after *luncheon . . .*

"No, I daresay she disagrees with you—I am dreadfully sorry to say it."

I am so sure.

He continued, "It wasn't because of anything she wanted at all." His voice drifted away, dropping to a thoughtful quiet, a searching wonder. "No, that look is not the lady's gaze but the heart of the artist . . . " Katherine found herself leaning in, Braxton's spell all the more effective due to its apparent sincerity. "This is how she would always look to him, in his aching heart—prim, perfect, and pretty. A loving look he would never receive staring back at him forever. He set her likeness in oils to smile back at his sorrow." Braxton stood a little taller, his blue eyes fierce where they had been jovial only moments before. "This painting is a wish, not a memory."

Katherine looked at the painting again, now with new eyes. The deep reds of the woman's lips and the fine arch of her brow were far more perfect than a lady could ever attain in life. She sat, the garland overhead with all but the glow of a halo and the porcelain skin of an Aphrodite. "Oh my . . . how did you see all that?"

He smiled with a sadder wink. "I understand the artist a little too well, perhaps." He bowed, his golden hair hanging down in front of his upturned eyes. Katherine felt her cheeks redden.

Oh yes, you will be troublesome . . . Then she continued aloud, "Perhaps we should continue on to luncheon, now . . . they might wonder where we went." Katherine turned away from Braxton before he could see her blush deepen at her awkward transition.

"Ah they can wait." He rose with renewed energy. "I will be honest, but I *do* like poking fun at Cousin *Allie*. He does hold himself so stiffly." Braxton executed an exceptional impersonation of Lord Alcott's frown and rigid bearing.

Katherine covered her mouth before she could be heard to laugh. She tried to turn her expression to one of distaste, but Braxton knew better.

"Ah well, I suppose we should get on then." Braxton extended his elbow once again. Katherine took it a little more readily than she did the first time, though she maintained an air of dignity as they walked past portrait and landscape after portrait and landscape. "You will review more of these old smudges with me sometime, won't you?"

"I think I should like that . . . very much."

Katherine saw one last painting of a dark horse and groom looking down at her from above the door to the dining hall as they entered. *I wonder how Mr. Francis is getting on with the mare. I wonder if his walks are lonely . . . without me?* Elizabeth's beaming face from across the room interrupted Katherine's thoughts, and she immediately went to join her. A phantom flutter in her chest dissipated as she joined in on the conversation.

The party had started eating already but had yet to start their puddings. So Katherine and Sir Braxton caught up on the main course. Lord Alcott would not look at Braxton until Katherine had made a point of speaking most of the meal with him, leaving Braxton to chat with the others at the table. Alcott was clearly displeased at his cousin, *if they really even are cousins,* but no longer pretended that he wasn't there. Elizabeth chatted mostly with Sir Braxton while Rodney played sadly with his gravy and Galloway discussed politics with the Misses Braxton with a self-important air. All-in-all it was a usual, unexciting meal.

After the plates were cleared, everyone excused themselves to rest and prepare for the evening. The estate was drafty despite the great fires burning in every room and so Elizabeth and Katherine napped together.

After waking, Elizabeth pleaded with Katherine to head back downstairs, exaggerating her duress. "Kitty! They are surely missing us! Why must we put them through such anguish—put ourselves through such agony? Please, it is my eighteenth birthday. How can I spend it cloistered like a veritable nun!"

Katherine tilted her head with a long-suffering look. "Eliza, it would behoove you to remember in situations like these that 'always toward absent lovers, love's tides stronger flows.' If you want the men to miss you, you have to *let* them miss you."

Elizabeth wobbled her head in reluctant agreement then flopped back onto the bed. "This room is so *dull,* why do we stay here when we could be in the music room, or the hall, or the—"

"Wherever Sir Braxton is?"

"*Exactly!* Did you see his beautiful eyes? Or his hair? Or his, his— well, everything?" Elizabeth bounded to her feet, twirling around the room. "Oh, he is the most *beautiful* creature I have ever laid eyes on!" Elizabeth plopped down onto the vanity's stool and fanned herself dramatically.

Katherine smiled despite herself. "How can you fancy a man you've hardly met? You fall too quickly. Love is not a subject you learn with a late-night candle and the *Encyclopædia Britannica.*"

"Love is the most *interesting* thing I have ever studied. And surely I am falling—if indeed you may call a mere fancy that—no faster than you did with William."

William's name struck Katherine's heart like a broken bell. "That—that was different. We had much in common and learned that quickly from our discussions in a properly conducive environment."

Elizabeth's eyes glowed with the rhetoric of her studies, forgetting her sisterly kindness after abstaining from debate for so long. "As have we! I know that he is Lord Alcott's second cousin on his mother's side, that he has two sisters. That he loves the color blue, and that he has a tan horse named George. That's quite a lot considering that we haven't spoken—" Elizabeth's face changed from the hunter to the eighteen-year-old lover. "Oh, imagine if we were to marry *cousins!* You here at Alcott, me at Braxton House. Oh, the balls we would throw!"

Katherine exhaled the sharp remark forming on her tongue. Then, the ever-responsible sister continued, "Elizabeth, I remember the feeling of being swept off my feet. I remember nature herself aligning with the glorious light within my breast—the birds singing at night, long past their usual hour, when I heard his voice. I do not want to deny you of this untainted ecstasy, but I fear that Sir Braxton is more interested in teasing Lord Alcott than in finding a wife."

Elizabeth scrunched up her nose, conceding to Katherine's logic reluctantly. "Oh, well, I *suppose* that he might be a bit of a rogue . . . but such a *beautiful* one that it would be worth a *pinch* of heartbreak to get it."

Katherine smiled sadly and sat down to embrace her sister. "Perhaps a little heartbreak might be permissible . . . but please do not throw your heart away. It's too sweet to be trampled under the foot of man—or *men* as it seems to be coming about." Elizabeth nodded and Katherine rested her cheek on her sister's hair. "And don't pretend to be silly to attract men either. If they are only interested in what is below your chin then they do not deserve the rest."

"Of course, you are right, Kitty . . . though it would be easier if what was 'below my chin' was not so appealing to them." Elizabeth raised her eyebrows with an innocent look. And Katherine swatted her shoulder lightly while shaking her head.

"Oh, what will we do with you?"

A few hours later, the Misses le Chevalier descended the stairs in their evening gowns. A handful of other guests had arrived, but otherwise the meal was quiet. Katherine heard the others exchanging niceties and learned that one new young man was a cousin of Sir Rodney's and the two new women were friends of Lord Alcott's uncle. Despite his earlier comments, Braxton did not return to his discussion of "warming up" the ballroom floorboards and instead incited a game of charades.

"I say, you are a goose!" Braxton yelled at Alcott's poor imitation of an Egyptian.

"I, most certainly, am not!" Everyone laughed as Lord Alcott scowled at Braxton who had managed to both volunteer the lord to perform first *and* had stolen the lord's seat next to Katherine in the process.

"He is actually a hieroglyph, I should think," Braxton whispered to Katherine with a wink. "I always wonder why he bothers listening to me. But he always does."

Katherine struggled to maintain the cool dignity that she suspected would send Braxton away. "I have a suspicion that most people have difficulty denying your whims and fancies." *He is incorrigible . . . bordering on delightful.*

Braxton nodded with a thoughtful look on his face. "You could be right. Well, look at you reading me like a book, when I can hardly say I know a single thought passing behind those pretty eyes of yours."

"You flatter me, William—I mean, Sir Brax—" Katherine looked down at her lap, too embarrassed to cover her pink cheeks and turning redder for the knowledge that her color was so evident in the lamp light.

I let my guard down too much with him. I am being foolish

Braxton continued to watch Alcott's continued attempts at performing a hieroglyph speaking comfortably. "You flatter me with the comparison to your late betrothed." He paused for a moment and continued, "It is quite all right to speak of him. I don't think it offends the dead to be remembered fondly."

Katherine looked up into those bright blue eyes and felt the tightness in her chest loosen slightly. "Well, I was going to say that I know you are flattering me with tired lines, because for all the compliments and kindnesses my William ever shared with me, he never listed my eyes as one of my leading features."

Braxton leaned in, his perfect face far closer than was proper, and looked deeply into her eyes. "Hmm, he must have missed them in his calculations, among so many. Personally, I find them to be lovely." He sat back in his chair as someone had *finally* called out the correct answer, relieving Lord Alcott. Braxton applauded politely but made no move to return the lord his seat. Braxton spoke again, "Also, I should say that I am truly sorry about your William. I knew him only by name, but it was terribly unlucky of him to go, leaving you at the mercy of lesser men."

"Yes . . . terrible." Katherine's cheeks had cooled from her earlier blush, and now felt even cooler as a thin wash of tears covered her cheeks.

Braxton pulled a handkerchief out of his jacket and placed it in Katherine's hand. "Miss le Chevalier, why are you *really* out? I see that you are distraught, and I can feel the rumors stirring in the rafters, waiting to descend upon the party guests tomorrow. What would make you face such pain and derision as all this?" Braxton somehow looked more settled and comfortable in his hard wooden chair than the ladies in their cushioned ones on the corners. His confidence acted like a shield, distracting anyone from noticing Katherine's tears.

Katherine sighed. "I assume that you will share what I say with everyone you meet?"

"On my honor as a rumormonger." He placed his hand solemnly on his breast.

She sighed again. "I mourned my William's passing like my own heart . . . but family responsibilities necessitate that I accompany my sister to this gathering."

Braxton tapped his nose twice with his index finger. "Ah, yes. *Familial responsibilities.* Excellent answer. I will be sure that it circulates, but may I guess as to the full story?" Braxton brushed an imaginary piece of fluff from his sleeve as he reached it around Katherine's chair at precisely the moment Lord Alcott *happened* to look at them from across the room.

"There isn't anything else to—"

"Oh, do let me have a go—these *responsibilities* might somehow connect with Applehill's near apple-less station for decades, yes? And your William's untimely passing has the creditors—the wolves they are—howling at your gates and demanding payment on loans that were only extended because of William's standing . . . more or less?"

The color leached from her face. "And we must sell the title to survive, if I do not marry quickly. Does—does everyone know?"

Braxton's face showed only concern for a moment before settling into a bleak grin. "Do they know? No, only the ones with superior intelligence, like you and I. The fools think you to be either improper or callous."

The room suddenly felt cold enough to cloud her breath. *I am betraying my William, for this?* "Are you saying that everyone either sees right through my situation, or they think me a heartless monster?" *I suppose I am one . . . why should they not see it?*

"Not quite. There is the third, much larger, group who will only care that you are handsome, noble, and unattached, and it is this happy majority you must focus on. Focusing on any of the members on the fringes will only lead to wasted time and unnecessary pain."

Katherine wiped her brow with the handkerchief that had dried her tears. "Sir Braxton . . . I feel that you know me better than almost anyone . . . and from the first, I had mistaken you for the shallow sort."

Braxton's booming laugh sounded over the several discussions in the room, drawing everyone's attention back to Rodney's rendition of a sea captain, which it seemed Braxton was admiring. He affirmed their supposition with a shout, "Good show, Rodney, good show." Braxton winked at Katherine and whispered the next bit under the applause Rodney was garnering with confusion. "Oh, I am *mostly* a shallow fop, but one must have his hobbies. You are a work of art and I have long prided myself on being able to appraise a masterpiece in moments."

Katherine paused, seeing Sir Galloway taking the stage now that the crowd was warm. Then she turned to look at Braxton's face. "And . . . how did you measure me?"

Braxton tapped his nose again. "If I were to tell you that, I would lose all mystery and intrigue and would be nothing but a fop in your eyes once again. Thus, I will only say that whatever I saw, it was to your compliment and to the aggrandizement of my insatiable wit."

Katherine rolled her eyes. "How do you manage to compliment yourself so extravagantly even while complimenting others?"

"I am so good at it, why *wouldn't* I do a little for myself?"

Katherine actually found herself smiling.

Chapter 8

March 15th

The pain comes and goes like a branch scraping my heart's window, a gentle scratch suddenly shrieking into a scream with the tempests of my longing. At moments, I almost remember what happiness felt like, but these feelings disperse like the blowing clouds of a storm.

The weight of your passing does not crush me like it did, but that is because there is nothing left to crush. All that remains is emptiness.

I had thought the pressure of heartbreak to be unbearable, but this distance, this absence, is far worse. I am yours forever . . . but less of me remains every day. Less of the love I shared with you reaches my shuttered heart, regardless of the branches that scrape.

—Katherine, Milford Manor

The dawn rose as Katherine's stomach sunk deep into her gut. *They come today.* The guests, the ball, the stares, the whispers, everything that Katherine had been dreading would arrive in the next several hours.

I cannot delay any longer, she thought as she brushed her long, raven hair. *The creditors are hindered while Father is away, but they will descend upon Applehill the moment we return.*

If Alcott was willing, he seemed the best option—a young, rich lord interested in her since before she had met William . . . *but is his welcome only hospitality, or is he interested in a union?* Katherine imagined their wedding day in greys and ashes, her gown blackened from the soot of her charred hopes.

Could Father bring himself to ask for help from someone as proud as Lord Alcott?

Elizabeth's voice broke Katherine's reverie. "All right. You've been mooning all morning and I have had it with the silence." Elizabeth turned on her stool until she could speak to her sister face to face. "You may not want to share with me, but I already know."

"What do you know?"

"That Sir Braxton has chosen you as his favorite."

Katherine's voice cracked with distress. "Elizabeth, he has *not* made any such thing known to me, in word, deed, or action."

Elizabeth lifted a shoulder and let it drop. "Well, he *certainly* spent the whole night fawning over you. I, and likely everyone else, think that he is *sick* with admiration."

"Oh, Eliza. What must I say to convince you? I have not won him. My reluctant conversations and awkward manner do not seem much to his liking—and that is *all* I was able to provide in my companionship yesternight."

Elizabeth rolled her eyes over a smirk. "Oh yes, the *demure* and cautious beauty—like *that* has not won the heart of valiant knights for centuries!"

Katherine's sigh sounded more like a growl. "Elizabeth Ann le Chevalier. I have *no* intentions of winning the heart of Sir Braxton!"

"And why not? He is handsome, and noble. And he's astoundingly rich—nearly four thousand a year, and heir to another five!"

Katherine's jaw dropped. "How do you know?" *He's certainly more pleasant to look at than Alcott.*

"I asked his sisters—like any lady would if she were not distracted by the undivided attentions of the quarry himself!"

The games of the young . . . I am so tired.

Katherine looked at her sister's face. "I do not want to compete with you, Elizabeth. If you want him, he is yours. I can hide up here for the ball and—" *but I can't do that!*

"That's silliness, Katherine. I need you there. It's just, you are so beautiful and talented, and you deserve to be happy . . . but how do we both find someone when we're fishing in the same pond?"

Katherine stood, placed her brush on the vanity, and rested her hand on Elizabeth's shoulder like their mother used to. "You will meet more suitors than even *you* could handle tonight. There is no sense in pining over men that do not see how wonderful you are."

Elizabeth nodded and turned the rest of the way to embrace her sister tightly. "I am . . . *terrified*. How did you do this without an elder sister watching over you?"

"Honestly . . . I did not know what I was getting myself into." *And now the consequences are far worse . . .*

How am I supposed to dance *with this hanging over me?*

⌘

The Misses le Chevalier breakfasted in their parlor to save their conversation for when Lord Alcott's final *specially* invited guests would arrive for tea. When tea was over, the guests would sup together and then ascend to their chambers to freshen up to greet the guests that had only been invited to the ball that evening. Lord Alcott made a point of making the differing statuses of his various guests' invitations and privileges known to all he conversed with at the ball. Some felt that the act of elevating the few was benevolent, but if Katherine were ever to be the mistress of Milford, she would train that rude habit out of the lord as quickly as she could.

After breakfast, Elizabeth asked questions about several of the lords and ladies who would be in attendance, and Katherine answered to the best of her ability.

"Honestly, I met William so quickly that I never knew most of them, except in name."

Then the sisters left their rooms and spent time playing cards with Lord and Lady Blakesly who had spent most of their time at Milford reading in the drawing room or walking near the manor.

Lord Blakesly laid his cards down and looked at each of his daughters in turn. "A good father must warn his daughters to be wise before every ball . . . and a foolish father might believe they'll listen." He smiled. "And thus, I commend you both to the frivolities and spectacles that these events always contain."

It is so soon! Katherine thought, anxiety blurring the cards in her hand. *I must tell him . . .* "Father . . . about our conversation in the carriage." She watched his face to know that he understood. Seeing him nod slightly with a quick glance to Lady Blakesly's and Elizabeth's faces, she continued. "I wanted you to know that I will be seeking to enjoy myself to the fullest at this ball . . . and you have no need to fear for my position." Katherine swallowed and looked at the forgotten cards in her hands once again. *Was I clear enough?* She looked back up to her father's face. There she saw a painful hope, a guilty acceptance—gratitude—as he nodded slowly.

"But you shall take a few turns with me, to see me through?" Katherine asked, the panic only a little evident in her voice.

Lord Blakesly smiled, the sadness still shining in his eyes. "I would be delighted . . . but perhaps your dance card will be too full?"

We shall see . . . "There will *always* be room for you, Father."

⟳

The clocks turned round, and the sickly sun rose behind the dreary clouds, passing its apex and teatime arrived. Elizabeth had decided since arriving at Milford that performing her song for this larger, but still incomplete retinue would be the best. This was a positive strategy in two ways: first, it would draw less undue attention to herself than at the beginning of the ball when others were wishing to dance; and second, if she performed well, her accolades would be worthy conversation pieces the original party could share with the newcomers. *Of course, that would also be the case if she performed poorly.* Katherine chose not to share *that* thought with her sister.

The Misses le Chevalier entered the ballroom where the tea was set and Braxton called across the room, "Ah! If it isn't the Misses le Chevalier!"

His voice rang over the muffled din of polite conversation. "We missed you at breakfast."

Lord Alcott scowled at his cousin, then turned to them and bowed. "Indeed, we are pleased that you are here now with the others of my *esteemed* guests. Please take a seat and enjoy the refreshments."

With his host duties accomplished, he returned to his conversation with Rodney.

The sisters sat together—another plan of Elizabeth's in keeping with Katherine's "absent lovers" sentiment—and they noticed the three new gentlemen and one new lady interspersed among the previous guests. The lady and one of the men appeared to be married and the other two men were officers of the Royal Navy. Elizabeth sighed at the striking red coats until they turned, and she saw their faces.

Elizabeth's wistful glance changed for shock in an instant. "What a shame! I see why they took up the uniform—*nothing* else could make them even the least appealing," Elizabeth whispered in her sister's ear.

Katherine frowned. "Don't be unkind . . . " *I might have to marry one of them if they're rich enough.*

Braxton ended his conversation with his sisters and Galloway and made his way over to the le Chevalier sisters. He bowed over both of their hands in turn and brushed his lips lightly over the delicate skin. "The room is so dull without you. I was worried Galloway's voice would be the only thing I remembered forever. If I were to listen to his stories one *moment* longer, I swear . . . " He wiped the agonized expression off his face with a single pass of his hand, leaving his usual pleasant one in its wake. "Do tell me something funny?"

Elizabeth rose from her seat with her serene demeanor belying the gleam in her eye. "I wouldn't pretend to know what your refined wit would consider humorous, but perhaps *you* could share something with me?" And she took his arm. Braxton's smile turned curious as the two of them strolled away. Katherine looked at the sweetmeats and other refreshments, and with a warning protest from her stomach, decided to walk the room herself. *I don't much feel like speaking with anyone yet . . . maybe I will feel more prepared when the ball begins.*

It was unlikely.

So, Katherine wandered the ballroom, watching the servants coming and going with new platters of delicacies. *Perhaps I should find a chair near the pianoforte for Elizabeth's performance?* She turned to walk there and found herself standing before one of the officers.

"Hello, my lady, it is a pleasure to make your acquaintance." He bowed low with military stiffness. "Are you the Miss le Chevalier?"

Katherine curtsied. "Yes, I am, and it is my pleasure as well . . . Mr.—?"

"Beamsley, Mr. Beamsley of Southampton. I should love the opportunity to take a turn with you at the ball tonight." He smiled confidently and reached for her hand with yellowed teeth.

"That would be lovely. Thank you." Katherine curtsied instead of offering her hand. *Perhaps the uniform* has *gone to his head.*

He bowed again, seeming to miss that he had been slighted in the routine. "*You* are lovely . . . I should say." He smiled again, his eyes lingering on her face longer than comfortable.

Katherine sat in the nearest chair with a small smile and picked up a book that sat next to it. Opening it, Katherine pretended to read with her best "*I am finished with this interaction*" posture. Mr. Beamsley did not take the hint, seeming content to stand in front of her for the rest of tea, but Lord Alcott—a white knight in the rescue—and just as flexible as a suit of armor—appeared to drive the sailor away. Then he sat next to Katherine.

"I see you have met my other cousin. I hope that he has not asked for the last spot on your card? I assume that Sir Braxton has monopolized most of it?" Alcott glared cooly across the room at Braxton who was howling at something the other officer had said. "Both cousins are so brash and in such different ways. I do *not* know how we are relatives."

Katherine put the book down as she could not truly read it with her stomach in knots. "I do not yet know Mr. Beamsley," *and am not at all interested in changing that,* "But Sir Braxton has been incredibly amiable."

Alcott tugged his moustache in a rare display of frustration. "He seems so to any of the reputable ladies that he graces with his presence." He performed a seated imitation of Braxton's flowery bow.

Katherine's eyes opened wide in surprise. "Why, Lord Alcott, that was a joke!"

I wasn't aware that he could make jokes.

Alcott crossed his arms in front of him. "Humph. He taints everyone he interacts with." He rolled his head over his shoulders, as if loosening himself from Braxton's influence, then continued, "Anyway, I wanted to see if your second dances are taken? I should have requested the first pair but felt I need ask your sister . . . as she is, technically, the guest of honor."

"I should be delighted." She thought for a moment, *perhaps I need to assist him.* She sat up a little straighter. "I should say that I could spare another set or two, if you wanted them. As it is, the only one who has asked for my card has been Mr. Beamsley. Otherwise, I am completely *unengaged* for the evening." *I am sorry William . . . but perhaps it was too forward for his tastes anyway.*

Alcott visibly perked up at the knowledge. Katherine could almost imagine him wagging his tail. "Then if it is not too much to ask, I should love to ask you to save another spot for me later in the night, after I have fulfilled my other responsibilities as host." His dog-like brows raised cheerfully, and at her delicate nod, he nearly bounded off to the refreshment table, his sideburns bouncing like floppy ears.

Katherine sighed, the feigned positivity draining from her bearing. *This is wretched work . . . I feel such a devil.* The art of the wedding chase felt an awful lot like tempting the hearts of men. She sighed again and retrieved the novel from where she had placed it. She read for the rest of tea, keeping to herself in a comfortable way, accepting the dance requests from Rodney, Galloway, the other officer, and Braxton in turn. She would only have a few remaining spots for any potential suitors that would arrive that night, but she would be on better display for all the men in attendance twirling around the dance floor than tucked away in a corner someplace. *I must present the bait to catch the fish—oh, I shouldn't think that way.* Gaping, sucking fish lips were *not* the image she wanted painted in her mind as she looked at the potential suitors.

When tea was nearing its end, Katherine heard Braxton's exclamation above the clearing of the china, "Why you simply *must* perform it for us!

Well played, Elizabeth.

Katherine turned to see Braxton leading a blushing Elizabeth toward the pianoforte. Braxton handed Elizabeth down onto the pianoforte seat and backed a short distance away to listen to the performance. Elizabeth began with shaky fingers, but within a few measures, she grew more confident, and the melody flowed with the beauty the composer intended. One of Braxton's sisters sang the familiar tune quietly in a pleasant voice and soon others joined in. Katherine felt her throat tighten at the melody in the air. *I can't sing!* Mr. Francis had commented in one of their treatment sessions that singing would likely free her from some of her pain, *but I do not* want *to be free of it. It is all I have left of him—besides Ebony, I suppose.* She felt her eyes stinging, but hoped it seemed due to the music.

At the final note, everyone applauded, Braxton the loudest. *"Brava!* Lady Elizabeth! *Encore!"*

Elizabeth stood and curtsied, a pleased pinkness in her cheeks. "Oh, no, thank you for listening, but that is all I care to share for now." There was a general sigh of disappointment but then the conversations continued. Elizabeth beamed across the room and Katherine smiled back. The dancers would be speaking of Elizabeth's accomplishment the rest of the evening. *Her plan is working perfectly.*

The refreshments and tables vanished like a flick of a duster and the party glided to the chairs set before the musicians preparing for their evening performance. Katherine looked around at the opulence of the rooms, and the dazzling costumes of the occupants, her arm on Alcott's as it seemed to be with every little journey, whether through the wood or from one chair to another. The past few days had given Katherine an idea of what life would be like if she were to marry Lord Alcott—dry and uneventful, but comfortable and secure.

He isn't all that *unattractive, perhaps bland . . . and serious but not repulsive.* No, for a man as rich as he, he could afford to be a little less handsome, and to maintain his eccentricities of acting two or three decades his own senior.

"Miss le Chevalier, what do you think of the room?" Lord Alcott asked, directing his attention to her for the first time in several minutes, despite having her on his arm.

"Oh, it is simply lovely. I am sure that Elizabeth is delighted to have her debut in such grand circumstances."

"Indeed."

That is that, I suppose. Katherine closed her pursed lips, sealing off the next question she had been planning. *If he doesn't like talking, all the better.* She simply drifted along, glancing from group to group and quelling the memories of the night she first met her William.

The herald cried from the door, "May I present to you, Lord and Lady Gillingham and Lord and Lady Blakesly." Two couples glided through the entrance to find seats at tables near the corners of the room. Lord Alcott bowed from where he stood but made no effort to greet them personally. The herald cried again, and another pair entered. They were the parents of one of the officers and therefore Alcott's aunt and uncle. Other guests then began to arrive, their gilded finery and vibrant colors in direct opposition to Katherine's mood. The band tuned their instruments one final time, causing Elizabeth to squeal audibly from across the room, followed by Braxton's loud laugh.

"I suppose I should prepare for the first dance . . . " Alcott looked at Katherine for a moment. "Do not forget our appointment." He smiled his wrinkly eyed smile and strode toward his animated cousin and the guest of honor. Katherine held back from following him, melting between the gathering couples lining up for the dance.

Beamsley must have assumed that she was already taken for her first dance as he was lined up with a young woman who had only recently arrived. Katherine would have to dance with him eventually, but possibly, just for a moment, she could allow herself to remember what it had been like when she was happy.

She sat down in a vacant chair, a ways behind the dance floor and those gathered to view it, and she closed her dark eyes. She imagined the warmth in the air that summer night and the colors of the dresses when William had entered her life—his dark curls—his cerulean eyes. The entire room had seemed to clear the path between them as they flowed together like winds over the waves. They had danced more dances than was proper—some may have even thought them engaged that very night. Perhaps they were in their hearts, but it had not been made official until three months later. The remembered love bubbled up into her eyes and she felt tears form and cool in the drafty air of the manor.

"Ah yes, I had thought I would find you here." Braxton's voice materialized out of the milieu. "I fear I have done you a disservice. Has Allie thought to scold me by spurning you?"

Katherine wiped the unshed tears from her eyes. "No, he felt that as host—"

"He should dance with the youngest sister? Odd if you ask me." He smiled, not truly caring about Alcott's reasons, but ready to make him regret them all the same.

"We are scheduled to share some dances later in the evening."

Braxton nodded then looked out over the guests with a discerning eye. "Would you like the pedigree of each of the eligible bachelors in attendance? I would ask you to dance, but as this one is almost over and I have been on my feet rather a lot already, I thought I might share some knowledge if it could be useful?"

Katherine nodded, the memories of the first ball crushed under the more recent memory of a handful of dirt and days of blurred agony. "I suppose."

"Where is the cut-off, should I only name men who garner more than . . . five a year?"

Katherine lifted a shoulder in indifferent acceptance, sitting forward in her chair to prevent the slouch seeking to deflate her posture.

"Well, besides Allie and I, you have Galloway who barely squeaks by, and Lord Inglemere is a little better off than that, though he owes me a *fortune*. There's Sir Humphries, Sir Templeton, Sir Pembroke, and . . . " Braxton looked over at Katherine. "And you are not hearing a word of this, are you?"

Katherine shook her head, trying to swallow the old familiar sobs that she had been *sure* had finally left her. "I do not want to be *out*, Sir Braxton . . . " she whispered through her pain, fighting the whine forming at the back of her throat. "I do not want to be worrying about who I should speak to or with whom I am to dance with next. I want to be sitting on a chair at William's grave side, mourning for the rest of my days."

"My dear Miss le Chevalier, I know . . . I know." He patted her shoulder softly, somehow conveying the kindness of an embrace without the impropriety. "I read people nearly as well as paintings . . . and yours is a truly somber artist." He patted once again, looking out at the swirling crystal-colored skirts and dark suits. "But we do what we must. Don't we?"

Katherine sat up with an idea forming, desperation in her voice. "You are looking for a wife, aren't you? I know I wouldn't be the best company, but I would be true—I would keep an orderly house and I would—"

Braxton laughed his loud laugh, but for once the others in the room were having as much fun as he was and took no notice. "My Lady Katherine, I am sorry to interrupt, but I have *no* doubt that you would make me a *wonderful* wife. I am flattered by the proposition, but I am afraid that aside from some light entertainment, I would make for you a terrible husband—for reasons that I could not share with you without shedding my own tears." The bitterness in his voice on the last word was too much for even him to mask with flamboyance.

Katherine's stomach clenched. *How could I be so foolish? So daft that pleading for his hand would make him ever want someone like me?* Katherine's white lips parted, her voice the picture of practiced propriety. "I am unbelievably sorry. I was shamefully forward. I would only excuse my weakness by explaining that your apparent, deep understanding of my predicament fooled me into thinking that—"

Braxton shook his head, a smile returning to his lips. "I beg your pardon for yet another interruption, but you are, indeed, the *perfect* opposite to weak, my lady. You need not excuse yourself for *that.*" All gaiety fled his expression as his blue eyes pierced Katherine's very soul. "You sacrifice an enduring love that most people have never experienced to save your family. You are willing to give your entire self— your very existence—so that your smart, yet somewhat silly, sister can have her time in the sun, sickly though its rays may be in these troubled times."

Braxton leaned in closer. "No, my lady, but you are the *strongest* woman I have had the chance to deny my hand in marriage." He winked and after a quick glance around, he wiped the last tear from her cheek. "I am not yet willing to sacrifice what you have, which is why I will remain unmarried for another season and perhaps forever. If somehow you could wait that long, which I don't suppose you could, I would be delighted to discuss this option again."

Katherine nodded, her mind unable to accept the truth of his words, but her heart hoping all the same that they were true. "I am so deeply sorry to have embarrassed you."

"Please—no more apologies." He looked out at Alcott who bowed to Elizabeth as the musicians played their final chord. "I will ease off my disruptive attentions so that Allie may feel surer of you . . . his money is good, and he's not altogether, completely *in*tolerable. So, if that should work out, as I think *he* hopes it does, I wish you all the happiness the heavens have to offer." Braxton stood, dusting imaginary specks from his arm, then extended his hand down to Katherine. "Though, making him a *smidgen* jealous, just once more, would likely be more for your good than your ill." The mischievous twinkle was back in his eye, and Katherine had no choice but to take the hand and follow him to the dance floor for the second song of the set.

⌒◝◠

The dance nearly over, only the most dedicated dancers still took turns around the floor as others trickled away to their rooms. Elizabeth was one of this last stand, fulfilling her intention of dancing with every available bachelor—*and the handsome ones twice.*

Katherine had danced with a handful of the men, most of whose names she could not remember, and she had danced with Lord Alcott no less than three sets. Even the densest socialites had marked the attention he was bestowing on the pretty, un-widow. No one would assume a man as high in standing as he, to be engaged after only *one* extra set with someone of her standing, but it put a tired hope into Katherine's mind that *perhaps he might be the substitute savior for her family.* Mr. Beamsley had taken his promised dance, but Alcott had scared him off before he could ask for any others. Now Katherine stood in Alcott's circle, waiting for the night to end and for the blissful oblivion of a dead sleep.

"Now presenting *Mr.* James Sterling." The herald announced with less gusto than he had welcomed the sirs and ladies hours before. Even before the "ng" trailed off, a man of middling height with steely eyes and dark curly hair entered the ballroom. He was hours late if he was invited and dressed more for a formal event at the House of Lords than for a ball at a country manor—no matter how large or how old. The man walked confidently into the hall, barely noticing those in attendance except to bow stiffly when there was no other choice.

"Lord Alcott, who is this man just arriving? I do not recognize his name."

Something seems . . . familiar about him . . .

Alcott's back became even more rigid than normal. "That is Mr. Sterling—a man of business. I did not think he would come." The lord's words were dripping with derision, old blood looked down on the merchant class, *even if they made them more money.*

Katherine watched Mr. Sterling stride through the thinner crowd and onto the dance floor, obviously making his way to Lord Alcott's circle. He crossed the room quickly until Elizabeth, enraptured in her dance with a handsome young lord, twirled into Mr. Sterling in an exuberant movement. He stood firm, catching her before she tripped, but releasing her quickly. *Oh Elizabeth, you must watch where you are going . . . but then again,* he *should have walked round instead of through.* Katherine watched as she blushed and curtsied and he bowed back to her. Lord Alcott scowled almost as deeply as he did for Braxton at his most flippant disturbances, though this scowl lacked the familiarity.

Katherine looked back to see Elizabeth's partner tap her shoulder and she was back into the dance with a last curtsy to this strange Mr. Sterling.

How do I know him?

Mr. Sterling drew nearer, and the color drained from Katherine's face. *It cannot be . . .* but the closer he came the more the uncanny resemblance settled in her mind. *It is not . . . my William?*

The man named Mr. Sterling arrived at the circle and Katherine took an involuntary step backward as he bowed his first truly cordial bow of the evening. "Lord Alcott, I am deeply sorry for how late the hour has become. I had matters to attend to in Town and had to ride post all night and most of the day to arrive at all."

Katherine's frame shook. *His face . . . his bearing . . . even his voice! Is this some spectre from the shadows? An apparition?*

Lord Alcott responded reluctantly. "Indeed. Well, there is some music left in those musicians. Why not ask a few of the young ladies to dance?" Alcott turned back to his circle, dismissing the man with his posture.

But Mr. Sterling did not yet leave. "Of course . . . " He turned to Katherine who stood frozen, staring at the phantom of her William in cold flesh before her. Mr. Sterling addressed her directly. "My lady, I do not know your name, but would you care to take this turn with me?"

He has come to punish me. Mr. Sterling's steely eyes, locked with hers, waiting for her answer. She inhaled a cold breath. Katherine was being asked to dance by her first love's doppelganger. *My shame on the night of his funeral must have halted his travel to the heavens.*

She nodded her acceptance. *I must see what he wants of me. I deserve whatever retribution he brings.* Mr. Sterling took her arm and led her onto the dance floor. Katherine's vision narrowed, darkness creeping in from the edges. *How can this be? He died. I saw him buried!* Katherine stood beside this man, his glove still icy from his ride to the manor, all evidence pointing at a spirit returned from the netherworld. If Katherine could have noticed anything besides the man leading her away, she would have seen Alcott scowl deeper, or Elizabeth follow them with wide eyes as she turned with her own partner.

Katherine shivered and slowly looked at the man standing next to her. His cheek, though winter pale, had pink circles from the wind, *a sure sign of life.* The longer she looked at him, the more she doubted that this could be her William returned, and the astonishment at the resemblance grew. The brow and jaw were the same, but the eyes showed no habit of smiling, the lips no love of singing. He was as beautiful as William—perhaps even more so, for not creasing his visage with something as frivolous as a smile—but this man was not the cheerful man she had loved. *He cannot be—it would be impossible.* Katherine swallowed and turned her eyes to the floor.

Mr. Sterling knew none of what passed behind the dark eyes of his partner and spoke as any new acquaintance would with a pretty young lady. "Thank you for accepting my request. May I ask you for your name, my lady?" Mr. Sterling stepped forward and back in the familiar steps that accompanied this melody. Katherine's feet responded before her lips as she matched his movements. She became aware of Elizabeth's craning looks and dropped jaw as Katherine's thoughts began to thaw.

She glanced at his cool expression and had to force herself to ignore her nagging feelings of illogical fear to answer. "I am Miss Katherine le Chevalier . . . of Applehill Cottage, and you are Sir James Sterling?"

"*Mr.* James Sterling. I am the second son of a fourth son. Not enough titles to pass along to ones like me." No bitterness entered his voice as he spoke, though his movements seemed stiffer as he spun her around himself.

Noble born, without a title.

He continued, his movements loosening back into familiarity. "I understand from the papers that your sister suffered a tragedy recently. I give my condolences to you and yours."

"My sister? I think you may be mistaken, sir. It was I who . . . am bereaved." Katherine swallowed, watching for rage in the man's eyes. *I do not see it BECAUSE HE IS NOT WILLIAM!*

Sterling's eyebrow arched in surprise, much the way that William's had done. *Oh, please do not be William.* But a part of her wished to be punished by him, if only to be with him again.

"My apologies, and condolences once again. I met your sister and had thought she was the eldest . . . " His ears turned slightly pink, the only indication of his mistake. He continued in silence for a time, the two of them forming up with another couple to walk in a star, and so their conversation was paused for a moment. Then when they split, Sterling continued, "I hesitate to ask, but . . . are you not *out* a little soon after such a tragedy?"

Katherine's flimsy assurance that this was not the ghost of her beloved vaporized in an instant. *Surely, he knows that I had to—that I never wanted—that I would be true all my days if I could!* A little part of her mind whispered about a cloak and long walks with a handsome commoner, *that was not out of responsibility—it was to warm your broken heart.* But her terror drowned out these niggling thoughts. She gulped down air, her stays tight against her ribs as she struggled to gain hold of herself again.

This cannot be William's ghost! Lord Alcott knows him—they have business dealings. Still her heart cried out for William's each moment her hand left this stranger's and her heart sobbed at the coldness in his fingers each time they returned.

Mr. Sterling raised an eyebrow, waiting for her answer.

Katherine shook her head. *I must focus—I look like a fool.* "I felt that—that I must . . . fulfill my familial duty." The words fell flat as they left her dry mouth. *I promised to never love again, even though I could not stay single . . . but was that enough?*

Despite her discomfort, Sterling simply nodded once. "Just so. I am glad to have made your acquaintance." They finished their dance in silence. Mr. Sterling bowed and excused himself from Katherine to pursue further business with Lord Alcott. She watched him go, the cold fist around her heart loosening some as he left. Then she reached for the nearest chair before she fell in front of everyone.

Elizabeth hurried over to sit beside her elder sister in a flush. "Why do you get all the *luck!* The *handsomest* man of the entire night enters like a Moses, parting the room like the red sea and *immediately* asks you to dance?!" Another song began as Elizabeth spoke, her eyes riveted to Mr. Sterling across the dance floor. The young man Elizabeth had just been with, stood back a little way with an uncomfortable expression, hopeful to have his second dance with Elizabeth, but she didn't even glance in his direction.

Katherine grimaced at the fellow, and he left with a nervous nod. Then she looked across the room at Mr. Sterling as well. *Handsome . . . I suppose he is that, but even knowing that he is not who he seems . . . I cannot help but see an icy reflection of William's likeness.* She cleared her throat. "Did you not notice that he looked a bit like—"

"Like a prince from a fairy tale? Yes, and I *also* noticed his *extraordinarily* striking face."

Katherine shook her head "Not that. Did you not notice that he . . . " Elizabeth was craning to see who Mr. Sterling was asking to dance next as Alcott looked too busy to speak with him. *Elizabeth will not hear me until she has learned more about this Mr. Sterling.* Katherine sighed. "Oh never mind. Perhaps we might speak of it later. I believe you are missing the second dance with your last partner." Thankfully, Elizabeth left with a hand squeeze and a promise that they would discuss it later "before they did anything else." Katherine closed her eyes in the hopes that she would appear tired rather than petrified.

When I open my eyes, will this have all been a dream?

Chapter 9

March 16th

I have betrayed my heart. I have no words for the terror I felt seeing those cold eyes stare into me. I am so deeply sorry . . . but that is not enough to expunge this sin against your love.

And yet, I will not turn away from my responsibility—no matter how it tears me up.

—Katherine, Milford Manor

Elizabeth had been far too tired to pursue her promised discussion and so Katherine had helped her undress. Katherine tucked Elizabeth in even as her breathing had slowed and her eyes blissfully closed. Katherine shared her sister's bed that night, too shaken to return to her own rooms. Still, she passed most of the night tossing and turning, seeing shadows of a dance with William in front of a room of strangers. The sun rose its sickly yellow through the distant clouds and Katherine rose and packed quickly. She considered packing Elizabeth's things too, but that would be too presumptuous.

I must escape this place. I will feel so much more of myself once I return to Applehill. A quiet sigh from the bed witnessed to the now stirring Elizabeth.

"Oh . . . what a night it was . . . "

"Indeed. What a night." Little could two people have such different perspectives on the same events as they. "I believe Father would prefer to leave early, so if you would like, I should be happy to help you pack your things . . . ?" Katherine said, her hands squeezing the fabric of her outer skirts.

"Oh Kitty, you needn't ask to do chores for me. I am only too happy to oblige you." Elizabeth stretched and snuggled into her pillow in remembered ecstasy from a night of attractive young lords twirling sophisticated young ladies, such as herself.

It was daft of me to have waited.

Once they each had finished their preparations, they descended one last time to breakfast with those who had stayed over after the events of the previous night. All but the original party and the two officers had retired to their own arrangements, and so the end was nearly like the beginning. Braxton and his sisters were happy additions, with the officers as less welcome inclusions.

Most ate in silence, the extra activity and refreshment from the night before not all the way worn off, but Braxton was as chatty as ever.

"I think you performed a great work on old cousin Allie. If Lord and Lady Gillingham were not in need of his constant attention, I should think he wouldn't be leaving you alone to talk to the roguishly handsome ones like me," he said to Katherine.

Katherine merely nodded.

Braxton slapped his knee. "Don't be sad! We will see each other again." Braxton put a fist to his heart and an arm out in front like a renaissance painting of a romantic hero. "I shall see you at your wedding!" He returned to his normal posture. "I shall have Allie make me his best man. It is only fitting."

Elizabeth chimed in, "You mustn't wait for such an occasion to visit us! Surely you must come sooner." Elizabeth did not seem so smitten as their first meeting, but genuinely content in his company.

Braxton tapped the side of his nose. "We will see what the stars have in store."

Katherine remembered her impromptu proposition from the night before and looked down at her plate. "I did truly appreciate your company this visit, Sir Braxton. I will miss our conversations." Katherine swallowed a lump in her throat, the only thing she had swallowed yet despite the bounty before her.

It was nice to speak so honestly with someone . . . someone who was not also tending my horse.

Braxton bowed in his chair. "As have I, Miss le Chevalier, as have I."

Lord and Lady Blakesly descended to breakfast when the younger guests were just finishing, and so the party decided on one last walk through the labyrinth before they separated. Katherine saw Mr. Sterling descending the stairs for his own breakfast as she put on her fur. If she looked long enough, she could almost imagine his hair curling tighter and his countenance lightening the slightest, but in the morning light he looked less like the William she had loved so dearly and more like a cold, yet handsome, young man.

I simply cannot see him up close again, or it will unmake me as before. She turned, took Lord Alcott's outstretched arm, and left the manor for the last time.

An uneventful turn about the labyrinth completed, Katherine placed her fur on the pile in a footman's arms before Lord Alcott handed her up into the carriage. There she joined her mother and sister. "I think that I would like to stop by your cottage in the near future, to see what environs raised such an exemplary young woman." He smiled his retriever grin.

Katherine suppressed an inward sigh. "Why yes, of course . . . that would be lovely." Katherine smiled back the sweetest she could, though it didn't quite reach her eyes.

"Thank you for lending your fine daughters to this event, Lord Blakesly. They were sought-after company." The young lord bowed with his usual gravity.

"And thank you Lord Alcott for being our gracious host." Lord Blakesly returned the bow and entered the carriage. Elizabeth waved at Rodney and Galloway who each stood beside one of Braxton's sisters. Then she waved even more warmly at Braxton, who waved with a wink. Whether Elizabeth noticed Rodney and Galloway's uncomfortable expressions at her diverted attention, one could not say. Though the mischievous twinkle in Elizabeth's eye spoke of something. She only pulled away from the window when Mr. Sterling exited the house.

Elizabeth looked a little out of breath as she peeked around the curtain. "I don't think Mr. Sterling would wave back, otherwise . . . " Elizabeth pulled herself away from the window as the carriage lurched to a start. The family took to the road once again.

The le Chevaliers ignored the vistas they passed for the varied and sundry concerns they each had on their minds: protecting her daughters, delaying the banks, finding a rich husband, and finding a handsome—*and rich*—husband, bounced around the carriage walls like the passengers themselves on their way to the Denton's home—Lady Blakesly's sister and brother-in-law.

Mr. and Mrs. Denton lived in a quaint abode, their little garden with barely enough room to house their cow and two pigs. Though their cottage was humble, it was clean and though they were not well off, they were comfortable enough. In all honesty, they were to be envied by their "richer" sister and nieces, as the Dentons could live their lives with a happiness that only the unentailed and untitled could afford.

The road turned from hard-packed earth to cobbles as the carriage pulled up to the edge of town. The horses sounded barely four "*clip-clops*" each before the driver stopped them.

Mrs. Denton came running out of the house. "Oh, my dearest sister! And Katherine! And Elizabeth! Come inside before you catch your death!" And with the help of the carriage men, the three women descended the step and hugged their beloved aunt and sister.

Lord Blakesly descended the steps, bowing to his sister-in-law. "It is a pleasure to see you, Mary."

"And a pleasure to see you too, my lord—as always."

After the small talk and catching up were accomplished, the le Chevaliers shared a hasty tea with Mrs. and Mr. Denton as Mr. Denton had some matters to attend to down at the parsonage. He was the assistant to the clergyman and in line to inherit the position when the kindly old man passed on. Unfortunately, the head parson was blessed with an abnormally long life and did not appear in the least bit close to exchanging his earthly position for a heavenly one. Thus, the Dentons lived on in pastoral simplicity.

How would it be to have a life so unrestrained, so carefree? Katherine thought as she looked at the laugh lines lovingly creased around Mary's eyes.

That is what life would have been like with my William.

Mrs. Denton looked up over her teacup to Katherine's sinking expression. "I've felt so dreadful for you, Kitty. Would it do you good to visit with us for a few weeks? We could certainly make room, and Lord Blakesly must have business in Town soon enough to collect you?"

Katherine looked up with love. "Oh Auntie, that would be lovely . . . but perhaps another time." *I cannot find a rich husband staying here . . . and if I do not find one, we may be living here permanently before long.* Katherine sighed and looked out the window at the little sty.

Perhaps the pigs could move out.

Mary nodded, kindly. "Well, be sure that you watch for my letters. I am composing some in my mind already." She smiled her congenial smile and began to clear the tea. Katherine helped while Elizabeth looked out the window at the small town.

"What estate is that way up on the hill over there?"

Mary responded over her shoulder as she removed the dishes to the kitchen. "That is Limeridge Hall. It's a bit severe—old you know—but Lord Harlow is fair enough with his neighbors, if he is a little severe himself. They have their own parsonage. Mr. Denton reviewed it when we first moved here but it has practically its own entailment, it's so coveted."

Mr. Denton chimed in. "Not *coveted,* dear. Why, that would break the tenth commandment!" His eye twinkled as he took his last sip, placing his cup on the tray his wife held out to him with a vexed expression.

"Well, perhaps *other* clergymen need to read the commandments as often as you do." She took the tray into the kitchen as Mr. Denton chuckled. Then Mary returned and spoke to her nieces. "If you aren't in too much of a hurry to get back on the road, I could walk you to the top of the hill and we could see a little more of the estate?"

Elizabeth nodded and exclaimed, "That would be lovely!" She tilted her head and squinted at the ancient stones, speaking again. "Auntie, is the lord of Limeridge very old?"

Mary nodded again. "Yes, he is. I don't expect that there will be much there to interest you save the gardens and the house." Now Mrs. Denton's eyes twinkled. "But it would do you good to stretch your legs before the rest of your journey, in either case."

Elizabeth wilted a little but nodded all the same.

Katherine had seen the view before on her visits with her aunt but could think of no good reason to turn down the invitation. Thus, the entire party left at the same time—Mr. Denton to the parsonage, Lord and Lady Blakesly toward the small group of shops at the center of town, and Mrs. Denton led the young ladies up the old, cobbled road. Each step led them incrementally higher up the steep hill and soon Elizabeth was huffing a little to keep up.

"Aren't we walking a little fast? The estate isn't going anywhere, is it?"

Katherine breathed as deeply as her stays would let her, yet she found that she was barely winded. *Perhaps all that . . . apple picking has done me good.*

"It's not too much farther, but let's slow a little. I forget how steep this hill is for how often I take it!" Mary slowed and her nieces matched her pace, Elizabeth holding a stitch in her side.

Finally, they crested the rise and the estate's commanding aspect opened before them like a living painting of medieval splendor. Even in the dreary greys of the lingering winter, the verdure of the downs and the neat rows of crops sat so primly by the stately wood and river that the steel-grey mansion on the hill was almost a second thought.

"My, my . . . I had forgotten how beautiful it is," Katherine said, wonder in her voice. "What a tremendous sight!"

Elizabeth looked wistfully at the vision before her. "Lord Harlow doesn't happen to be looking to make a young woman his widow, is he?" Elizabeth asked, almost sounding like she meant it. *For a manor as stately as this, I could hardly blame her.*

Mary chuckled. "The old lord makes for a good neighbor, but I shudder to think of you as his wife, no matter how fast he left you in your 'widowhood.' The only things he loves are propriety, notoriety, sobriety, and his son and grandson—likely in that order, though perhaps that is unchristian of me to say." Mary fixed her apron and cleared her throat. "No dear, admire the grounds all you like, but that old widower is one I would avoid. He has quite the temper."

At least Lord Alcott doesn't have a temper . . . he doesn't seem to feel much more than irritation and grudging contentedness. He's so different from William—or Mr. Francis, for that matter. Katherine sighed and descended into her thoughts.

"Goodbye, Mary! Oh, I do hope you will make it down to Applehill this summer?" Lady Blakesly kissed her sister's cheek and took Lord Blakesly's proffered hand, entering the carriage.

Elizabeth hugged her aunt's neck. "Goodbye, Auntie. You will write to me if Lord Harlow's grandson comes to visit, won't you?"

"Oh, Elizabeth, he is not yet sixteen! He might be a little young for you."

Elizabeth shrugged with a mischievous smirk. "Well, if I'm not married by the time he's old enough—*highly* unlikely though it is— then *perhaps* I will consider him, despite being his senior." Elizabeth walked regally into the carriage, accepting the footman's hand, and waving like a queen before disappearing inside.

Mrs. Denton shook her head smiling. "She walks slow and plans to marry fast, it seems."

"Like many of her contemporaries," Katherine responded, embracing her aunt. When she went to release, her aunt hung on more snuggly.

"I pray for you, Katherine. I pray that your heart will be filled with light once again."

"Thank you, Mary . . . we will see." Katherine ended the embrace and entered the carriage.

Late in an already dark afternoon, the night conquered the sky quickly. Katherine feigned sleep to ward off the reiterated questions about who at the ball suited Elizabeth best—"Braxton was fine, but Sterling was *finer*." Elizabeth chatted to her dozing mother for hours before finally falling asleep herself. Then Katherine looked out at the dull grey ceiling above her and imagined what stars William would be telling her stories about now if he were here.

The carriage pulled to a stop in front of Applehill early in the morning, so Katherine guided her bleary sister up to their room and they slept well into the day.

⁓

For the first two days after returning, Katherine all but returned to full mourning, spending as much time alone as she could without worrying her parents. "Thank yous" and greetings from the ball trickled in by the day, a near constant reminder of her mission, but she wallowed in her sadness for all the time she still could.

The third full day at Applehill began with her descending the stairs as always and eating her breakfast. Elizabeth was preoccupied with the mountain of notes she had received via the sisters and female cousins of the men she had met, and Lord Blakesly was out early on business. *Probably related to my "promising" prospective suitors I told him about.* Bile rose in Katherine's throat. She was doing what she must for her family, *but if it only did not have to happen so soon.*

Lady Blakesly watched Katherine lift and lower her fork for the third time, and she cleared her throat. "Kitty dear . . . before the ball, you had taken to walking every morning and it seemed to do well for your constitution. Will you resume the custom?"

I suppose that would be all right . . . if mother is recommending it. "Why . . . yes. Would you care to join me? We would not have to go far, perhaps just through the garden?"

"I would only slow you down . . . " Lady Blakesly saw Katherine look back down at her plate and hesitated. "Well, perhaps I can walk the garden with you, and you may continue on without me afterward."

"Oh, thank you, Mother! Elizabeth, would you like to come?"

Elizabeth only shook her head, her nose almost touching the note with a finely flourished "R" on the back. *Sir Rodney, no doubt.* The mother and daughter accepted the warm cloaks placed onto their shoulders by the attendants near the door and the two of them walked round to their modest garden, seeming all the smaller after the visit to Milford. The buds had only just started to show, despite being so late.

In the garden, Lady Blakesly paused before a stone bench, but seeing the ice still sulking in its shadow, she walked on. "Katherine . . . are you all right?"

"Yes, Mother, the ball was truly diverting."

"I know your father well enough to recognize when he is concerned. Do his concerns have any reason behind why you went to the ball?"

She always sees straight through me. Katherine looked at her mother but didn't answer. Her throat tightened. *I will not cry again.*

"Ah. Yes." Lady Blakesly needed no other indication.

They rounded the corner, and the wind blew stronger without the shrubbery to shield them. Lady Blakesly wrapped her fur around herself tighter, and they hurried to enter the next section of shrubbery. There they came to a wooden bench and Lady Blakesly sat down immediately.

"Well, I do not know how you can resolve the bad luck and misfortune of, now, three generations, but I must say thank you for trying." Lady Blakesly lightly moved a strand of hair behind Katherine's ear.

Katherine only nodded, looking at the gravel as she sat beside her mother. They spent a quarter hour huddled together against the cold before Lady Blakesly excused herself. Katherine wanted to sit there forever, to allow herself to freeze solid and stop her racing thoughts and aching chest from hurting any longer. But an obscure force pulled her slowly from the mires of her melancholy until she stood and walked the frigid trail to the stables.

It will be good to see Ebony.

When she arrived, she saw a sour look from the stable master accompanied by a swipe at the young stable boy. Thom shook his head when she neared the opened stable doors.

"Welcome back, ma'am, but the black one is out. That horse doctor is walkin' her down thataways." He pointed vaguely off past the paddocks.

"Do you know when he should bring her back?"

The boy scrunched his face then shook his head. "No, miss. It's always different. He's usually gone by midday though, I think."

So, he will be here only an hour yet . . . Katherine turned away from the stables and the boy scurried into the warmth. Katherine repositioned her cloak and meandered toward the paddocks. *Perhaps it would be kind to relieve him of her. Besides, I should ask for the news of her treatment whilst I was away.*

She passed the two large paddocks, seeing six handlers leading around various unfamiliar horses. *Perhaps Father could sell a few of these. We never ride them.* Of course, they couldn't appear too desperate, or no one would pay what the horses were worth.

Katherine arrived at the third and smallest enclosure and paused before continuing. Her horse, *and its handler,* were nowhere to be seen. The day was cold, and each breeze reached wintry claws between the folds of her cloak and swiped at her stockinged ankles. *How did I ever manage to make it to the stables that night wearing what I was?*

Her cheeks warmed despite the cold, remembering again his arms around her. The agitation at Milford had mostly superseded that memory but standing there on the windy green she might as well be in her night clothes with the doctor's chin by her ear. Her thoughts stilled as she reached the old stone marker that signaled the halfway point between the cottage and the orchard, having still not met them. A little dirt road led off toward the village where carts of apples used to be directed to become sauces, pies, and preserves.

Perhaps I will turn back if I haven't reached them by the time I reach the orchard. Katherine's toes were numb but with the occasional unladylike stomp, she kept some of their feeling. That same force implored her to walk on, despite the discomfort.

Katherine walked on to the orchard, then through the orchard, and back out onto the green without seeing either Ebony, or Mr. Francis. The force inside her withered with the likelihood that she had somehow missed them, and she made her way back. She paused at the stables to be sure of her estimation.

"You there, was the black mare returned from her exercises?" Katherine called to one of the unfamiliar grooms.

The man frowned, it seemed to Katherine that he was as unfamiliar with her as she was with him. He answered regardless, "Which one are you looking for, my lady? The tall one or the filly?

I didn't know Father had two other *black mares. I suppose Father may have been searching for a replacement, in case Ebony didn't make it.* That answer did not sit right, given their current situation, but she did not know the estate's dealings well enough to say why.

Katherine spoke again. "I do not think it is either of those. There is a pitch-black mare with a hurt front leg. Did the doctor bring her back to the stables recently?"

"Oh, yeah. He dropped her off a quarter-hour ago and left. Said he had some business to attend to, but he'd be back tomorrow. He's here most days. *That* mare is inside to the left, down three stalls." He turned to leave.

"They have moved her? Why would they do that?"

"Oh, some of the newer stallions don't get on too well and they had to be separated—usual stable business." He walked into the stable and off to the right. Katherine raised an eyebrow at the dismissal but went to the specified stall. Ebony whickered when she smelled Katherine and butted her hand looking for apples.

"I am truly sorry, my dear. I will try to get some for you tomorrow." Katherine patted Ebony's muzzle and she whickered again. "Were . . . you well while I was away?" Katherine looked at the fresh bandage on Ebony's leg and was pleased that no blood was seeping through. "Mr. Francis is taking good care of you, isn't he? Well, it looks like we each took our walks separately today, so till the morrow, I hope you enjoy the warmth and quiet—" A stallion whinnied and kicked two stalls away, shaking the wooden walls several compartments in both directions. The kick was echoed by another across the way with another angry whinny. "Well, the warmth, anyway. Good day, Ebony." Katherine patted the horse once more then prepared herself to enter the cold once again.

"Miss le Chevalier, it is a pleasure to see you back safely," Mr. Francis said, walking out of an empty stall with his doctor's case.

Katherine stood up straighter, brushing at but failing to dislodge some of Ebony's hair from her skirts. "Oh, I thought you had gone." Katherine gave up on the skirts and looked up into his dark eyes as he drew near. *He really is tall, isn't he? And broad-shouldered . . . from tending horses, of course.* She cleared her throat.

Mr. Francis tipped his hat, acknowledging her words with a mirthful grimace. "Yes, I am rather late to a horse birthing in town, but in my haste, I managed to leave my instruments behind. So, I had to make a return journey and am thus, even later. Are you headed up the cottage-way? I have a phaeton waiting and would be delighted to update you on Ebony's progress along the way."

Katherine nodded and raised her arm habitually as if to offer it to him. She dropped it quickly as she realized what she was doing. She imagined the *preposterousness* of him escorting her up to the cottage for a moment, then spoke. "That would be perfectly—well—perfect. I came to hear how she is doing, but I never caught up with you—or Ebony." *Until now . . .*

Katherine snapped her jaw closed before saying anything else and nodded once to the smiling doctor, who gathered up his case and motioned for Katherine to lead the way out of the stable door. Her arm twinging, expecting to be escorted, left her thinking. *Why is it so wrong for common men to escort ladies? It is not more intimate than dancing and the servants' ball every year mixes the up and downstairs.* There always seemed to be roguish tales of noblemen marrying common women and making their wild fairy tales come true. *I suppose men just get away with more.*

Mr. Francis disrupted her musings with a question. "Did you enjoy your time away?" He spoke with a calm voice of a dinner party guest though he walked with the surety of a man with someplace to be. He seemed comfortable without permitting his conversation to be casual.

I would have enjoyed it more if I had found a husband . . . or if my dead betrothed had not visited me. She veiled her thoughts with a painted smile. "Oh, well, I should say that I did."

He nodded, an amused tone coloring his otherwise professional demeanor. "Are you saying that you *should* say that you enjoyed yourself, or that you truly did so?" He matched her pace, staying a step or two ahead so as not to appear to be walking *with* her.

"The second one. It was a delightful holiday." What else was she to say? *I have already shared too much of what I* actually *think with him.*

Mr. Francis smiled, looking on ahead. "I'm glad. As a doctor who once practiced on his fellowmen, I cannot help but check in on the guardians of my current patients. Old habits die hard, I suppose." He looked back over his shoulder with the same smile, but with a searching eye. Katherine remembered Braxton looking at her this way, but somehow, Mr. Francis's gaze was both briefer and warmer, like a beam of light through a morning window gone with the movement of a cloud.

He continued, "Regarding Ebony, she is markedly improved. She can walk much farther, though she favors her foot if she's out for too long. The wound is mostly scabbed over and has managed to evade infection, one reason to be thankful for this unseasonably cold temperature. All things considered, your horse is doing splendidly."

Katherine paused. "Do you think that she will ever truly heal?" *Can I?*

Mr. Francis paused as well, despite his schedule, and thought for a moment before responding. "Well, that is hard to say. There is still a long road for her to travel. I cannot, yet, promise a full recovery, but at the least I feel that your investment would be returned if she became well enough to bear foals. In my professional opinion, I believe it is worth staying the course with the treatment as she has responded well thus far."

Katherine nodded and looked down at the frozen cobbles. *I suppose she and I are the same that way . . . it is all right that we are broken, so long as we can bear children.* She tried not to allow the bitterness to overwhelm her. *Especially not in front of* him. "Well, that is something, at least."

They walked on, entering the courtyard one after the other. Mr. Francis bowed quickly before hopping into the awaiting phaeton. Katherine walked up the front steps but turned to watch the phaeton disappear as it curled its way up the drive. With him went a little of the energy she had found in her walk, a little of the hope she had renewed. Then she walked into the twilight of the house, leaving behind the dim light of day. On a whim she passed down the hallway and entered the music room.

With the ball over and the potential for demonstrating her fledgling talents again slim to none, Elizabeth mostly left the pianoforte to collect dust. So, Katherine sat down at the instrument and played an old ballad she used to when she was young, a song she would sing and dream of the man that would one day take her hand and her heart forever.

It sounded sadder now when she played it, but with the aching familiarity of an old friend—changed, but eternally hers. She played another song and another, her voice box tensing at the imagined notes she would have sang but remaining still. Tears fell silently down her cheeks as she remembered William's hand sitting softly on her shoulder. The weight she bore felt a little lighter for it. The magic of melody and rhythm, tempo and harmony, washed over her soul in beautiful waves of healing light. So long as she played, the pain hovered around the corners of the room even as the memories sat and turned the music sheets beside her.

The song reached its ultimate resolution as Katherine played with skill remembered after pain. Then Elizabeth came sliding into the room on her stockinged feet.

"Kitty! Rodney, Galloway, and *Lord Alcott* are coming to Applehill *tomorrow!* Oh, I have so much to prepare—will my Christmas dress do? Perhaps I should buy a new one—but it wouldn't be done in time! I must go tell Mother!" And she skidded out of the music room once again, leading away the peace that Katherine had been feeling only moments before.

Katherine exhaled, her worries taking their place in the now vacant page-turner's chair.

"Tomorrow . . . he is coming tomorrow." *If he should ask for my hand, I will give it to him.*

But never my heart.

Chapter 10

March 20th

It truly is a Wednesday. The weary weight of the week piles upon my chest so that I can hardly breathe. Lord Alcott is coming to see Applehill, and I do not want him to. I need him to—we need him to, but I feel the dread of it like a peasant waiting to be thrown into the colosseum.

I long for your smile—that would see me through these darkest of days.

But then it would not matter where Lord Alcott was.

—Katherine, Applehill Cottage

The le Chevalier daughters remained in their quarters past breakfast for different reasons. Elizabeth had not one but three handmaids helping with her hair, stays, dress, and perfume. Katherine sat and watched, wanting to be invisible as long as possible.

"Oh Kitty, *imagine* if they are *all* coming to *propose!?* We could both be engaged before the day is out!" Elizabeth had spent the evening reading their mother's gossip news from Town to learn all the newest etiquettes, slang, and flirtations. *She really should be an academic in the subject, her bibliography is astounding*

"Eliza, there are three of them and only two of us. Do you suppose that you should have two husbands?"

Elizabeth laughed. "Of course not! Though that would remove the difficulty of choosing" Elizabeth paused habitually, waiting for Lady Blakesly's scandalized gasp, but she simply received a giggle from the youngest maid before continuing. "No, I imagine that Rodney will best Galloway in a duel for my hand. That seems the most likely, the more I think of it."

Katherine asked on, recognizing one of her sister's daydreams and playing into it more out of kindness than actual interest. "What if Galloway bests Rodney?"

Elizabeth turned to Katherine so abruptly that two maids nearly collided as they tried to readjust. "Then I will have to marry *him* instead. *Unless* Sir Rodney is able to convince him to a tournament of three duels and then bests him on the next two."

Katherine shook her head, *that's enough whimsy for one morning.* She picked up a novel only to stare at the unintelligible symbols inside. The calm demeanor she exhibited for the maids and even for her sister belied the twisting concern that ate away at her insides. She could barely stop her knees from shaking, and the cold seeping through the windows was not helping.

Around luncheon, the sisters descended the stairs together and ate a belated breakfast, as well as either could with their nerves. It wasn't long after the tables were cleared that the young gentlemen were announced. Elizabeth leaped out of her chair then thought better of it and sat back down on the front edge, picking up a book to "read" with a fetching tilt to her chin, displaying her elegant neck. Katherine just looked at the ceiling.

"Presenting Lord Alcott, Sir Galloway, and Sir Rodney." The foot-man stepped aside and the three men walked in. Each eyed the small dining room with mild disinterest but all eyebrows raised at the sight of the two young women. The men bowed as the sisters rose to curtsy.

Lord Alcott spoke. "Miss le Chevalier, Miss Elizabeth, it is an honor to see you both."

Katherine nodded and spoke, formality ringing in her tone. "We are likewise pleased to receive your noble selves. Could we interest you in a brief tour?"

Lord Alcott and Sir Rodney nodded as Galloway spoke. "I should think it *would* be brief. And interest will be sparse. There is hardly enough house to tour!" He chuckled at his joke, and though the others felt similarly about the cottage, neither joined in.

Maybe Rodney could simply strike him down instead of dueling him fairly. Katherine maintained the calm face of the hostess even as she imagined Rodney's sword hovering over Galloway's heart. "Yes, well, right this way gentlemen." Katherine directed them out of the hall and Lord Alcott took little time in offering his arm to escort her, even as she led the tour.

"Here are the portraits of each Lord Blakesly going back five generations. This was the seat for an ancient duchy granted by the Conqueror himself. But that title and most of its lands have been distributed and entailed away, all that is left now is the grounds. The stables to come are original to the great medieval duke."

Katherine led them through the house, the kitchen, the court-yard, the garden, then down to the stables. Galloway was silenced by looks from Alcott more than once but appeared genuinely impressed by the size and utility of the stables. When even Rodney and Alcott seemed to be losing interest in the tour, the small group returned to the cottage. Sir Galloway made a point to duck as he entered the front door, though it stood a full foot above his beaver hat. He chuckled to himself again and Katherine was disheartened to hear Lord Alcott cough to cover what was likely a chuckle.

She then led them to the music room to allow Elizabeth to dem-onstrate her only other song, but Elizabeth insisted, with eyebrows raised almost to her hairline, that Katherine must have a go first. So, Katherine sat and played a popular song that Sir Rodney sang to with some ability. Katherine occasionally looked over at Lord Alcott, who sat through the first, second, and third songs with a thoughtful, and somewhat craving look on his face.

Perhaps all is not lost with him. He seems interested enough . . .

After the songs, Elizabeth piped up. "Tea will be served in the drawing room, if you would follow me." She should have let Katherine continue to lead the party. Still, aside from that little breach of con-duct, she performed the hostess duty with skill and prowess, things that men like Sir Rodney (and potentially Galloway, though he was showing himself the less gallant of the pair) looked for when spouse hunting.

Good show, Sister, I hope to be out of your way soon.

They entered the drawing room and found seats near the tea table. Tea was laid out by the servants and Katherine indicated to Elizabeth to pour the tea. She performed this domestic action with exceptional poise and Katherine was reminded that for all of the flighty thoughts she shared, Elizabeth had also been raised by Lady Blakesly and could show her mettle when the occasion arose.

"Would you like anything in your tea, Sir Rodney—Sir Galloway?" Elizabeth looked down demurely.

"No thank you, excellent biscuits like these deserve the honest leaf without any additions." Sir Rodney said.

Galloway made a face. "Excellent, you say? I would say *good*, or perhaps satisfactory."

Alcott rolled his basset eyes. "Galloway, not all fare can be as good as Milford Manor's. Perhaps you eat there too often." He stared with that sober canine look until Galloway gulped and looked down at his plate. Katherine appreciated the censorship, though saw that it did not in fact negate Galloway's statement.

I am almost ready to throw them all *out . . .* Still, she smiled and lifted the tea pot. "Thank you all for coming. Will your return trip be far?" Katherine poured another glass for Alcott who smiled at her dexterous service.

Alcott responded for them all. "No, not too far. We will ride to a friend's north of here to spend the night then head back to Milford in the morning."

Elizabeth paused with her biscuit halfway between her dish and her lips. "Did you come for any . . . particular reason?" She took the daintiest of bites, returning the biscuit to its place.

Mother's magazines, no doubt, said that hungry women are more appealing to men.

Rodney spoke up. "Simply to enjoy your company, Miss Elizabeth—and Miss le Chevalier." Rodney smiled. He seemed to be showing some interest in Elizabeth, even if Galloway seemed not to care anymore. Still, from each of the men's interactions over the past few hours, Elizabeth's prediction that both sisters might be engaged by day's end was looking less likely.

The men finished the dried fruits and biscuits before walking with the sisters to the entryway. As they waited for their horses to be brought from the stables, Elizabeth led the two sirs to the front window to point out the distant wood and to draw them close enough to smell her perfume. *Another magazine recommendation.* Katherine stood in regal silence with Lord Alcott, until he cleared his throat.

"Miss le Chevalier . . . I would be lying if I were to say that you had not impressed me with your abilities as a hostess, your accomplishments in the arts, and in your generally appealing . . . " She felt his eyes linger on her shoulders. "Demeanor." He cleared his throat again. Katherine nodded slightly, unable to move or speak for fear of disturbing what might be coming next.

Oh, please just get it over with!

Alcott hummed and mumbled a bit to himself before continuing. "Well, as you know, men get to an age where they seek companionship . . . someone to spend their days with and uh . . . their lives with." He shifted his feet, the regular stately rectitude replaced with the slow-moving discomfort of a hound laying on a pebble.

Here it comes . . .

"Well, I would be lying . . . I already said that part, but I would be lying if I did not say I was drawn to you."

Katherine nodded, a cold buzzing feeling at the base of her neck descending down her back and around to her collarbones.

"But . . . "

Oh no.

"I was speaking with my aunt . . . "

Oh no!

"And she reminded me that the year of mourning after a woman's tragedy fills at least two purposes . . . "

The cold buzzing pierced through her skin to Katherine's very heart, wrapping her in a cold panic—drowning in worry.

"The first being sadness, appropriately so, of course, but the second being a way that society can be sure that . . . well that there would be no confusion with, well, any future heir's . . . lineage—descendancy as it is."

Katherine's jaw dropped. "*Surely* you are not saying that you think I—" She couldn't finish the sentence. *The presumption—the insolence!*

Alcott blanched. "Oh, of course not—I am sorry to—well, I *know* that none of . . . well, *that* occurred. Like I have said, I have been very impressed with your propriety, given the circumstances."

"The *circumstances?* My lord, I would *never*—how could you think such a thing about me?"

Lord Alcott had never looked so uncomfortable in his life, but still, like a hound on a scent, he would not budge. "Yes, *I* know, but despite what I know, my aunt was right to say that *others* in society might *not* know—through no fault of your own, of course. But the implications are *completely* avoided if the full period of mourning is accomplished." He smiled at himself for completing such a convincing argument so articulately. He continued, "Therefore, I wanted to make you aware of my intentions, that I should be very interested in seeing more of you come February eleventh."

The cold gripped tighter around Katherine's chest as her thoughts whirled. "But my Lord Alcott, that is too long!" Seeing superficial torment in his eyes at her words, she added, "Too long to be—well, to be apart from each other, isn't it?" *I cannot wait until next year! I need to have been married already!*

Alcott patted her lightly on the hand. "Yes, yes. I know, I know. It pains me to say it, and I feel that the year will pass all the more slowly knowing that you would have me sooner, but it is what shall set us up the *right* way. And that is what makes it worth it."

Katherine's thoughts tumbled over each other, none of the arguments surviving the birth of her own counter arguments, every word vanquished by her feelings of defeat. Through the noise, she felt words whisper past her lips. "We cannot wait that long."

Lord Alcott placed his hand over his chest, as if Katherine was speaking from love and not from desperate need. "You must keep your heart guarded, and your mind firm. This little hour of loneliness will breed an alliance that will last a lifetime." He reached his arm to the ceiling in a near-perfect re-creation of Braxton's parody in parting the week before.

Katherine didn't have the ability to acknowledge the irony as the dread of the damage this foolish decision would cause mounted up like ocean waves, crashing over the bow of her feeble attempts to overcome his pomp with logic. The other three were listening now, but unsure of what was occurring, Elizabeth had her hands clasped before her in a forgotten gesture of excitement even as her head tilted in confusion.

Lord Alcott, now with an added audience, stood with an even stiffer neck. He lowered his arm until it extended toward her, and he spoke with more fervency than ever he had before. "To defend ourselves from the temptation, I ask that you send no card and make no visit to Milford Manor until February eleventh."

No hope . . . no way . . . nothing but to sink into despair.

He continued, taking her silence for feeling moved. "We will never need pass another day of Saint Valentine alone . . . here come the horses. I must go, excuse us, Miss le Chevalier." Alcott bowed low and strode out of the house with the gentlemen in his wake.

Katherine stood rooted for a moment, Elizabeth staring at her with a mixture of worry and confusion on her face. Then Katherine rushed out after them. "Lord Alcott! Don't go, please!" Her voice gasped out of her as sobs fought to take hold. "I cannot wait! We have to marry—please!" *You are my family's last hope!*

Alcott waved as he reached his steed, a joyful look upon his mustached face. "Keep your heart true! I will see you in eleven months!" And with a spryness forgotten in most of his usual habits, he leaped upon his piebald gelding and galloped off down the drive with the gentlemen galloping behind him.

Katherine looked on in horror as her only chance to save her family bounced and trotted merrily down the lane. *Where did I go wrong?*

She stood in the cold for what felt like an eternity before reentering the house past her dumbfounded sister. Her feet barely touched the floor as her fears pulled her to her father's study. The door opened before her, and Lord Blakesly lowered his paper.

"What is it, darling?" He rose from his favored leather wingback.

Katherine closed the door quietly behind her, turned around, and fell into her father's chest as the sobs finally escaped. "We are ruined! All is lost! Our only hope is dashed!"

Lord Blakesly held on tightly to his foundering daughter. "Calm yourself, my dear, calm yourself . . . Do you mean that Lord Alcott did not propose?" he whispered, trying to sooth her fraying nerves. "I had hardly thought he would so quickly—he is not a rash man."

Katherine was nearly too tired to speak, wanting to drift into the painlessness of sleep. Still, she soldiered on—*I must tell him before I faint.* "He all *but* proposed but insists on waiting until February eleventh to begin courting me . . . " Katherine felt her father's arms slacken slightly with the news.

"The assurance of his heir's parentage . . . "

"Yes." Katherine cried into her father's chest again.

"Ah . . . yes. I see."

This is the end of us!

"Father, what is left? I cannot find another wealthy suitor to marry before the debts are due—please tell me that Mr. Stewart had some luck with the London firm?"

Lord Blakesly lifted Katherine's chin, patting her cheek with a sad smile. "It would be my greatest delight to tell you that . . . but I have always tried to be truthful with you."

"Oh, Father . . . "

Lord Blakesly's voice warmed with a little seed of hope. "It's not all bad news. Mr. Stewart managed to get an extension until the apple harvest in autumn."

"The trees have not given us saleable apples for decades! How could we ever pay the bank by then?"

"Mr. Stewart knows, but London does not. It gives us some months to arrange our plans so we are not tossed out like common beggars." He smiled again and patted her cheek once more. "You have borne too much of this burden. I should not have asked you to. Return to your mourning in peace my dear—let your tears be for William, and not for your foolish father." Lord Blakesly pulled his handkerchief out of his pocket and placed it in her hand.

Katherine embraced Lord Blakesly once more, her heart longing for the freedom he offered, to bury herself in sorrow. But her resolve hardened within her. "Thank you, Father . . . but you will not see me in black. I still have the rest of spring and summer to find a husband, and I will do whatever I can to see it done. I can mourn when I have failed, or not at all."

I am sorry, William. Katherine wiped her eyes with the handkerchief and left her father standing alone in his study.

Katherine set about the rest of her afternoon with a resolution to work through her melancholy. She ate her meals with determined bites and reviewed her cards from the ball with unblinking eyes, seeking to discern any hinted regard written in the thank yous and well wishes. She went to bed with the knowledge that on the morrow she would begin to solve this ultimate problem. But the morning came, and breakfast passed with little added hope for success.

Her list of potential suitors was short, and the prospects discouraging, but Katherine responded with her best paper in her best hand, even passing the letters over her unstopped perfume bottle. Spraying the letters would be too forward—bordering on indecent—but the hint of aroma from a quick sweep would be a modest reminder of her feminine graces.

Sitting at her writing table, Katherine heard the door open.

"Kitty . . . are you all right?" Elizabeth was herself again now that the men were no longer there to beguile her. "Lord Alcott left rather abruptly . . . and you haven't spoken with me since."

Please do not ask, Elizabeth. I cannot hide the truth from you.

"Yes, I am quite well, Sister. Lord Alcott is insistent on keeping with certain traditions, and I am insistent that I will not. But thank you for your concern." Katherine turned back to her perfume bottle, stopping it before the scent all escaped into the room. Without looking back at her sister, Katherine continued, "Was there anything else?"

Please just go . . .

Elizabeth seemed to read her sister's thoughts as she began to back out of the room. "No, no there isn't . . . just, please do not carry a burden alone that you can share."

"Thank you, Eliza." Katherine sealed three short letters with the family signet and stood to leave. Elizabeth still stood outside the door, her brows furrowed with worry. Katherine smiled and patted her sister's arm, but the latter's expression only softened a little. Katherine waved the letters and walked down the hall.

Upon depositing the letters with a footman to be delivered to the post on the next trip, Katherine wandered to the front door and out into the courtyard. She had missed her appointment to participate in Ebony's treatment, so she continued off toward the hamlet for a change of scenery. Elizabeth didn't seem convinced that Katherine was well.

I can barely convince myself *that I am well at the moment.*

So, she walked through the aged trees lining the path to the village. They were still winter bare, not yet putting forth their young leaves. Katherine touched the cold stone of the low sheep wall, its familiar roughness whispering reminders of years walking this same path to the parish. Sheep grazed unconcerned of the bundled passerby and Katherine paid them similar attention, her eyes on the ground before her shoes and her thoughts elsewhere entirely.

Will any of them respond? Are they even rich enough to consider?

Katherine stumbled on a near-frozen wagon rut and was forced to observe her surroundings a little more. The sheep fields continued as far as she could see to her left and right, hugging the edge of the Applehill estate. Before her the small hamlet sat snuggled into the hillside and surrounding wood. The chapel bells called with a friendly toll of the half-hour mark and so Katherine made her way to the little stone church.

The garden surrounding the modest parish was smaller than Applehill's, but the parishioners kept it orderly. The parson here gave Katherine's favorite sermons of any congregation south of Town. *This is our home. How can we let the bank take it from us?* Katherine sat heavily onto a wooden bench at the side of the garden and stared out at the turned earth that lay waiting on better weather, fruitlessly, to be planted. Each passing day made the possibility of a successful vegetable crop less likely.

A voice broke the sanctuary's silence. "Hello, Miss le Chevalier. I don't mean to interrupt." Mr. Francis stood under the arbor entrance on the other side of the garden. "Ebony missed you today. I swear she looked over her shoulder every time she might have heard you."

Katherine covered her face to hide her quiet tears. *How does he always find me at my lowest?* She answered through her hands, "Hello, Mr. Francis . . . I am sorry to have missed it. We had some lately announced visitors we needed to entertain." Katherine removed her hands, hoping her tears did not leave streaks. Then she smiled politely and turned to look at the dull stones and the lifeless plants, a polite cue to be left in peace.

Mr. Francis either did not get the hint, or refused to acknowledge it, continuing with another question. "Was it a pleasant visit?"

Katherine sighed internally. *Does he not see that I am trying to be alone?* "Yes, it was—it was not unpleasant."

He smiled, nodding. "Good. I've just been looking in on one of the parson's ewes. He was worried that she had taken ill, but it appears that she simply refuses to eat turnip greens." He chuckled and took a few steps into the garden.

"How unsympathetic of her, in times like these." *I will likely be eating nothing* but *turnip greens soon.*

"Indeed. The parson was almost worried sick himself." He took a few more steps, pausing to snap a stick from an untrimmed hedge. "It would be an imposition to ask why someone is visiting a church outside of regular parish hours, so . . . how are you finding the weather this afternoon?" He smiled, twirling the stick between his fingers.

Katherine sighed aloud this time. "The weather is as it has been for weeks—dreary and unseasonably cold. As to your implied question. I was seeking solitude if I am to be honest."

Mr. Francis tossed the stick into a compost pile. "As a doctor who once practiced on people, I am always willing to listen, if that is useful to my *current* patients' owners?"

"I am sure that you are," Katherine said with a long-suffering look.

Mr. Francis took the hint the second time. "Well, good day then, Miss le Chevalier," and he turned to leave the garden the way he had come.

Katherine sat as the good doctor made his leisurely way out, but as he passed under the arbor, she blurted out the words, "He was supposed to propose." Her face dropped as she tried to stem the tears that cooled on her burning cheeks.

Mr. Francis paused and turned around, an indiscernible look on his face. "Is that so?"

Katherine wiped her tears as more fell, her shoulders rising slightly up then lowering quickly with her stifled sobs. She could act for her sister, and she could pretend for her parents, but she could not lie to herself about how she was doing. And for some reason, she found she couldn't hide anything from this man either, as words flowed unbidden from her lips, past her palms and through the frosty March air to his ears.

"All of our problems were solved. I had my William, and he had the rents we needed to save Applehill. Then he was gone, but then Alcott seemed the solution, but he will do nothing until the customary year and a day." Katherine swallowed the tears from the back of her throat. "And so I am, once again, without a husband to save my family—and the chances of acquiring a suitable one before summer is out are implausible, bordering on impossible. If I cannot do this, my sister's chances will be dashed along with my parents' living. I am the eldest. I should be able to manage this." She raised her head, wiping the tears from her eyes with the heels of her hands then placed them on her shivering knees.

"My mother and father have always been Lord and Lady and are not built for the labors of common life. If my sister is not married before our ruin, then all her prospective matches—all her undeniable beauty—will be for naught and she will die a spinster or the wife of some country bumpkin of no land or title . . . it is too much for one family to bear!"

He listened with an intent expression. "Certainly too much for you to bear alone—but did I hear you correctly that you are the eldest? I had thought that you were the second."

Katherine sighed. "Yes, I am the eldest. Though you are not the first to make this mistake." *Maybe that is why the stable master disrespects me*

Mr. Francis's brows furrowed, a worried look taking over. "I meant no disrespect . . . " He hesitated, likely waiting for some further reprimand, but seeing Katherine look up at the bells chiming the hour, he continued. "About the other matters, I've long appreciated the adage, 'It is always darkest just before the day dawneth.'"

Katherine turned her head and looked at Mr. Francis with tired eyes. "How apt that you quote a theologian at a church. I want to believe it, but when do I know I have reached the dregs? Or that things are indeed as dark as they will get? If I was assured that *this*, everything we've been through, was the worst, then perhaps the adage would bring me peace. But the hope of the rising light is only more pain when the night lingers on—like this blasted winter and our continuing trials."

Mr. Francis nodded. "What you say is true. My adage does not solve any of your problems—but I still believe that hope is worth the pain. I feel that you will see Providence bless your efforts as you continue in your hopes . . . but then again I'm a doctor, not a parson."

Katherine let her head drop. *Hope is worth the pain?* She slowly looked back up at his inviting face. "Why are you here, Mr. Francis? You must have understood that I wanted to be alone—so why do you teach me these garden sermons?

A fervent look grew on his face, a resolution forming behind his eyes. "Well . . . it is because I luh—"

The old parson walked quickly into the garden, interrupting Mr. Francis. "Oh, *there* you are! I wanted to be sure to pay you before sunset, as the Bible states, 'Thou shalt give him his hire, neither shall the sun go down upon it,' Deuteronomy 24:15." He chuckled and counted out a shilling and a few pence while humming a hymn. He turned and saw Katherine. "Why, Miss le Chevalier! What a pleasure. Were you in need of anything?"

Katherine shook her head, feeling exposed for some odd reason, like the parson had walked in on a secret. "No thank you, Father. I am only here for some solitude." *What was Mr. Francis about to say?*

"Just so. Well, I had best be off then—I must prepare a sermon for the Sabbath!" The little man left the garden with a heavy silence that his disappearing humming could not penetrate.

Katherine cleared her throat, her eyes locked with Mr. Francis's. "What . . . what was it you were going to say?" *Surely it was not—*

Mr. Francis's regular charm was back, no sign of the fervency remained. "Oh, I was only going to say that I looked over here and it seemed like you might need some help."

Something about his words fell flat. They were not insincere, but they felt incomplete, *unsatisfying.* "You needn't worry about me. I am not your patient. You do not care for me."

Mr. Francis smiled, something akin to sadness touching his eye, then he shrugged. "Oh, well perhaps you are right. A *common* horse doctor isn't the right man to care for one such as yourself . . . but, like I said, I am always willing to lend a listening ear." With that the young doctor bowed low and turned, making his way slowly out of the sleeping garden. As he passed under the arbor, he paused and spoke without turning around. "I would not presume to expect you, but if you happened to be on your stroll tomorrow around 10 o'clock, we might cross paths." Then he exited the garden.

Katherine watched him go, a strange confusion within her breast. *Why is that man wherever I am when I most need someone to talk to . . . to hold on to?* She fumbled through these new perturbations, struggling to sort her earlier sadness from this *other* emotion rooted inside her. Then she rose slowly, a familiar pull drawing her steps along the path that Mr. Francis had taken. She paused under the arbor and peered out, *to be sure that he was not standing just around the corner, speaking with the parson.* She looked left and right, seeing nothing but the cobbled street and the thatched roofs of the town—no sign of the young doctor.

And somewhere deep down, she felt *disappointed.*

Chapter 11

March 22nd

Some days are better than others . . . but what "better" means is never the same. Occasionally I can smile, and other times I can speak. Still others, I feel that I pay the balance of those "better" days with tears and cries. How I wish you were here.

Old pains, with their deep ruts and sodden tracks through my heart, dry up only for new pains to replace them. The journey continues every morning, no sign of ending—no horizon past the clouds of my misery. I trudge on with little hope of anything more than this forever.

Could hope truly be worth the pain?

—Katherine, Applehill Cottage

Each day that passed was one day closer to the end of the world. Lord Blakesly's apocalyptic newspapers did not touch Katherine's terror at what would happen to her family. She tried to hide her fear, never crying where anyone could see her, clenching her shaking hands in her skirts when others passed. Still, life continued. Elizabeth received a near ream of notes each morning, and the occasional indistinct, and disinterested cards came for Katherine. Nothing spoke of potential suitors.

Katherine walked toward the music room after breakfast as Lord Blakesly was seeing Mr. Stewart and Mr. Banks out of the cottage.

Katherine waited, thinly masked anxiety gnawing at her chest. When her father returned to his study, she asked in a whisper, "Are there any developments, Father? Is there any chance for another extension?"

He only patted her cheek, his eyes sorrowful. "Isn't it time for your morning walk?"

"Well—I, I suppose it could be . . . "

"Very well, see to that and I should like one of those sorry excuses for an apple to gnaw on if you should happen across one." He smiled as he closed himself into his study, his eyes remaining unchanged.

"Yes, Father," she said to the closed door before turning to the entryway and the morning cold.

Perhaps I should only walk the garden, I just saw Mr. Francis at the parsonage and . . . She felt almost as ashamed of her behavior for this most recent encounter as the first. *He must think me an utter fool.* Despite her thoughts, she continued the familiar path down to the stables.

After the familiar bite of the March air and the same murky light from the obscure sun, Katherine walked into the stables without needing to ask the bustling grooms where to go. She walked down the stalls reading the chalk names scratched onto slates hanging by each gate. *Swindler—tawny gelding . . . Midnight—grey mare . . . St. Vincent—white stallion . . . Madeira, roan gelding . . .* she read down the aisle until she came to *Stormy—lame.*

"Humph." Katherine shook her head in irritation, the curls by her temples flicking like a cat's tail. Then she walked back to the records table near the door to retrieve a cloth and chalk, her back stiff with distaste for her horse's treatment . . . and *a little* that she hoped the stable master wouldn't be there to ask what she was doing.

Returning to the stall, she erased the disparaging monikers and replaced them with "*Ebony—black mare.*" Tilting her head at her careful script, she smiled. "If the grooms are going to ignore you, at least they can think of you by your name."

"I agree."

Katherine swallowed a squeak and turned to see Mr. Francis standing with his hands clasped behind his back, admiring her handiwork.

He stepped forward, maintaining his inspecting stance—like a lord reviewing a painting. "I changed it once, but the stable master commented that I might be willing to 'waste my time on a lame horse,' but he wouldn't be wasting chalk on getting its name right. I had thought chalk was rather inexpensive, but I am just a doctor, not an *Adam Smith*."

Katherine nodded, not trusting her voice enough to speak. *He does look noble when he stands like that . . .* She shook her head slightly and cleared her throat. "Hmm, well, I should hope that he will at least heed the eldest child of his lord, if not your doctor's orders." She went to return the chalk, but he stepped slightly forward, his proximity stopping her.

"May I return that for you?"

Katherine suddenly felt that the cool stables were *perhaps just a little stuffy.* She held her skirts to prevent pulling on her collar. "Y-yes, please do," and she placed the chalk and cloth into his two extended hands, watching him walk briskly to the table. Her fingertips pulsed through her gloves where they had touched his palms, and she rocked once on her heels, nervously. She stopped herself before rocking again. Her governess had scolded her out of that behavior before she had turned twelve. *Why must I feel so out of sorts when he is near?*

Before Katherine could answer her own question, Mr. Francis returned with a smile, a saddle, and other riding tack. "I thought it might be good to equip her for the next few sessions, so she does not forget how to carry it." Mr. Francis walked carefully around Katherine, opening Ebony's gate. The mare clip-clopped a few steps forward, revealing her dark face. At the sight of the saddle, she whinnied and backed herself quickly into the corner with a hobble.

Mr. Francis placed the saddle carefully on the ground, raising both hands before him in a calming gesture. "It's okay, beautiful . . . It's all right, Ebony. I won't be riding you today . . . this is all you will carry . . . " He picked up the heavy equipment, squeezing it under one arm with ease. Then he approached her slowly, crouching lower than his substantial height, keeping one calming hand forward. As he drew close, Ebony made a weak kick, scuffing the grey wood and causing it to show its blond self beneath. Mr. Francis paused and spoke without turning back. "Miss le Chevalier, would you speak to your horse while I prepare to put the saddle on?"

Katherine caught her breath, as nearly under his soothing spell as Ebony. "I am willing . . . but is it safe? She seems to be discontent."

"She will not harm you or me, but she could harm herself if we are not gentle."

"Well, all right then." Katherine mimicked Mr. Francis's hand gesture and walked slowly into the stall a little behind him. The floor was surprisingly clear of any unsavory debris. *Did he come early to prepare this for me?* Still, she took another step forward and looked into Ebony's eye.

Katherine placed her hands lightly underneath Ebony's muzzle, feeling the mare quiver as her eyes rolled back toward Mr. Francis. "What should I do? She is terribly frightened."

Mr. Francis's voice dropped to a whisper, causing Katherine to lean toward him as he stated, "Speak to her like you would a child that has lost her way. Stroke her cheek and tell her everything will be all right. After that, you can tell her whatever you like, just be sure to keep your tone smooth and soothing." He watched Katherine lightly rub Ebony's cheek then nodded. "Just like that—once she is ready, I will give you the word to lead her out of the stall like you have led her before, but keep her focus on you until then."

Katherine lowered back down onto her heels and looked back into Ebony's eye. "Well hello, Ebony, lovely girl. I am here to tell you that everything will be all right. The doctor cares for you and will be sure to keep you safe." Katherine's eyes flicked up to where Mr. Francis was slowly raising the saddle high enough to lower lightly onto Ebony's back. The muscles in his arms and shoulders strained under the controlled lift, but his face did not reveal significant exertion. *Will his sleeve burst?*

Mr. Francis's eyes met hers and Katherine looked back at Ebony. "I—well I just improved your name plate. It had you listed as lame, which I think is both rude and increasingly untrue. A pretty lady such as you should have the right name on her dance card, after all." Ebony whickered and her eye rolled back toward Mr. Francis as he finally lowered the saddle into place, but Katherine rubbed her forehead and kept talking.

"For all the apples you've eaten out of my hands, I feel that we are not too well acquainted . . . so," Katherine performed a slight curtsey.

"It is a pleasure to meet you at this fine equestrian establishment. I am not sure if you were aware, but I am indeed Lord Blakesly's *eldest* daughter. I have a sister named Elizabeth and no brothers or cousins to speak of. I know, it is not ideal, given common entailment practices but we had a way worked out until . . . well, perhaps you know more of that than even I do. So, we will speak of something else . . . "

Katherine looked back as Mr. Francis reached under Ebony for the strap. The horse stomped a back hoof, but Katherine held the reins and continued in soothing tones.

"Mr. Francis believes in you, and you have been taking your treatment so very well. If I were your governess, I would give you full marks on your studies. This is merely the next step, and you will do marvelously. Mr. Francis will see to it, if my name isn't Katherine le Chevalier."

Mr. Francis nodded to Katherine. "All right now, lead her out slowly."

Katherine stepped backwards, keeping Ebony's eye locked on her own as Mr. Francis tightened the belly strap a little at a time. As they neared the gate to exit into the aisle, Mr. Francis threaded the belt's needles through the holes in the leather and walked forward like every other walk they had been on. Katherine led Ebony calmly right out of the stables.

"Should we head to the orchard? Or where were you hoping your walk would take you this fine morning?" Mr. Francis walked with the same stately posture as before, looking out over the greens and greys.

"I think Ebony deserves at least *one* apple for her patience," Katherine said.

"Then lead the way, my lady." Charles directed forward with a bow.

Katherine nodded and led Ebony down the aisle and out onto the pavement. She walked with her arm holding the reins down at her side, while Mr. Francis walked off to her right, close enough to be nearby, but not so close as to be escorting her. Glancing over at the young doctor, Katherine's mind saw a brief image flash through her mind of her arm wrapped snugly in his as they walked through the green. She looked ahead, down the cobbled road as far as she could see and felt the cold wind carrying off the heat from her cheeks.

Over the subsequent days, their walks saw them sometimes silent and sometimes speaking, discussing memories, philosophy, and music. Mr. Francis learned that Miss le Chevalier was not fond of the little lap dogs common among ladies of high standing, but rather of the hunting dogs her father kept. Katherine learned that Charles was an accomplished fencer from his time at Oxford and an amateur composer. Katherine found that on the days she went on her walks, the weather and her memories did not pain her as much.

Each day they seemed to meet a little earlier and walk a little longer—always for Ebony's benefit, of course. This morning was no different, seeing Katherine hurrying to the orchard with the sun barely over the trees. She had scoured most of the branches for remaining fruit and was now forced to glean the edges that had been passed over even when the trees were healthy.

So with only a few small apples, she stepped lightly onto the green from the path, a smile forming on her lips. "Hello Mr. Francis, it is a pleasure to be seeing you."

He smiled and the sun seemed a little brighter through the drab clouds. "Yes, it is always a pleasure to cross paths with you . . . " He passed the reins to Katherine, his hand lingering on the leather strap for an extra moment. He waited for Katherine to begin leading Ebony then he followed. "You know, you needn't call me Mr. Francis. You may call me Charles, if you like." Before she could speak, he added, "You call your other attendants by their names, after all."

Katherine pressed her hand against the fluttering in her stomach, then smoothed the fabric to cover it. "But you are not one of my attendants."

"I am, of a sort. Perhaps not *exactly* like one of your attendants . . . "

Katherine looked forward as she considered his argument. "*Mr.* Charles then . . . that would still be proper, yes?" Her blithe expression was betrayed by the question in her voice.

He smiled and nodded, then asked lightly, "And may I, perchance, call you Miss Katherine . . . like one of those attendants?"

Katherine's back stiffened at the impropriety . . . but hearing her name on his lips *did* set her chest humming. She swallowed. "I am not sure if that would—" She stopped herself.

Many of the maids call me that already and even Mr. Banks does on occasion . . . She stopped walking, turned resolutely, and said, "Yes, I suppose that would be acceptable." She nodded once and turned back around, hoping that *Mr. Charles* would attribute her trembling to the weather.

Chapter 12

April 13th

I do not much feel like writing this morning. The clouds hide the sun, and what little peeks through the heavy gray curtains gives no warmth. If not for Ebony's treatments I feel that I would simply return to bed and wait for a new day.

—*Katherine, Applehill Cottage*

Katherine chewed her scone with little vigor, the jelly adding flavor that her tongue didn't register. It was early for tea, but it was a welcome warmth against the drafts that snaked their way into the manor from door cracks and window seams. Elizabeth looked nearly as miserable, as she had slept poorly and barely managed to get dressed and prepared to breakfast with everyone else.

"Elizabeth, are you quite well?" Lady Blakesly asked with a look at Elizabeth's barely brushed hair and somewhat wrinkled gown. "You appear as if you were waylaid by vandals."

Elizabeth's face remained somber as she sat straighter in her chair. "Perhaps I was mother, in a way. I had a horrible dream that Sir Galloway and Sir Rodney had fought a duel over me." Elizabeth paused, a dramatic rise to her brow as she waited for someone to ask more about it.

Katherine sighed but was smiling all the same. "I thought you said that you *hoped* that they would duel, and that you would marry the victor?"

"Yes, but seeing it was absolutely *horrid!* All the most handsome young men tried to speak to me—Mr. Sterling, Sir Braxton, and more—but whenever *they* tried, Galloway and Rodney took turns destroying each of them to the last. Finally, when only the two remained, I walked toward them and then they rammed their sword into the other's breast." Elizabeth mimed the action, a glint in her eye betraying her supposed disturbance at the vision. "I was left all alone in a ballroom with dozens of beautiful corpses that—"

"That is quite enough for the breakfast table, my dear." Lord Blakesly had been reviewing his mail on the platter borne by a footman but had heard enough of the dream to comment. "You will have plenty of young men battling over you in the wakened world to satisfy even your most bloodthirsty affections. Perhaps, we might eat together in peace for now?" He smiled kindly, despite the strength of his words.

Elizabeth sighed. "Yes Father . . . " She lifted her fork. "At least something *happened* in my dream, pleasant *or* unpleasant. *Nothing* exciting ever happens here, good or bad."

If only you knew. I hope that your lack of prospects does not prove prophetic.

Katherine walked in silence as Mr. Charles led Ebony behind them. Some days were gloomier than others, but however she was when she came, Mr. Charles always knew how to lighten her proverbial skies— if the ones above maintained their dour appearance.

"Mr. Francis . . . " Katherine hesitated, unsure of what she had wanted to share, but knowing that she wanted to converse.

"Call me Charles if you would, Miss Katherine—or Mr. Charles . . . but yes?"

She paused a moment longer. "Do you think this winter will ever end?" *The weather? Can I not think of something other than the weather?*

"They always do, sooner or later. I don't expect that we will *never* see the warmth again." Ebony whickered, pausing him mid step. Then he continued up to where Katherine had paused waiting for him.

Katherine began walking again. "But what if these are truly the last days, and everything is coming to an end?" *An end of ice instead of fire.* A wave of sadness flowed into her heart as she turned to look up the green to Applehill Cottage, its old trees swaying in front of the winter-waiting ivy. *Even if the world doesn't end, this life of ours will.*

Charles extended his hand to her with that same look on his face that he had when the parson interrupted. Katherine's eyes left his and fell to his hand, as she took a step back. Even with her retraction, he held it out like a sailor ready to pull his shipmate out of the raging sea.

His hand left her hovering like a compass needle between two magnets, one pulling her forward and the other back. The tension tore at her heart as she held her hands together, preventing them from darting into his awaiting palm.

Before she could speak, Charles's expression changed to his usual jovial smile. "Let us continue up to the garden today," he gestured with his outstretched hand, as if he was only ever pointing the way.

Perhaps it was *only in my mind . . . he* would *think it improper to hold a lady's hand . . . ? Either I misunderstand him, or I understand him too well.* Katherine nodded quickly and turned toward the garden before the color of her cheeks rose to a beacon in brilliance.

After only a few steps Katherine stopped dead and turned again. "Mr. Francis—"

"You know to call me—"

"Mr. *Francis*, I speak to you as one knowing my family's situation, and you *know* that my father should not be spending the money he must be on his horses—even if it is for his daughter . . . " An old pain renewed splintered in her chest as tears rose in her eyes. "On your word as a doctor, do you *truly* believe that she is worth it?" Katherine's tears fell as she looked at Ebony staring out into the wind.

"Miss Katheri—Miss *le Chevalier,*"

Hearing him almost say her name again sent chills down her trembling back.

"I believe *she* is worth it all and more. She has heart, and more strength than even she knows. Though she has been hurt, I see her improving every day." He spoke without letting his eyes fall from Katherine's. He concluded in a near whisper, barely audible over the early April breeze. "I wouldn't miss a chance to see her for the world."

Katherine paused, enraptured by the moment, tingles spreading through her entire body. A few loose strands of her black hair flew on the wind that played with the hem of his jacket. Despite the space between them, they breathed the same air.

Ebony whickered and stomped, eager to continue, and the moment was gone. Katherine coughed and turned toward the garden, forcing down the same insistent feelings.

Nothing has happened. But something had. *We've done nothing wrong . . .* but why did she feel like she was lying to herself? *William is still . . . he is still . . .* Katherine couldn't finish the thought.

Charles—*Mr. Francis*—seemed content to track the wind's touch on the leaves and the grass as it flew out over the green, so they walked again in silence. The pair, now with the mare between them, meandered up the green, the wintry hedges rising to meet them until they could enter the sparse cover of the bare branches. Still, they walked in silence, Katherine unsure if she could ever broach the divide.

Mr. Francis looked around at the sad, freezing stalks and cold-blasted buds dead on their twigs. "Well, there's not a flower to speak of, is there?"

"No . . . no there is not." Katherine had nothing more to add, so they walked the slowly turning paths to reach the center of the maze, Ebony's flanks nearly touching the hedges on either side. A few minutes later, Katherine sat down on the cold bench while Mr. Charles stood rubbing Ebony's nose.

A crunch of boots on gravel sounded behind the hedge, heralding the arrival of some unknown visitor. Katherine moved slightly further away from Charles and Ebony. *No one will think anything of this . . . why would they?* The grinding stones drew nearer when the man turned the corner. Once again, William's ghost entered the reflection circle as he had so many times before his death.

No! Not William! Sterling—yes, James Sterling. Oh, let it not be William! Katherine inched all the way until the bench's stone arm dug painfully into her ribs. *Please do not look on me with such coldness!*

Mr. Sterling, unaware of the reasons for Katherine's apparent fear, offered a customary greeting. "Ah, Miss le Chevalier. Lady Blakesly said that she thought that you might be in the labyrinth. I apologize for startling you."

Katherine's knees quivered as her shoulders fought to hunch down on themselves. She felt colder in her heart than she had out on the open green. "It—it is all right . . . Mr. Sterling. I—I think the cold is disagreeing with me, is all."

Mr. Sterling nodded curtly. "Then let us retire to the cottage." He turned to Charles, acknowledging him for the first time. "Thank you, groom. Please return Miss le Chevalier's mare to the stables." He flicked a shilling to Charles who caught it with a wry grin.

Mr. Francis tossed the coin once with a thoughtful look, seeming to take in all that Mr. Sterling was with a look. "Thank you, sir," he flicked the coin back to the newcomer. "But my services are all accounted for." Charles turned to Katherine. "Miss le Chevalier," and he bowed formally with a more genuine smile. Then he led Ebony away. Katherine saw something like sadness in his final glance as he turned the corner, but he was gone too soon for her to be sure.

I'm sure that he only looked *sad . . .* Katherine quelled the sympathetic pain inside of her.

Mr. Sterling tossed the returned coin up and back down to himself a moment, looking after where Charles had just been. Then he pocketed it and turned back to Katherine. "Would you give me the honor of escorting you back to the cottage?"

Katherine turned from where she had watched Mr. Francis leave, her empathy chilling to disquiet once again. "Yes, yes of course." Katherine accepted his outstretched hand, and rose to her feet, only really needing the support due to the proximity of William's doppelganger. As it was, Katherine leaned a little more on the man's arm than she normally would with a near-stranger.

The familiar images of the garden and the cottage spun before Katherine's eyes. Her heart beat like the futile flapping of a bird struggling to escape a fox's jaws. She could barely look at the man beside her for fear of fainting. *He is not William! I* know *he is not.*

The footman at the cottage door took Katherine's fur then Mr. Sterling led her to the sitting room, clearly having received the tour before retrieving Katherine from the maze. Elizabeth sat, pretending to do some needlework, as it was easier for her to pretend with than a book. Her eyebrows soared high over her eyes in barely contained excitement.

Mr. Sterling's eyes passed over Elizabeth for a moment before turning to Katherine. "I must beg your pardon once again, Miss le Chevalier. I know that my appearance must have been a surprise."

"It was indeed . . . but, it was no less a pleasant meeting, despite that." The fogginess in Katherine's head cleared some, enough for her to remember some semblance of her manners. "Did you travel long?"

He helped her sit down in a chair. "Not too long, no. I had some business with a lord a day's ride north, and when I saw that he would not be interested in my proposition, I thought that I might turn a bad deal into a good trip by calling on you." Mr. Sterling looked down at his coat and removed a stray leaf from the lapel. "I regretted speaking with you so little at the ball."

"You regretted not speaking with me?" Katherine asked, her chest constricting further than her stays' tightness.

"Yes, you, and your sister," he gave a small bow to Elizabeth, "were the most interesting young women there."

Elizabeth flushed in delight, hiding the roses of her cheeks behind her stalled floral needlework. Katherine turned her head in neither acceptance nor disagreement. "Perhaps the most interesting had already left before the hour of your arrival, but won't you sit?" *His words sound flirtatious . . . but his manner is so formal as to be unidentifiable from stated fact . . .*

"I would be most pleased. Thank you." He sat with the dignity of a lord, though much more vivaciously than Lord Alcott—who did nothing with animation save scolding people for lacking manners. The longer Katherine spoke with him, the more his uncanny resemblance to William dwindled through his unfamiliar mannerisms, *but still his gaze haunts me—accuses me.*

"If you do not mind me asking, what business did you have this far from town?"

"Oh, that would be of little interest to ladies such as yourselves . . ." Mr. Sterling looked like he would change the subject, but both ladies were *very* interested in business deals and their accompanying rents.

So he continued with a grimace. "Trade dealings between here and the continent . . . "

The ladies nodded, with "go on" all but written across their foreheads.

"Well, with Louis restored and Napoleon ousted again, there is a scramble to acquire factories on the continent. The old lord has had some historical success in the region, and I was looking to purchase his factories from him. Unfortunately, he was not interested in selling them to me—no matter what I offered—and so I must continue with the small clutch of factories I currently possess and pray they hatch laying hens." He sat a little taller, his grimace changed for his usual coldness. "I fear that we are in near direct competition, he and I. I would much rather have unified our efforts to defeat the French in an economical Waterloo, but 'self-interest' won out once again."

Just how many is a clutch . . . ? She daren't ask.

"Are you an economist, then?"

He smiled his first smile, pleased to see Katherine recognize commerce-related terminology. "No, not really. I dabble in it as every businessman should when choosing where to invest and the like. I do not have the luxury that most men of my standing have to receive their living from ancestral rents. I must make my money work for me." Mr. Sterling's brows knit together in a scowl for a moment, scarring his smooth face with displeasure. Then he smoothed his features once again.

He seems to mask his emotions . . . but he feels them deeply, if only contempt for the easy life of lords.

"I am sorry that your proposal was denied."

"As am I, but there is nothing to be done. I am sorry to carry my gloomy dealings into your home like so much mud on my boots. Perhaps we could speak of something more cordial."

Elizabeth chimed in, her pretense and needle both forgotten. "Indeed, perhaps Katherine could play us a song?"

Of course, Sister . . . / will play along. "But Elizabeth, you have been working on your song far more than I have been of late."

Elizabeth beamed in thanks. "Oh, *all right* then, I shall play you a song." Elizabeth stood, dropping the framed fabric and for the first time Katherine noticed that she was in one of her best ball gowns. Mr.

Sterling had come late to the party, and so Elizabeth's song would be as fresh for him as it had been for the other, timelier guests.

"Yes. I would love to hear you *both* play . . . if you feel up to it, Miss le Chevalier? I have heard tell that you are quite the master."

Is he truly *that interested in me?* Katherine nodded "Of course . . . I should be happy to."

Elizabeth was across the sitting area with her arm looped through James's almost quicker than he could stand. By the time that Mr. Sterling turned back around, to help Katherine stand, she had already risen and extended her arm for him to take with his free one. The three walked to the music room as Elizabeth chatted about the cottage, filling the hostess role that Katherine had for Lord Alcott. Katherine was left to bear her thoughts alone.

Young, rich, and handsome, if cold . . . could he truly be here to see me?

Chapter 13

April 24th

Being near one like you, I have never felt so far away.

—Katherine, the darkest depths of my heart

⌒⌒

The stable boy kept his eyes turned down whenever one of the men, especially the stable master, was nearby. He did his chores well. *It wasn't his fault that he got them done so quickly that he had spare time.*

His father had taught him the horse business when *he* was stable master and if he hadn't ridden off to Waterloo, he still would be. The first Lord of Wellington himself had used the boy's old man to watch over his horse. Sadly, that honor had not saved his father from an eight-pound Gribeauval cannon a mile away. Since the arrival of the terrible news, Thomas had stayed on under the new stable master, trying to support his mum and two sisters the best he could.

"Fill these buckets and scrub out stall fourteen. You're lucky it was mucked before the lord picked up his horse last night." The groom turned without a second glance. Thom was the last person who had worked the stables before the current master. He would have been turned out if Lord Blakesly hadn't forbidden it. The others that had been there then had slowly been replaced by men that suited the stable master's fancy, and unkindness, better.

Thom set about his task, his mind floating out the window and past the sheep fields to where he would sometimes see Annie Cotts leading her cow home from the public pasture. *Maybe he could save up enough to get her a nice ribbon for May Day.*

It was unlikely, but a boy could dream.

The images of Annie smiling at him with a red ribbon in her braid were interrupted by the doctor fellow tapping him on the shoulder. "Excuse me, Thom—that is your name, isn't it?"

Thom nodded, nervous to be within arms' reach of any man in the stable, even one that spent time trying to help a lame horse.

Seeming to sense this, the good doctor took a step back and bowed his head in greeting. "Thom, I have noticed that you often find yourself *available* between tasks, and I was wondering if you could do me a favor."

"I'm fast, not lazy. They won't let me do groom stuff, so I do all the running and cleaning they can find." Thom crossed his arms to look tougher than he felt. It worked on some of the smaller grooms at least.

"Indeed, well the favor I will be asking is similar in action, but perhaps a bit more lucrative. I have several of the town's animals to watch over in this belated calving season and I will not be able to visit my ward as often.

"Your ward, sir?"

"Excuse my medical language—the black mare, Ebony. The hurt one."

Thom nodded that he understood, so the doctor continued. "Well, I will not be able to visit her as often and I would like for you to walk her if I do not. Would you be able to do that for sixpence a week?"

"Certainly sir! That's what I get to work here! But Doctor, sir, I already do that stuff . . . Why are you going to pay me more to do the same thing?"

Charles smiled sadly, tapping the side of his nose. "I knew you had a quick wit. I have another *little* favor I would ask of you. It will be harder and might get you into a little trouble."

"For sixpence a week I could get into all sorts of trouble for you."

Charles laughed. "I simply ask that you keep a lookout for me. If Miss Kath—I should say, if Miss le Chevalier comes down to walk her horse, I want you to run and let me know. I will come post haste and you will get an extra two pence whenever you do."

Thom very nearly jumped for joy—he was going to be *rich*. "Yessir! I will do that! And I'll be sure to brush and feed the horse every day!" The boy looked around to be sure no one could hear, then continued in a whisper. "Is this so the lady wouldn't know that you haven't been watching the horse for a bit?"

Charles hesitated, but his smile returned. "Yes . . . if the horse wasn't doing well, I would need to come more often, but as it is, she seems somewhat secure on her own. I would only hate to miss the lady when she comes down."

"That's smart, sir. I'll do what I can and walk the mare some days too. The lady won't ever know that you left." Thom tipped his floppy work hat to the doctor.

"That's my boy. Here's your first payment." He pulled a shilling out of his pocket and placed it carefully into the boy's outstretched hand. "This is back payment for the times you've assisted in caring for the horse when she was forgotten, and the rest to cover this week."

"Thank you, Doctor, sir. I was only doing my job."

Mr. Francis patted his shoulder again; this time Thom didn't flinch. "Thank you, Thom. I know that you are a resource that the stable master is underutilizing. My uncle has often said that you can tell a lot about a man by the way he treats those that he feels are beneath him—horse or man alike." Charles touched his finger to his lips once with a serious expression, then smiled and left the stable with only a brief glance at the empty stable master's table.

Thom looked down at the shilling in his hand and smiled. "Maybe I can get Annie that ribbon after all."

Katherine lay with her eyes closed waiting for her sister to stir. They had stayed up late playing cards with Mr. Sterling and Lord and Lady Blakesly, but Katherine couldn't sleep. Troubling dreams had disturbed her peace all night. She walked through visions of torn earth over William's grave and William—*or was it Mr. Sterling?*—chasing after her with dead eyes. She had others where, happily married to William, his dark-eyed twin walked into the room and stabbed him through the heart.

Of course, there were the regular dreams she had of standing in her night clothes in the stable, knowing that someone could see her. Waking brought little comfort as Lord Blakesly had invited Mr. Sterling to "finish out the week" at Applehill, and so there would be no respite from Katherine's anxiety for some days yet. So, she waited for her peacefully sleeping sister for hours, wondering if Mr. Sterling really had come only for her. He and Elizabeth seemed to have an easier time talking, but he always seemed to find his way back over to Katherine. Elizabeth stirred, with a happy sigh.

Finally.

Katherine sighed as well, affecting a yawn that was quickly overtaken by a real one. "Good morning, Eliza."

"Good morning to you, my sister-dearest. How did you sleep?"

"Well enough, I suppose, and you?"

"Never better! I can't *believe* that *Mr. Sterling* will be staying for two more days! I couldn't be more delighted!" She crooned into her pillow. "Well, I would be a *bit* more delighted if he were here to visit *me,* but you take what you can as the second."

Katherine blushed. "I am not so sure that he is here to visit me. He seems to get on far better with you."

"Men are *always* more comfortable with the one they aren't pursuing," Elizabeth stated, likely gleaning the thought from their mother's magazines.

"It seems that men are always more comfortable with *you,* no matter whom they may *or may not* be pursuing."

"Well, I can't help it if I am amiable." Elizabeth batted her lashes, earning a wry smile from her older sister. "But, we can't dally *all* morning. We must get ready for another day with Mr. James Sterling!" She hopped out of bed, displacing a handful of economics, music theory, and French history texts.

Mr. Sterling stood in the antechamber inspecting the family portraits and apple blossom scenes painted by generations of le Chevaliers. One of Katherine's was hung somewhere in the house, but she had made it a game of moving it for William to find, and it hadn't returned it to its place of honor after . . .

How I still miss him.

Elizabeth had made it to the top of the stairs first, but seeing James below stopped her like a witch's enchantment and sent her skipping back with pink cheeks to let Katherine descend first. Though Elizabeth looked older, she still maintained the animation of her eighteen years.

Katherine felt Mr. Sterling's eyes on her at the same time as she noticed Elizabeth's eyes on him. Katherine felt a little like a rabbit under the searching stares of two hawks only with less hunger. *Do not trip . . . do not trip . . . do not trip.* The shallow steps, designed for women in gowns, did not fail her feet. So despite the cool grey eyes aimed directly at her, and the barely contained boisterousness of her sister behind her, Katherine was able to maintain the poise and unaffected air expected of the eldest daughter of a lord.

"Good morrow, Miss le Chevalier. Would you do me the honor of escorting you to breakfast?"

Has he been waiting here this entire time for me?

"Certainly, Mr. Sterling. I would be delighted."

"As would I," Elizabeth said, stepping in beside Katherine as her foot barely touched the main floor. "If that is not too presumptuous of me to suggest." She took James's other arm the instant after Katherine had taken his right, and the three of them proceeded to breakfast. Plates and sweetmeats were already arrayed for the three of them and they ate in respectful silence. Elizabeth lifted her brows at Katherine, prodding her to strike up a conversation with him, but Katherine maintained her silence, ignoring her sister's ever more insistent glances.

Mr. Sterling dabbed the corners of his mouth with his napkin and spoke. "Would you fancy a walk about the garden this afternoon? I have some business correspondences I must post, but I would love to better make your acquaintance later, if I may?"

Katherine's stomach tightened, the scone she had eaten turning to stone. "Yes, of course. I would be delighted."

"Excellent. Miss Elizabeth, you are, of course, more than welcome to accompany us." He rose and bowed to each of them and continued. "I am sorry to be such a brief companion for this meal, but I hope to be more attentive once these matters are seen to." He bowed once again and then exited the hall.

Elizabeth dropped her spoon back into the dish and turned quickly to Katherine. "Now there is *no* doubt that he is looking to court you! Do you think you'll say yes when he proposes? I know I would. He's rich, smart, and incredibly handsome!"

Katherine closed her eyes, the scone threatening to come back up. *He is all that . . . to someone other than I. Would William haunt me through Mr. Sterling the rest of my days?*

Elizabeth moved over into the vacant seat left by Mr. Sterling and opened her mouth to ask another question when a maid hurried into the dining hall.

"Deepest apologies for the rude interruption my ladies, but *another* young man is pulling up on a horse. He sent his footman before to say that it is a Sir Braxton calling." Judging the young lady by the flush in her cheeks, she must have run straight from the court-yard to let them know.

Or she had caught sight of Sir Braxton—he would be the kind to wink at every young girl and set her heart aflutter!

Elizabeth squealed as she jumped out of the seat she had only just occupied, tugging on Katherine's arm. Katherine's body felt numb, if a little less tense than it had moments before. Braxton would make for an excellent conversationalist to speak with Mr. Sterling about "men's" exploits and take some of his attention from herself. *But what is he doing, calling here?*

"Aren't you excited Katherine? Not one but *two* of the most *beautiful* men in all of England at *our* little Applehill!"

Katherine covered her mouth, pressing her lips together against the pressure from her stomach. When she felt the scone settle, she spoke. "Yes . . . indeed."

"Oh, come now! Nothing excites you save your walks with the doctor these days!"

A cold draft swirled around Katherine, stiffening her spine and sending goosebumps up her arms. "What do you mean by—"

"Oh, *come!* He will already be in the entryway!" And she dragged her pale sister out of the hall. Sure enough, Sir Braxton was handing his coat to the unfamiliar footman who stood with the other household servants.

"My dear Miss Katherine! *Bon matin!* I am sorry to visit so early, but I simply *had* to come!" He looked around the antechamber with a smile then stepped forward to take Katherine's hand to kiss it.

Katherine allowed him, though her stomach clenched again. *Too much all going on at once!* She welcomed him all the same. "Sir Braxton, you would be welcome at any time or season. What brings you to our humble lodgings?"

Braxton smiled, glancing quickly at the servants and lowered his voice. "I dropped by old Alcott expecting to hear of my cousin's impending nuptials but learned that he had put you off!" He took an arm from each young lady and led them down the hall like he had lived in the cottage for years. "I said that if you were available, perhaps I should give you a visit." He chuckled. "If only you had seen his face when I took off at a run and vaulted my horse that had only just been handed to a groom. I half expected him to ride me down, but he never gave me the satisfaction of seeing that."

Katherine took the lead and brought them all into the sitting room, then Braxton continued,

"So, my ruse turned into truth and here I am. I don't mean to stay long but thought I had better take back *actual* news from you if I am to torment my cousin sufficiently on this trip."

"Oh, so you are not looking to court my sister? But you get on so well," Elizabeth asked, sitting down a little heavier than usual.

"Alas, my beautiful *mademoiselles*, I am not. Though, if you wanted to draw a quick sketch of me and sign it with a heart, it would truly assist a dear friend in his extremely important game with his old cousin." Braxton winked so that only Katherine could see.

"Katherine doesn't have much time for drawing, she and *Mr. Sterling* are to take a walk this afternoon," Elizabeth stated with an arched brow, looking like the knowledge might change Braxton's mind. "If you don't stay, you will miss the opportunity to steal her away."

Katherine looked at her sister. *Why does she drive me toward Braxton so much?*

"*He* is here? My, well perhaps I have better news to share with Alcott than I had hoped!" Braxton raised his brow at Katherine then turned a renewed smile at Elizabeth. Katherine took the hint, "Elizabeth, would you ask the maid to fetch our guest some refreshment?"

Elizabeth pouted theatrically but still went to ring the bell. Braxton spoke without moving his lips, keeping his pleasant smile still all the while. "Is he a true prospect? He seemed a little cold to me, if sufficiently well off."

Katherine, lacking his skill in ventriloquism, looked down as she spoke, masking her lips behind a hand. "I do not know . . . he came to visit unannounced, and he seems to, perhaps, be showing some interest. I had thought that Lord Alcott would propose too, but in his absence, Mr. Sterling could be a 'true prospect' as you say."

"It pains me to say it, but he is a good match. He is driven by his 'business,' but that is the only affair I have heard of in his life. I never like to admit virtue in a rival, but he seems to come by his money honorably, if less respectably than my old cousin. Are there any others you are holding out for?"

Katherine thought about the cards she had sent and then slowly shook her head. "I had about given up hope—honestly I have still given up hope. I don't believe that he is interested, but Elizabeth seems to think so."

Elizabeth, likely sensing that she was missing gossip, hurried back from speaking with the maid to sit beside Katherine. "Any news from Milford Manor? You didn't happen to see Sir Rodney or Sir Galloway while you were there?" She seemed to cringe at their memory—*perhaps the dream really* did *affect her.*

"Sadly, no. I barely managed to say hello to *Lord Alcott* before I came here. My sisters send their regards—or at least, I imagine they would have, if I had stayed long enough to hear them say so."

The same maid who had notified the sisters about Sir Braxton's arrival entered with a tray of bread, cold meats, and warm drinks. The maid curtsied and blushed as she served cups to the sisters and Braxton, then she scurried out with only one glance back at the gorgeous nobleman. *She did catch sight of him it seems.*

Braxton smiled after the maid, taking a single pastry. "I really should return to Milford Manor soon, since I was expected to pass the entire week there and have instead spent a full day gallivanting through the country as a show."

"Oh, but you must stay for dinner?" Elizabeth voiced Katherine's own thoughts.

"I am a terrible man to blow in and weave out like a broadsheet in a winter storm, but I cannot. My fractured honor can only support so much flippancy before society falls down upon me. Though, I should *love* to accompany you and Mr. Sterling on your walk after luncheon?" His eyes twinkled as he looked at Katherine. "I think there is *much* I will have to share with old Allie, if I may."

The forgotten scone gave a final flip in her stomach as she nodded her assent.

Chapter 14

April 24th—Again

Braxton ate luncheon, and Mr. Sterling is leery of him, I think. He looks less like you when he is suspicious . . . but I could never love his cool intelligence like I did your warm cordiality.

—Katherine, Between a fop and a hard place

The sisters each accepted the offered furs. When Braxton turned his down, Sterling was quick to return the one he had taken reflexively. Sterling held his arms stiffly at his sides even when the icy wind made the women fold their arms across them. Braxton seemed warmed alone by the game he was playing.

"It is cold, but I will be riding again soon, so I feel the need to acclimate myself to the weather," Braxton said over his shoulder at his "new friend" as he had been calling Mr. Sterling all lunch. It seemed that Mr. Sterling's eyes narrowed a little further each time he mentioned it, which was exactly the reason why Braxton continued to use the term. Braxton then extended his arm to Katherine. "I thought that perhaps we could daisy chain our way through the garden, Miss Katherine taking one of each of our arms and young Miss Elizabeth taking the arm of whichever she finds more suitable."

Katherine spoke quickly, before Mr. Sterling need stake his previous claim. "Actually, Mr. Sterling requested to walk with me first, so I must honor our arrangement." She spoke politely, even while twisting her hands inside of the fur muff. She would feel less nervous if they *were* all walking together.

Sir Braxton bowed his head slightly, lowering his arm. "Ah yes, I could not disparage a woman who honors her engagements. You are as principled as you are beautiful." Then he bowed lower. "Would that I had arrived but a little sooner and had earned your promise first." His eyes twinkled and he gave a wink for only Katherine to see.

He certainly can play this role well.

The act clearly affected Mr. Sterling. A faint bit of color showed on his ears and on the back of his neck, too quickly appearing to be from the brisk environment outside of the cottage. To his credit, or perhaps to Braxton's delight, Mr. Sterling held his tongue and accepted Katherine's awaiting arm.

"I suppose I am a paltry consolation prize, Miss Elizabeth, but would you honor me with your arm?"

Elizabeth laughed, long over her sour mood from missing the gossip between him and her sister. Mr. Sterling then led Katherine at a quick but reasonable pace until a respectable distance fell between them and the other pair—not so far as to be scandalous, but not so close that they could easily hear one another.

Except for Braxton's booming laughs, of course.

"Miss le Chevalier, I do not mean to hold you to my request if it is objectionable to you?"

"By no means! I am happy to better make your acquaintance. Sir Braxton passes his time by ruffling feathers." *Or preening his own.*

"It seems most women's feathers *ruffle* simply from being in the same vicinity as *Sir* Braxton." He nearly spit Braxton's prefix as he looked back at him. "He has a title that he cares so little for. He games and flirts with the nobility, but none of their nobility rubs off on him." Mr. Sterling turned into the labyrinth and slowed so as not to enter so far as to be considered alone, even though the top of his head was above the shrubbery.

Mr. Sterling visibly calmed himself with a deep breath through widened nostrils. "I apologize for any disrespect . . . your *guest* reminds me of my shortcomings as a suitor."

Katherine's acceptance stuck in her throat at the word "*suitor.*" She nodded with the raising of her eyebrows the only sign of her surprise.

Sterling noticed and nodded. "Yes, if I could see myself as such . . . I will admit that I came here with uncertain intentions, but while here, I have been greatly impressed with you and your sister and Lord and Lady Blakesly. You have been raised well and show it in every movement." He spoke each word so matter-of-factly as to make the statements indisputable.

But still so cold.

" . . . Thank you, Mr. Sterling. I have enjoyed your company," *though Elizabeth may have enjoyed it more.*

He bowed. "And I yours. I want to be sure that I am not placing myself in between you and any . . . *arrangements* you may have with Sir Braxton?"

Katherine shook her head and he continued, "You are objectively beautiful and indeed, principled, if I am to borrow words from my rival. I disbelieve and would disavow any who intimated that you left mourning too quickly due to the need to conceal . . . " Mr. Sterling looked up into Katherine's eyes with his sharp grey ones, before coloring a little in his cheeks and looking away. He cleared his throat and paused for a moment.

I have seen a larger range of emotions from Mr. Sterling in the past hour that Braxton has been here than in the previous twelve.

He cleared his throat and spoke again. "I have a proposition for you."

Katherine's reveries shattered. "Y-yes?"

"In the short while that we have known each other, I know that it would be impossible for you to have come to love me, or I you, but I have a respectable annuity which I am actively working to increase, and I would be a faithful husband."

The cold wind blew, shaking the skeletal branches against each other and cooling the tear forming in Katherine's eye. *How can he look so like you, and be so different?* William had filled a room with roses and dropped to one knee sharing the deepest thoughts and purest love for her when he had proposed. Katherine knew that there had been a chaperone and even a quartet playing one of her favorite songs, but to her the world had been empty except for the two of them. The music had been nothing compared to the angelic tones singing through the very chords of her being as she had whispered, "*Yes . . . my dearest, my love—my William!*" That embrace driven by an unspeakable bond between them had changed her heart forever.

How could this be so different?

"I understand that Braxton has a title, and I do not. So, if you are waiting to see his intentions . . . "

Katherine shook her head. "No."

Sterling's face remained mostly impassive, even as his shoulders fell. He released the arm he was holding and stepped back. "Ah . . . I see—"

Katherine stepped forward and caught his arm again. "Sorry, not 'no.' I meant to say that 'no,' he does not *have* intentions . . . at least not for me. He is a friend who likes to play games. Towards me, he feels only the charity one gives another of God's children."

Mr. Sterling nodded, the creases in his forehead smoothing out to their usual marble. "Excellent. Then may I be permitted to share my proposition with you?"

She nodded, the moments between each breath seeming to slow even as she felt her heart beating faster.

"I have received word of some disturbances on the continent that might affect my holdings and so I must away with haste. I should not expect to be detained more than one month, but upon my return, it is my intention to ask for your hand. With your title and my resources, I feel that we will be a strong match . . . and I feel that, in time, our mutual interests will grow to mutual regard, and perhaps, even love." Mr. Sterling stumbled over the last sentence as if it had been rehearsed, but his eyes looked as if he wanted it to be true, if he was not himself altogether convinced.

Father's title retains some value it seems . . . at least to some.

"I will tell my father that I happily await your return."

"Wonderful, I too look forward to our reunion." Mr. Sterling stood straighter and bowed formally. "And now that our arrangement has been discussed, I must excuse myself. I ride immediately to town, but will return some time after May Day, perhaps closer to the opening of June." Then he turned on his heel, and strode back toward the house, leaving Katherine feeling reassured, but somehow empty. *This will solve everything . . . so why don't I feel relieved?*

The bare branches afforded some cover that she should use to compose herself, but she found that her breathing was easy, and her heart had slowed. So, she simply walked in his footsteps left in the gravel with a straight back and dispassionate look as her betrothed-to-be made his way back toward the cottage. Exiting the labyrinth, she caught sight of Mr. Sterling inclining his head to Braxton and bowing to Elizabeth.

"You're leaving too!? But who will dine with us tonight?" Elizabeth's pout seemed genuine. She had lost not one, but two handsome dinner guests. She folded her arms across herself and looked away, making even the incorrigible Braxton pull his collar. Mr. Sterling flushed and bowed deeper, speaking at a normal volume, and thus leaving his comments inaudible to Katherine.

Elizabeth extended a hand to Mr. Sterling, her position and volume enough to carry with the wind. "Then you owe me an apology when you return." It was clear what her intention was, and James acquiesced with a quick kiss on her hand, somehow going redder in the process. He bowed to them both and scurried away, barely maintaining his usually impeccable posture. Elizabeth then turned her attention on Braxton, her eyes fierce though her cheeks had a little more color in them as well.

"He gave me a kiss for his sin, and what will *you* give me?"

Katherine hadn't chosen to start moving, but somehow after Mr. Sterling left, she found that she had closed half the distance between herself and the pair.

"Oh, my dear, dear girl. I have already given you more than *that!*" Braxton turned to Katherine. "I have given you a brother! James, 'the supplanter,' what an apt name. I'm sure Allie would think it. Is that not so, Miss le Chevalier?" Braxton smiled and Elizabeth's mouth dropped open, the color fading from her cheeks in her surprise.

"Is it true? Are you engaged in the little second you hid from view? Can it truly be?" Elizabeth looked more shocked than when she had learned that most books used to be written *by hand.*

Katherine wobbled her head "No . . . and yes. He has urgent business to attend to on the continent until May, but he has expressed his intent to ask for my hand once he returns."

Elizabeth's jaw dropped as she placed her hands on her cheeks. "What gorgeous nephews I shall have!" She lowered her hand to her chest. "He loves you so quickly." The last sentence floated away on the cold breeze. Katherine's heart was already too iced over to freeze any more. At Katherine's silence, Elizabeth's thoughts seemed to turn inward, replacing her excitement with something else.

Oh Elizabeth, you would not be so excited for me if you knew that I could never love him.

Whatever her musings, Elizabeth nodded to them both and trailed back toward the house on her own. Braxton watched her go with consideration in his expression. Then he extended his arm to Katherine who welcomed it, the truth finally reaching her now shaking legs.

Leading Katherine after her sister, Braxton spoke in a hushed tone. "I should apologize for my behavior, but I admit that despite my good intentions, I had devilish fun." He chuckled to himself, still looking thoughtfully after Elizabeth.

"No, I must thank you. I do not know if he would have been as keen on expressing his intent this early if it had not been for you." Katherine squeezed his arm like she would a brother's, with no less feeling for not having any natural brothers to compare it to. "You have been my Cupid twice now, though I have done nothing to deserve the assistance."

"Ah ha! Cupid, the blindfolded disturber . . . I suppose it fits. I always did like to make matches that most would disapprove of." His expression turned dark for a moment but was replaced with his usual cheer quickly. "But I disagree that you have done nothing to deserve it! You are an honest woman in distress, in a world chock full of silly and wanton women—and men—who seek for discord. Even a 'cupid' such as I cannot allow an innocent to suffer."

Katherine squeezed his arm again and he nodded. They walked in silence for a moment before he spoke again.

"I don't suppose you'd like me to tell Lord Alcott about your agreement? He might change his mind about how long he's willing to wait if he was afraid you might not be available." Braxton looked into

Katherine's eyes, watching each near-invisible emotion flash through her eyes as she considered.

Alcott is much richer . . . and has a title, but he would wear the unneeded shame of my early venture from mourning for the rest of his days. He still might not *change his mind and wondering would be so much the worse. A bird in hand, as they say . . .*

"No . . . I feel it best that he did not know until the announcement is made. I am sorry that you will not have your fun."

Braxton chuckled. "Oh, I can bother Alcott in *so* many ways, it barely dims my prospects. I was thinking of referencing the several times I had to greet and leave you in my short visit and how each meeting and parting demanded a kiss on your hand. Perhaps I will rub my lips with salt to chap them and see what he thinks of that!"

Katherine swatted his arm lightly. "You will have him riding here *without* knowing of my arrangement!"

"Ah ha! Yes, perhaps that would be too much, but I will think of the perfect game on the ride." They came to the front door that hung ajar from when Elizabeth had recently entered.

Katherine slowly removed her arm from Braxton's and turned to him, extending her hand. "I suppose you must leave now as well?"

Braxton took her hand mildly with a small smile. "Yes, I think it best. But I must take *one* kiss, if only to lord over my Lord Alcott." He lightly brushed her hand with his lips in the definition of propriety. "Fare thee well, *ma chere amie.*"

Elizabeth stepped out of the cottage closing the door behind her, unshed tears glinting in her eyes. "Are you certain that you cannot stay, even for tea?" Braxton nodded and Elizabeth nodded in return. "Then, tell Rodney that he had best visit soon or I will marry *you.* He doesn't have to believe it for it to work—I think."

"Ah ha! Just so." Braxton bowed and the sisters curtsied, and whether by design or by astuteness, Braxton's footman appeared with their two horses and the men mounted and trotted away, Braxton waving over his shoulder until they turned the corner and were lost in the trees.

"What will Father say when he sees the spread I ordered, with no one to serve it to?"

Katherine smiled and hugged her sister. *He will not be worried when he learns who it was intended for—who is now my intended.*

❧

Later that evening, after the ample remainders were removed from the fine dinner, Katherine stood brushing her sister's hair as the younger sat at the vanity. The long strokes through her locks calmed them both for sleep.

Katherine thought back over the events of the day, and like a forgotten ember in the dry grass, a memory raged to life. "Eliza . . . you said something earlier today that gave me pause."

"I did? What was it?" Elizabeth had her book on economics that she had been turning though half-heartedly.

The mental conflagration still raged, but Katherine fought to keep her voice disinterested. "Yes, you said that I only looked excited when I . . . when I am to go on a walk."

Elizabeth snorted as she closed her book. "Oh that. Don't be worried. Mother and Father haven't noticed, and I wouldn't confirm it if they asked me."

Katherine's spine stiffened again like it had that morning. "What . . . exactly are you intimating?"

Elizabeth turned on the stool and touched Katherine's hand to stop her brushing. "Sister, I do not assume anything untoward—only that you are sweet on the handsome horse doctor."

Katherine's jaw dropped as low as Elizabeth's had earlier at learning of Sterling's pseudo-proposal. "I am not! Elizabeth, he is in Father's employ and a *commoner*! How could you think that of me?"

She is not right. She cannot be right. But Elizabeth's eyes pierced through the fogs and shadows that Katherine had allowed to weave around her mind and her heart. Katherine stood stock still, feeling more naked before that gaze than she did in a night shift in a stable one February night.

Elizabeth smiled knowingly. "Oh please, you think I—or any woman with eyes and feelings—have never noticed one of the more handsome footmen or villagers? I've heard of a clergyman in Town who has nearly ninety percent female parishioners!" Elizabeth laughed and Katherine crossed her arms.

"A man of the church? Really, Eliza that is too much"

"Why? It is not wrong to see that a man is attractive. Providence *made* them that way for a reason—like birds with colorful plumage." She pointed at one of her natural history books on the shelf, then continued. "I daresay that it is not even wrong to take an *extra* look, being young and unmarried as we are . . . " Elizabeth saw that biology was not soothing her elder sister's concern. "Look, I shouldn't have said anything—I've caused you unneeded worry." Elizabeth turned back toward the mirror and sat up straighter, ready for Katherine to brush.

Katherine did begin again, stiffly, but the silence was tense for a moment. Eventually Katherine could glance up from her sister's hair to look at her in the mirror. There she saw only love and unmasked admiration in Elizabeth's eyes.

"I—I was just happy to see you excited about *something*, in all of this." Elizabeth wiped her eyes with the side of her hands.

Katherine nodded and looked down, wiping quiet tears from her own eyes with her left hand as her right continued to brush.

Chapter 15

April 27th

I have one month remaining.

I can be true for one more month.

I can keep my promise for one more month.

—Katherine, Applehill Cottage

"Any news from the bank, Father?" Katherine asked, standing just inside the closed door of his study.

"No word on whether a promise of engagement is sufficient for the extension I am afraid . . . and there is a payment due the end of this month that I—well, I suppose I do not need to share that. You are doing far more for your old father than you should need to, by rights." Lord Blakesly's eyes fell to the papers placed neatly on his desk, sadness folding creases into his kind face. "Are you sure that you want to go through with this?"

"Yes, Father. He is a good match and will represent our family's legacy with honor."

"You do not love him." His eyes showed hope that maybe it was not so.

Katherine swallowed the lump forming in her throat. "No . . . but I *have* felt love in my life, in many of its varieties, and if that is not enough to support me through . . . then perhaps it will be the beacon that leads me back someday." *Or the constant reminder of what I have lost.* She didn't share the thought with her father.

Lord Blakesly nodded, with a solemnity more common at a wake than a wedding. "Thank you, my dearest . . . thank you." He rose and embraced his daughter in a rare demonstration of his deep affection. They parted, and Katherine curtsied her way from the study.

I must deal with the doctor.

Katherine kept her eyes straight to avoid meeting anyone's gaze. Elizabeth might see where Katherine was going, and she could not face her until she had accomplished her design.

She walked down the familiar cobble road to the stables with the usual sounds and scents of horses blowing past her dark hair. *I will thank him for his service and say that we are looking for another doctor to fill the position.* She would be cool and proper like she *should* have been from the start . . . *but not so cool as to make him mad and share what he has witnessed of me.* Katherine exhaled slowly and walked a little faster to get it over with.

The stable doors stood open, and several horses were led in and out, the regular bustle of the stables even greater than usual. Katherine saw Thom sprint off as she approached, but otherwise things were as they always were. Katherine entered between the large beasts and caught sight of the stable master.

"Is the doctor here today?"

The man squinted but responded. "I haven't seen him."

"Oh . . . " *Well, that won't do.* "Has he been here recently?"

"I don't watch him that closely . . . " He saw that she wasn't going to go anywhere, and he *actually* sighed. "It seems to have been some time."

Perhaps the problem has solved itself then . . . if only the stable master might do the same.

But what to do with dear Ebony? Katherine would love for her to go to a good home, but William's last gift might be to help her family survive until Katherine could be dutifully wed, and Mr. Sterling's estate could be joined with their own. The stable master was losing even his normal semblance of patience, but Katherine was enjoying making him wait a little. "While I am here," she pointed down toward

Ebony's pen. "How much do you suppose I could get for my mare, if I were to sell her?"

The man sniffed. "You'd be lucky to get four guineas from the factories. Maybe seven if it was sold for meat on the continent. I told that 'horse doctor' that it was pointless."

Her face fell. "Not to sell her to a factory! If I were to sell her as a horse . . . perhaps as a present for a young girl?"

The stable master shook his head in disbelief. "Ma'am, no one in all of England would take her 'as a horse!' Like me, they wouldn't trust that the ankle wouldn't sprain again." He folded his arms and tapped his foot. As he did, a white stallion pranced inside, led by a groom.

Katherine ignored his foot and pointed at the noble animal. "Well, what about that one, or any of the other fine horses in the stable? What would they go for?"

"Much, but they're not the Lord's to sell. They're here as guests, favors to other lords."

Oh . . . these must be payments of personal debts. Katherine nodded, hoping it looked like she knew all along. "Of course. Thank you for your time." And she turned to leave quickly. In her haste she almost ran into the doctor coming around the corner. As it was, only her hands touched the lapels of his cloak. *That cloak.* She retracted her hands as if burned.

He smiled like she *hadn't* almost bawled him over. "Hello, Miss le Chevalier. May I speak with you?" Mr. Charles—*Mr. Francis*—had not been this formal since they had first met. *That should not make me sad. I will not be sad.*

"Yes, of course."

The doctor bowed and turned to head back toward the cottage. Once they were out of earshot, he paused, and Katherine stopped just outside of the reach of his arms. *When did I begin measuring distance based on the space between us?* That was not a question she was willing to answer.

Mr. Francis bowed again. "I am sorry to intrude on your morning, my lady, this will take but a moment."

Oh no! "Is it about Ebony's treatment?" *Perhaps he stopped coming because there is no hope for her! But she can't be sold to a factory!*

He tilted his head thoughtfully. "In a way, I suppose. I would like to make an offer for her."

"That is very kind . . . " *Did he hear my conversation with the stable master?* "But I have it on authority that she is worth next to nothing. Far less than you have already provided with your services. I could not ask anything of you and if you truly are interested in her, I gift her to you." *At least he would care for her.*

Mr. Charles—*Mr. Francis*—shook his head with a wry grin. "She is worth far more than 'authority' may see. Regardless, as a professional in my field, it would not bode well for my prospects to accept beasts as payment." He laughed. "No, I would like to offer one hundred guineas for her, and I would offer more if I could."

"One hundred guineas! Mr. Charles, there is *no* way that I could accept such a sum! She is an invalid and will possibly never recover!" *He has done too much already.*

"I know that better than anyone. Yet, my offer stands. Will you accept?"

100 guineas . . . What one hundred guineas could do for her family raced through her mind, and how much time it must have taken for Mr. Fra—*Mr. Charles!*—to save that sum from his country practice.

It is an answer to prayer, but how can I accept such kindness from a man I planned to turn out only moments ago?

Katherine pressed her hands against her stays. "I—I accept your gracious offer, but how could I ever repay you?"

He smiled again, bowing low. "That is the beauty of a sale. The payment is for something of equal or greater value."

Tears welled up in her eyes and she very nearly closed that arm-length gap between them to embrace this kind doctor. *But it must be a clean break. I cannot keep fooling myself into thinking that I am only walking with Ebony.* "Thank you, *ever* so much . . . " Katherine found herself at a loss for words. "Has the stable master paid you your due yet? I cannot accept your money unless I know that you have been dealt with justly."

He only nodded. "My lady, our accounts are completely settled. I only ask that you care for Ebony until I send for her. I have included a note for you to cash at the local bank for her board for the next week.

I shall pay the difference when I return." He pressed a bank note into her hand. She allowed her hand to linger a moment longer.

Thank you, Mr. Charles . . . you might not be a savior, but you have been my guardian angel. She didn't say those words aloud.

Then something he had said struck her. "Where . . . where are you going? I had thought you had taken up residence nearby."

Mr. Charles clasped his hands behind his back and looked past the buildings to the green beyond. *Where we used to walk . . .*

He smiled and responded. "My uncle is in need of some assistance." Charles paled slightly at the mention of his uncle. "He is not feeling well and, as I have some little skill in medicine, I am to attend him . . . for an unknown duration."

There it is, everything I could have wanted to happen . . . but why don't I feel relieved?

"I see. Then it is goodbye?" If she did not already have tears in her eyes they would have come now.

"Not forever, I hope. When my uncle improves, perhaps you might see me this way again. Perchance I will see you when I come for my mare." He smiled and looked back toward the stable where Ebony was still safe inside her stall. "You needn't tell the stable master of our arrangement. I have already enlisted the assistance of the boy who works in the stables. I know the business of training and boarding horses is busy and I would not want to interfere with the revenues the stables garner."

"You needn't worry about that. The stables are mostly services rendered without profit to my father's friends."

Charles's eyebrows rose. "Oh, I had misunderstood . . . no matter. Our arrangement still stands and all the best to you and yours."

"Yes, fare thee well . . . Mr. Charles." Katherine looked down at her clasped hands, afraid that if she were to look into his warm brown eyes again, she would fall to pieces.

With a smile in his voice, and something else, he bid her adieu. "Miss Katherine." He gave one final bow and strode away down the dirt path to the village. Katherine looked up, watching him go. She just stood for a moment with the bank note clutched over her heart. Then she rushed back to the cottage.

Trying to keep her breath under control, she raced through the entryway and dashed to her father's study, pulling the door open after barely a knock.

She held up the bank note with new tears streaming down her face. "Father, we are saved!" Then she collapsed, sobbing into his arms.

And he is gone.

⌒⟲⟳

"Your father seems in a state." Lady Blakesly stated, sitting with her needlework beside Katherine.

"Does he?" Katherine of course knew what the flurry of guests—Mr. Stewart and Mr. Banks among them—and the scrambling to the village and back had come from but was unsure of how much she could share. So, she focused on her shoddy sketch of what was meant to be a horse but had turned into a water buffalo somewhere after the exploit had begun.

Elizabeth did not hear the other ladies' conversation as she sat at the pianoforte, leafing through music. She had become more diligent with her musical studies ever since the two handsome men had come visiting. *Perhaps she thinks that men prefer the musical arts over needlework.* Her focus had been such that she hadn't noticed the hubbub that morning, or at least she had not commented on it. If she continued to work as diligently as she was, she would have at least two more songs prepared for her next ball. *I will be married by then . . .* Regardless of Elizabeth's intent on finding a new piece of music, Lady Blakesly and her eldest daughter continued to converse in hushed tones.

The lady continued. "Indeed. He kissed my cheek when he passed. He usually reserves such demonstrable affections for Christmas and New Year's . . ."

"Is that so—"

"Or when he is extremely relieved." Lady Blakesly looked directly into Katherine's eyes with the clarity of one who knows more than she lets on. "I wanted to tell you thank you . . . I know that far more is on your young shoulders than you deserve, yet you carry yourself with the poise of a true lady." She leaned her head over and rested her cheek on Katherine's hair.

Katherine gave up on the worsening sketch and closed her book and leaned into Lady Blakesly. "Thank you, Mother." *We all do what we can.*

Elizabeth groaned from the pianoforte. "Kitty! How do you know which piece is easy enough for what you can play, but *interesting* enough to entertain!?" Elizabeth laid her forehead down on her crossed arms across the discordant keys.

Lady Blakesly smiled and nodded toward Elizabeth. Katherine smiled back. "Coming, Sister. Perhaps I can help you."

❧

The next several days were spent the same. Katherine saw to Elizabeth's instruction at the pianoforte and was even prevailed upon to practice dancing, etiquette, conversation, and the other necessary skills for an eligible young lady. Katherine also visited Ebony most days, taking her on ever longer strolls. The bandage no longer looked red when it was changed and Ebony even pranced on the odd trip.

Perhaps Mr. Charles was right about her.

She hoped that he was.

Besides the usual employments and sisterly duties, Katherine spent most of her time in the sitting room listening for any visitors to be announced. For certain, Katherine employed her time reading, sketching passably, painting poorly, playing the piano, and anything else she thought might distract her, but really she never truly stopped the first labor on her list. May Day came and went with the colors and fun which that holiday always brought, but with a foreboding that was Katherine's alone to bear. *Soon Mr. Sterling will return . . . and I will be engaged.*

Part of her hoped that Mr. Sterling would arrive with the parson in tow, and they could marry quickly in front of her parents and have done with it. Part of her wished that Mr. Charles would return before she was married, and—*like the roguish common man he was*—steal a kiss from her *completely* unwilling mouth . . . though these fancies tended to only play out when she was asleep or distracted . . . very seldom when speaking or being spoken to. Thankfully, her nightmares about William and Mr. Sterling had mostly been replaced with these more enjoyable if only slightly less concerning visions.

It would be better if I allow the grooms to do their work and not see him. It is an unkindness to us both, and possibly an embarrassment for all.

Yet with each ring of the servants' bell, she sat higher in her seat and extended her neck to its fine length. When it was only the post, *again*, her back would slump, as much as years of training and her unyielding stays would allow. Even Elizabeth's regular boisterous attitude was eclipsed by Katherine's restless spirit.

Elizabeth squinted over her economics book, a recent favorite, when Katherine slumped *yet again*. "Sister, I think you should walk your horse longer than you do."

Katherine looked up from her same smudgy water buffalo. "Why is that?"

Elizabeth smiled. "I think you need to burn off more energy than the horse!"

Finally, after the fifth, and the tenth, and the fifteenth of May had passed with little respite from the poor weather, and no news from the continent, *or* from the charming doctor, Lord Blakesly visited Katherine before she came to breakfast.

"Good morning, my dear daughters. Eliza, would you be so kind as to excuse us?"

Elizabeth squinted suspiciously like she used to when she was young. "Of course, Father. I will practice my scales until breakfast is ready." As she left, she raised her eyebrows over her father's shoulder at Katherine, making it clear that Elizabeth would be asking for details later. Then Lord Blakesly pointed to the chairs in the small sitting room, and he waited for Katherine to take hers before he took the other.

"What is it, Father? This feels somewhat ominous."

Lord Blakesly's brows furrowed, not helping alleviate Katherine's feelings. "Have you heard from Mr. Sterling since his departure?"

What could this be about?

"No, Father, we are not yet engaged so we cannot write . . . is something the matter with the bank? He is meant to be here soon, he said, perhaps nearer to June than May Day."

Lord Blakesly continued, concern still etched into his face. "Did he say where he was going? Perhaps Paris?"

"He did not say—please, Father, you are giving me a fright. What is the matter?"

Lord Blakesly cupped his daughter's face with his hands for a moment and looked gravely into her eyes. "There was a fire . . . it razed several English factories in Belgium . . . I heard that a nobleman had died."

A cold chill slid down Katherine's spine. "How . . . how did this happen?"

Lord Blakesly tapped his paper. "Diplomatically, it has been ruled as an accident. But I heard other reports whispering that it was the Napoleonists exacting revenge on England for helping restore Louis to the throne . . . " He shook his head, unsure. "But there is such discord in France that it could have been any number of factions—or even an accident as they say."

Perhaps this engagement is more like the first than I had thought . . . Maybe it is not him?

Katherine exhaled the mounting weight of losing the love of her life, now almost two betrothals, and two financial saviors, breathing in a surprising calm.

We do not know yet . . .

"Thank you for telling me, Father. I do not know where this leaves us with the bank?"

"They have not made any connections yet . . . and we are not certain ourselves who the nobleman was who perished. I pray that it was not him, for all of our sakes."

We only pray that someone else's loved one died instead . . . but still, we must.

Katherine's anxiety grew each day that no news came. She told herself again and again that it wasn't him, *but how would they know if it was?* Many nobles likely had holdings on the continent . . . but the shadow hanging over her took more than hopeful thoughts to dispel. Katherine did not love Mr. Sterling, but mingled with her fears for her family were true feelings of concern for the man willing to be her husband and stand by her as a helpmeet. Elizabeth had not pressed to know what the meeting was about after seeing the fear in Katherine's eyes. Katherine's dark mood the following days had led Elizabeth to stop asking for assistance with her courting practice. It made the waiting all the harder, but she couldn't bring herself to offer again.

Will tragedy after tragedy befall me and my family until I have mourned the full year and one day that my heart had demanded? Or will these pains continue forever with no respite until I am laid to rest myself? I want to find Providence's light and blessing—the way I had felt with my William, but all I find is darkness.

Lost in these thoughts, Katherine nearly missed the message she had previously been so desperate to receive.

"Ma'am, a man has come to pick up m'lady's horse," the footman said with a bow, and before she knew what she was doing, Katherine was up and rushing to the front door.

Katherine spoke to herself as she rushed. "If anyone will be able to make heads or tails of this, it will be the good doctor." *Maybe . . .* She passed by the proffered furs and stepped into the belated winter without even a shawl.

An old husbandman bowed low. "G'day, ma'am. I've been sent about a horse." He bowed again, his hand raising high with his simple hat.

He didn't come . . .

Katherine stood straighter, her composure settling into place around her aching insides. "Yes . . . of course. Did the doctor say . . . anything?"

The man nodded vigorously, clearly unused to speaking to an *actual lady.* "Yes'm, he says that he's sorry he couldn't come himself, but that I'm to lead the filly at a right slow pace all the way back." He bowed again.

He probably didn't want to see me again. Smart of him. "Just so. Thank you. She took a shilling from a hidden pocket and held it out to the man. "See that she is cared for well, and I will be ever so grateful."

"Oh, no need for that, ma'am. The doc's got me right paid, well and good. If one of your men here can show me the horse, I can be on my way and out of your hair."

"I will, my lady," the footman said as he stepped forward and directed the husbandman toward the stables.

"Thank you . . . " Katherine watched as the last chance for happy news followed the footman down the cobbled lane.

He said he would come. Katherine stood in the cold, too dazed to even shiver.

After several minutes of this paralysis, Katherine turned and walked up the stairs to the door. Then the sound of loud hoofbeats rang out from up near the main road, coming quickly down the drive. Katherine looked up and saw a pair of horsemen riding the cobbled turns only moments from the house. The first man hopped off his horse as the servants scrambled around to receive his coat and hat. Before walking another step, the man dropped to one knee.

"Miss le Chevalier! Will you marry me?"

Katherine covered her mouth in shock at the man kneeling before her. One minute he was dismounting, the next proposing in nearly the same brisk manner. "My . . . how you have startled me, Mr. Sterling." *Now you are twice resurrected it seems.*

His ears turned pink as he stood and bowed. "Yes, I am sorry for my rudeness. I was simply overwhelmed with anticipation. Could we speak somewhere more privately?"

Behind the still-mounted footman and Mr. Sterling's gelding, Katherine saw the old husbandman leading Ebony past the carriage house as he headed down the twisting drive.

He was never going to return . . .

Katherine's frame stiffened with resolve. "There is no need, I will give my answer here. Yes, Mr. Sterling. I will marry you." The servants looked at each other in surprise, but withheld their whisperings for when they would be out of sight of the guest—their lady's *betrothed.*

Katherine smiled, pleasantry covering the emptiness in her heart. "Would you come in for some refreshment? I am pleased that you weren't harmed in your business on the continent." She walked into the house as if she had merely said good day to the gardener.

Chapter 16

May 28th

Tomorrow is Oak Apple Day, the day the country celebrates the restoration of King Charles II. We used to celebrate by handing out apple preserves to the villagers when I was young. Now my hopes have shriveled like the apples on the branches. There is no chance of restoration for the King of my heart.

I don't even know who that is now.

—Katherine, Applehill Cottage

Lord Blakesly had Mr. Sterling wait outside of his study for a moment while he took Katherine inside.

"Lights above, he is well—is he here to do what he promised . . . ?" Lord Blakesly wrung his hands in an uncharacteristic showing of nerves.

"Yes, Father. He has already asked me, and I have indicated that I am disposed to do so. He merely needs to receive your blessing and the papers are all but signed." Katherine said these words with the cold exactness of a businesswoman. *Perhaps he is rubbing off on me already.*

Lord Blakesly seemed not to notice her coldness in his relief. "Oh, my dearest daughter. This is *wonderful* news. The banks have granted a brief extension with the knowledge that you are promised to Mr.

Sterling—they have many dealings with him themselves and are aware of his standing. They have stated that if any other 'incidents' or 'disturbances' were to happen, they would call the loans. That would be the end of us—oh, but it doesn't matter because *our prayers are answered* just in time." Lord Blakesly sat down hard into his reading chair, wiping his brow.

Father hides it well, but he is nearly as excitable as Elizabeth. Katherine continued standing, pleased for her father, but unfeeling of anything else.

"Should I send him in then?"

"Yes . . . but do give me a moment to collect myself. This has been quite a strain."

I suppose it is good that the doctor did not come.

Katherine nodded and saw herself out. Mr. Sterling stood outside, looking a little nervous despite his strong status as the family's financial savior.

"He said he will call for you in a moment."

Lord Blakesly invited Mr. Sterling into his office with a stern look that to any who knew him was clearly masking a jovial mood. Indeed, if Katherine knew her father well, he would put on an intimidating act while discussing the terms, as if he was not desperate to sign the deal under nearly any circumstances. If Sterling was smart, he would see through the facade, but if he was wise, he would settle the agreement without offending the lord's pride.

Sure enough, not long after entering the study, the two men exited and bowed to each other with a look of mutual respect. Katherine, Elizabeth, and Lady Blakesly all rose from the seats that the servants had brought into the hall for them. Lord Blakesly stretched his arm out to Katherine who stepped forward to take his hand.

"My beloved eldest daughter, Katherine. I am happy to approve your betrothal to this fine young man." He led Katherine forward and placed her hand into Mr. Sterling's. "It is a day to celebrate!" The servants cheered as Lady Blakesly dabbed tears. Elizabeth smiled and nodded, though the smile did not seem to quite reach her eyes.

"When will be the day? This year without summer could use some happiness," Lady Blakesly asked.

Mr. Sterling cleared his throat and the servants quieted down. "I see no reason to delay. Would three weeks be enough time to prepare?" A seamstress in the back nearly fainted, but the rest of the servants cheered again.

Lord Blakesly clapped his hands together. "Splendid! Tonight let us celebrate and let us begin preparations tomorrow!" The lord very nearly clicked his heels, though with a raised eyebrow from Lady Blakesly, he transformed the motion into a step toward the dining hall. Everyone but Mr. Sterling trailed after him, though Elizabeth hung back close enough to be a chaperone, but not so close as to pry.

Mr. Sterling looked at their joined hands with mild interest. "You have said very little . . . is three weeks enough . . . my dear?" The pet name came mechanically from his lips, but with a determined set to his brow like he would become used to it, *so help him.*

"Yes. Three weeks is enough time . . . hopefully without killing the staff . . . though I had fancied being married at home. I suppose that is not enough time to petition a special license." Katherine was surprised to find Mr. Sterling's hand warm around hers. For how cool Mr. Sterling acted, he was only flesh and blood like her William had been—*or the doctor was.*

Mr. Sterling nodded in his usual curt manner. "If you want to be married here, then that is what will happen. I have a friend close to the archbishop who can arrange it for us. He owes me a favor."

Katherine nodded. "That would be delightful, thank you. And Mr . . . I should say, J-James . . . I wanted to ask about the terrible rumors I heard regarding an accident on the mainland. I was worried that it had been you."

He nodded gravely. "It was not a sight for the faint of heart. There were many trapped inside when the fires began . . . but we have done what we could to not allow that tragedy to hold back England's eternal progress."

Katherine's head tilted as they began to walk. "What do you mean?"

Mr. Sterling's face remained grave, but an animation buzzed in his voice. "The man who died was the son of my business rival. That man's young son was also with him for the factory inspection." His eyes darkened. "If he had sold me those factories as I had hoped, I very well could have been the one burned." He put his other hand around the one of Katherine's he held already and looked into her eyes with his steely grey ones.

"It is a tragedy, but I have been able to provide employment for many of the displaced workers in my factories and I have purchased the remaining materials from the old man. I have nearly doubled my wealth—our wealth, and the . . . challenges your father has faced will barely scratch what we shall gain."

Someone else's loved ones . . .

Katherine swallowed. "I am so very glad that you are all right." She meant it, if not quite as a lover.

Elizabeth left the post she had been leaning against and extended her hands to the couple. "Come sister *and* brother-to-be," Elizabeth's smile looked strained. *Perhaps she heard what we have been sharing.* "Let us celebrate your impending union."

Katherine stepped forward and took her sister's hand. "Thank you, Elizabeth, you are preparing well to be the new Miss le Chevalier." Elizabeth curtsied deep and smiled, the tension leaving her eyes.

Even without unreasonable demands for what the dress, cake, and ceremony were to look like, there were suddenly dozens of things needing to be done all at once. The papers and local churches had to be notified of the engagement and ensuing wedding, the dining hall needed to be decorated for the honored guests at the ceremony, and the parson had to be booked.

Miss le Chevalier, the soon to be Mrs. Sterling, threw herself into the plans, plates, and pleats with a fervor that surprised even herself. For her first engagement, she and William had wanted to spend as little time with the preparations as they could, so as to spend as much time together as possible. Mr. Sterling, James, was busy solidifying his business deals in Town and so had only stayed in Applehill a day before returning. Dutifully, he sent a brief and informative letter each day.

All is well, and I hope all is well for you and yours. My apologies that I am still held up and unable to assist with any of the wedding efforts. I trust that the selections you make will add to the day's success.

My dealings go well. I have had more offers of contracts in the past week than I had in the previous six months. Lords are always looking to increase their rents, and now that I will be one of them, they are most comfortable discussing these prospects with me.

Ever yours,
James Sterling

Katherine had long dreamed of love letters before she was engaged to William, but they had been so inseparable that they had sent very few letters to each other in that short precious time. Now she had the necessary distance for correspondence, but the emotional distance between their hearts prevented anything but crisp and sterile communications.

Katherine rarely thought about the doctor anymore, and only the faintest memories of her frequent fantasy survived the late bedtime and early rising of a woman with less than a month to her wedding. No, there was little left of the foolish fancies she had afforded herself in any part of her life. Soon she would be a wife, and likely soon after that, a mother. She would run their new household with acumen and dedication such as Mr. Sterling would expect from a woman of her breeding and would find happiness in the repetition of a pleasant routine, like so many married couples had done before her.

She would have none of the late nights talking by a dying fire or the passion so strong in her heart that it hurt to spend even a day apart. No, she would live with a simple happiness, a comfortable complacency filled with a sure foundation of mutual respect and a shared vision for their family. Yes, she would find happiness in her marriage like a farmer in his fields. Seeing it grow and bearing its proverbial fruit would fill her heart with satisfaction.

I can almost feel the roots forming already.

A maid broke her reverie with a tap on the door to the sitting room where Katherine was looking over the cook's final menu.

"Enter . . . Yes, what is it?"

The maid curtsied. "There is a lord here to see you, my lady."

"Mr. Sterling?"

"No, ma'am."

A jolt passed through her. "It's not Lord Alcott?" Katherine imagined the man blubbering and asking for her to reconsider her decision. *He must have seen it in the papers . . .*

The woman's head tilted. "No, m'lady . . . he says you'd best know him as 'Mr. Charles.'"

Chapter 17

May 29th

His name is Charles, and it is Oak Apple Day . . .
How blind have I been?

❦

Katherine blanched. "Did you say 'lord'?"

"Well, he didn't call himself that, miss . . . only he looks like one. He has a deep black horse there with him and he says he won't come in—" Katherine dropped the menu, smoothed her skirts and pinched her cheeks before walking stately past the maid, out of the sitting room, and down the hall to the entryway. For the second time in as many weeks, she eschewed the furs offered and strode out of the opened front door.

There was Charles—*the Charles*—standing in fine clothes and a beaver hat, holding the reins of an unbandaged Ebony who stomped and bobbed her head for an apple as if her ankle had never been hurt. Charles removed his hat from his parted hair and bowed with the same expertise of his earlier days, only now his clothing fit the motion.

Katherine shivered but ignored the servant who had followed her out with a coat. "What—how—why have you come?"

Charles rose from his bow. "Things have changed . . . Miss Katherine." He looked at the servants then fiddled with his hat. "Miss

171

le Chevalier, Ebony is healed, she rode beside my horse the whole way for days."

Katherine pulled her eyes off of Charles's commanding frame to Ebony. "She is beautiful. Thank you for letting me see her once again, but she is yours. Why have you brought her all this way?"

Charles took a step forward. "Miss le Chevalier, *my* situation has changed as well. My uncle, or great uncle as he is, suffered an immeasurable tragedy and he is left heirless . . . " He spread his arms to show his regal clothing. "He has selected me to fulfill this duty."

"Is your uncle?"

"He is a lord."

A lord . . . he is now the heir to a lord.

"Oh . . . " Katherine's heart ached within her, a longing she had never experienced before, even in the deepest throes with her love of William.

But the banks said, "No more incidents" . . .

Katherine cleared her throat and stood taller. "I am happy for you."

Charles began to kneel. "Katherine, I have come to ask for your—"

Katherine stepped forward. "Mr. Charl—*Sir* Francis, I must stop you." Charles's face fell and before he could say another word, Katherine continued, "I have recently become engaged to the honorable Mr. Sterling, and though I appreciate the great lengths that you have taken to demonstrate your skill as a doctor of medicine, your honor as a man, and now, a noble, I am afraid that I cannot accept the offer you are extending." The words flowed out of her mouth with surprising coolness as her heart screamed within her. Memories resurfaced of a potential future that could never be—images of kisses and touches she would never know with her cool and *sterling* betrothed.

Charles's face reflected all the pain within Katherine's breast. "But Katherine, I lov—"

"*Do not say that!*" Katherine's form trembled as the words echoed through the courtyard. Several servants poked their heads out from around corners but disappeared quickly when they saw who had shouted. *I cannot hear him say it . . . I will not have the strength to . . .* She whispered, "It is not to be supported . . . I will not hear those words from you."

Charles stood with white lips pressed firmly together, but he made no move to leave.

Katherine's heart ripped deeper each moment she did not fall into his arms. *I must send him away—but he won't go! He knows that I . . . that I too . . .*

Katherine drew a shaky breath. "How could you—how could you be so *mad*, so—so *crazed* to think that you love me? You know next to *nothing* about my heart or my mind, and you are overstepping if you think that *anything* had passed between us that would make me fall into your arms once offered. A nobleman would know that I was lost to him forever once I had signed the wedding agreement—a marriage is a *duty* not only a whim for young lovers."

Charles's fist tightened firmer around the reins with each word, but Katherine saw no change in his eyes. His fervor and mission had not changed. *Oh, please don't make me do it!*

Charles spoke. "Perhaps one that did not love you as I do, would be so easily swayed from his passion. Kath—*Miss* Katherine, I will only relent when I do not see regard for me in your beautiful face. Then, and only then, would I desist—if not in my heart."

"Then look upon this, my gorgon face and feel your heart turn to stone." She steeled her will and smoothed her expression to that of an uncaring statue. *Not only Elizabeth read Mother's magazines when she was young.*

Concern wrinkled Charles's brow, but he did not turn away. "You are talented beyond belief, but I am not fooled by your apropos performance."

Please don't *make me do this . . .*

Katherine let the steel of her expression sink like a dagger into her heart. "Sir Francis, it seems that you have taken a great deal of time *intimating* my feelings about you. Yet you have been mistaken." She swallowed the bile rising into the back of her throat. "To me . . . you will always be a *filthy . . . muck-shoveling . . .* commoner."

That rare mix of pain, sadness, and anger flashed through Charles's expression—a concoction of emotions only accessible to one who has the feeler's own heart in their hand. Charles loosened his grip on the reins, the leather of his gloves creaking as they eased. His voice escaped his lips in a near whisper, his bearing and tone that of a man bred since birth to hold his current standing. "I never found making my patients' lodgings more sanitary and comfortable to be beneath me . . . my only object was to see them well cared for."

When love is turned to ire, oh how deep the fires can burn!

"And am I one of your patients, sir? Does it please you to find every broken creature and bandage them up, and make them feel like they might be well someday—if they only follow your instruction? Am I to be just another animal in need of your doctoring the rest of my life? Led and bidden by the steady hand of a glorified groomsman playing the martyr?" The bile rose higher, burning her throat and gagging her. The words dripped and steamed like poison scorching the very stones upon which she stood.

Charles's face fell, like a man taking an arrow to the heart. "You were never *just* a patient to me . . . "

Both stood staring, a rift deeper than the English Channel now between them. Their gaze was broken by the thunderous sound of a horse galloping down the drive at post haste.

"Is everyone in such a hurry these days?" The servant with Katherine's coat spoke for the first time since the altercation had begun. He had not been able to escape and had opted to play a fawn camouflaged in long grass, rather than to move and draw the attention of these two young patricians.

The valet rounded the corner and hopped off his horse. He bowed quickly to Katherine, and then bowed to and addressed Charles, saying, "My Lord Harlow has sent me with the news that he is *en route* and that he is most displeased with you for running off without his approval."

The same Lord Harlow of Limeridge?

The valet continued. "He 'suggests' that you meet him in the inn, one town north of here." The valet clearly paled at the mention of his lord and paled further at Charles's hard expression.

Charles bowed his head to the man, "Thank you, Tim, but I have not finished my business here, so I will not be able to meet him."

The valet dropped to his knees. "Oh, sir, please don't send me with that message. I fear that his carriage would run me over in his haste to apprehend you here."

"I am sorry, Tim, but I am—"

Katherine raised her hand. "There is no need for further delay, Sir Francis, your business is complete. I refuse you, and as this has been a disruption from my wedding preparations, I must bid you good day." She turned away and covered her mouth, forceful breaths threatening to turn into sobs. *He cannot know how this kills me or he will never leave . . .* "Please give my regards to your lord."

Charles's brow softened. "All right, Tim. I will do as the lady says." He turned and patted Ebony's neck then released her leads and stepped over to his stallion.

I should just walk inside . . . but she couldn't. She had waited too long for him to come, and her heart wanted to see him as long as this last parting would take.

I will never see him again . . . at least not as Miss Katherine. I will be Mrs. James Sterling.

The valet rose from his knees and mounted his horse. Then Charles hopped up into the saddle. The two of them began a slow walk up the drive, but Ebony remained standing in the courtyard.

Katherine's voice cracked as she called, "You are forgetting your Ebony!"

Charles paused and turned back in the saddle. "She is yours. She was never truly mine, no matter what I offered for her." He turned back and Tim led on.

Katherine called again, taking an involuntary step after his retreating form. "Then—then I must repay you for her! I will not want to be indebted to you." *I am too attached already.*

Without turning back Charles spoke over his shoulder. "My lady, our accounts are completely settled. Always and forever. Consider her a wedding present."

The pain in her heart exploded, yet Charles continued, "Please care for her . . . and for yourself, as I will not be permitted to any longer." And he trotted around the hedge.

The cold wind rose, flicking and fluttering the hem of her gown like laughing demons prodding their next meal. Yet, she did not feel nature's cold any worse than the icy grip of despair. *If he had only come earlier, perhaps . . . perhaps things might have been different.*

Katherine entered the house. There she saw her father skipping along as he was wont to do, now that his worries were very nearly over. "Hello, my dear . . . what seems to be all the commotion?"

"Mr. Francis . . . Sir Francis returned my horse . . . as a wedding present."

Lord Blakesly nodded thoughtfully. "It is a rather generous gift, given the circumstances . . . but then it seems that generosity is his greatest virtue." He went to continue on to his study, but Katherine stopped him.

"What do you mean by that, Father?"

Lord Blakesly shrugged. "Well, I first met him when he returned my pistol of all things—somehow it ended up at the stables . . . " Lord Blakesly frowned a moment yet continued. "He had been commissioned by one of my friends to review his stallion but seeing your mare he offered his services . . . I had told him that, of course, we would not be able to afford such treatment for a horse that likely would not improve."

He didn't . . .

"But he said that he would see to the mare—"

"Free of charge?"

The lord smiled. "Precisely. He said it was a worthy exploit for his own education as a horse doctor and that alone was payment enough."

Katherine nodded, the tension in her spine that had kept her back stiff and head high sagged. *He was my savior . . . All along.*

The heavens would not be the heavens if they did not deny me entry for this.

She had never truly believed that she was cursed for dishonoring her heart, until that moment.

Chapter 18

June 12th

I have betrayed my heart twice. This pain will live on in me, unbidden and unsupported by any will, effort, or endeavor . . . until my last aching breath whispers my love for him—for my Charles.

Until then and forever.

—Cursed Katherine, Applehill Cottage

Servants muttered in the halls, maids gossiped in the passages, and doubts whispered in Katherine's ears. Still the wedding preparations marched forward like Napoleon's troops into ruin. Katherine found no solace in industry, no peace in sleep, and no comfort in conversation. Like a wight, she flowed from task to table, from bed to board, leaving barely a shadow in her wake. The usual rose of her cheeks traded for the common yarrow, white and splotched with patterns as varied as the hues of sadness.

I did not know that a broken heart, but little healed, could rend so much deeper.

Elizabeth tried everything to comfort her sister, but beside the faint smile or the nod of her head, Katherine gave little acknowledgement of the proffered consolation. Elizabeth even offered to brave the ever-gloomy environs to walk Katherine's now healthy horse, but walks did not rouse Katherine as they once had. *When I would see my Charles . . .*

I did not see it until it was too late.

Elizabeth finally had enough. "Kitty, you are scaring me!"

Katherine looked up from her nearly untouched meal and at the four-day pile of Mr. Sterling's correspondence that she had been unable to bring herself to read and spoke to her sister, "I am sorry to trouble you, Eliza, what seems to be the matter?"

"I don't know what the matter is because you will not tell me! I can barely sleep each night, fearing that I will wake next to a statue or a pile of bones. Katherine, won't you please tell me what is troubling you?!" Tears fell down Elizabeth's cheeks as she wrapped her arms around Katherine.

Katherine shook her head slowly, too tired to explain. Too sad to articulate her misery.

Elizabeth's eyes were round with unshed tears. "Oh Katherine, please tell me what is wrong—I only want you to be happy."

Katherine stared at her plate, seeing instead Elizabeth's disturbed eyes at hearing the shameful events of the past months from her elder . . . 'respectable' sister. Her mind's ear heard the hurt—the shame—the betrayal in her voice. *She would never look at me the same.*

Elizabeth touched Katherine's shoulder, turning her until their eyes met. "How can I make it better?"

"Thank you, Eliza . . . but you have not wronged me. I have wronged myself." Katherine speared a piece of ham. "To make it better . . . I am afraid that it is impossible." Katherine lifted her sister's hand off her shoulder, then she set to spearing, chewing, and swallowing each bite of food mechanically.

⸎

"Because I did not give my permission!" Lord Harlow roared from his couch. Since losing his son and his grandson, his health had deteriorated. Though Charles was seeing his improvements demonstrated even at that very moment with the force of the old lord's lungs. "You are my heir, a provision which I have been hard pressed to keep this last month, and I do not need to hear of you being thrown from your horse in your foolish, boyish, love-sick pursuits! You are a nobleman now, and it is not only *imperative* that you act like one, but also *mandatory*—so says your stipend!"

Charles would have had money of his own if he had not been working almost for free and living off what he had planned on using one day as an engagement present for the last several months. He had spent the remainder on Ebony's "purchase." He had never intended to keep the mare, though she was certainly worth as much as he had paid. Everything had been for Katherine . . . *my Katherine.*

"Yes, yes, Uncle. You have the right to name me foolish. I was a fool indeed."

Lord Harlow frowned. "Well, it's no good when you just take it." He settled back down under his covers. "What did she say?"

"She is already engaged to one Mr. Sterling."

"*Sterling!*" Lord Harlow nearly leapt to his feet only to spit and recline back down on the couch trembling. "He rises from the fires of my family's destruction and lights upon your little apple picker, eh? The money he is making at our expense must delight them both. Pfft." He went to recline but sat back up. "She's beneath you! But you had the right idea—it is best that you start looking for a suitable match. I want my succession secured before I head to my grave."

"Beneath me? She says that she will always see me as . . . as a commoner. How will anyone else not see the same?"

I have never hurt as much as when her cold eyes stared into mine.

The old lord waved his hand dismissively. "They've never seen you as a horse doctor, so they will have no reason to see you other than for what you are—a nobleman, an heir to an immense fortune and Limeridge Hall. Best if you forget about this little Miss Horse Apple." Lord Harlow nodded to himself, seeing the issue as settled, and laid back on his couch. "Now fetch me my medicine, *doctor.* I plan on returning to Limeridge by tomorrow morning at the latest. I detest these small-town inns."

"Yes, Uncle . . . my lord."

Goodbye, Katherine . . . I wish you every happiness.

The thick quilt did little to warm Katherine's rooms in the northwest corner of the cottage and despite laying down for an afternoon rest, no sleep had come to grant her reprieve from her pain. Elizabeth laid beside her, likely awake, but saying nothing.

If only Elizabeth knew . . . then we could cry into each other's shoulders like we used to.

Katherine laid in silence a moment longer. *But what would she think, knowing her elder sister fell in love with a commoner . . . or that I took Father's pistol to the stables in my night clothes . . . that he saw me?* Katherine shivered, more from her thoughts than from the cold. Elizabeth had looked up to her their entire lives—it would hurt to lose that regard. *At least I will soon be married, and no longer a dark mark on the family.* Katherine rolled over and closed her eyes.

Elizabeth spoke into the silence, "Katherine . . . may I ask you something?"

Katherine cleared her throat in the affirmative.

"I've been thinking . . . We are *very* poor. Aren't we?" Katherine said nothing, so Elizabeth continued. "You and Father meeting . . . you leaving mourning so early when you obviously didn't want to. I feel blind to some great conspiracy . . . Would you tell me now?"

Katherine laid on her back, sleep fleeing from her eyes. *Dare I share it?* Katherine remembered the secrets they would keep as girls, the broken plates and the stolen tarts. *It would be so* good *to not suffer alone . . .*

And Katherine's mouth opened.

She told of her shame standing nearly naked before Charles, then her worry about confronting him. She spoke of his honor in not disclosing the scandal. She shared her discovery of Applehill's near bankruptcy, and she described her decision to leave mourning early to find a suitable match. The more Katherine spoke, the more words appeared from the deepest reaches of her soul, finding freedom in confession to her dearest sister. All the while Elizabeth laid still and barely blinked.

Katherine stemmed the flow of her thought with these final words, "Now he is gone, and I am consigned to endless misery for lying first to myself and now to him and to everyone else."

Before I knew him, or anything about him—in the pit of my darkest night—I felt something stir within my heart. And even then, he cared for me. She squeezed her eyes against the burning as silent tears slid down her cheeks to her pillow.

After a moment of silence, Elizabeth spoke. "Whew . . . and I thought that nothing happens around here."

Katherine wiped her eyes. "Knowing the depths of my shame . . . can you ever look on me with fondness again?" Katherine's face screwed up against the tears that wanted to come, biting her lips in a heartbroken grimace.

Elizabeth looked surprised, but not disturbed. "Kitty, *my* Kitty. There is nothing that you could do that would take my love away from you."

Elizabeth extended her arms and Katherine fell into the embrace with gratitude, relief turning her joints to liquid. "Oh, thank you, Eliza—I am so deeply sorry, and thank you." In the dim light of the moon, her sister's face held a thoughtful look.

Elizabeth released Katherine then propped herself up on her arm. "So you *don't* love James—Uh, Mr. Sterling?" Her voice sounded more excited than conspiratorial.

"No, I do not . . . but he is aware of this already—"

"And *he* doesn't love *you* either?"

"No, he has said as much . . . but Elizabeth, what are you driving at?"

"No, one moment . . . " Elizabeth laid on her back with her fingers to her temples like she used to when working through the mathematics problems the governess gave her. "You do *not* love *each other* . . . but *Charles* . . . " She sat back up. "Katherine," she took her sister's hands, "Kitty, then do you *truly* love this Sir Francis?" There was a hopeful light in her eyes nearly brighter than the dim sun streaming through the windows.

Can I say it out loud to her—to myself?

Katherine looked down for a moment, feeling a warmth rise from her very core and spread throughout her entire body. "Y-yes. I have lied to myself over and over that being with him was only a pastime, a distraction, when really it is *everything* . . . " The warmth faded as she released her sister's hands. "But why do we speak of this? I am engaged to Mr. Sterling. We have signed our agreement and the banks will revoke our extension *and* call the loans if that were to change . . . "

Elizabeth nodded, closing her eyes and putting her fingers to her temples again. "Yes. I am working on that . . . " Then her eyes burst open. "Yes! Katherine, do you trust me?"

Katherine was a little startled by her sister's sudden animation, but she spoke. "Well, I did just share my deepest secret with you . . . "

"Good, then I am going to need you to trust me just a little longer. I think I have a solution to *everything.*"

"What?"

"There are only *days* until the wedding—oh! I don't know if it is enough *time!*"

"Enough time for what, Elizabeth? I am at a loss for what you are talking about."

Elizabeth grabbed Katherine's hands again. "Consider me your fairy godmother because I am going to make your dreams come true! You need to go to Charles's manor and bring him here."

"Now really, why would I do that?"

"Because you love him, and you want to spend your life with him!" Elizabeth seemed to be getting even *more* agitated if that were possible.

Katherine shook her head pulling her hands back once again. "This is not a children's book of princesses and knights. I have responsibilities. We would be ruined, and—and even if we could live with the same, what if Charles's uncle is unwilling to connect himself to a shamed house? Or if Charles does not have enough money to assist Applehill?" *What if he doesn't want me any longer?*

Elizabeth stuck her tongue out and blew. "Pish posh. Any man who would change his heart that easily isn't a man. Oh, I think I can do it . . . but *how.*" Elizabeth put her fingers once more to her temples, and Katherine very nearly ripped them off in grabbing them.

"What do you mean?!"

"My plan isn't finished. I need to do more research, but I know enough that you *need* to go to him!" Elizabeth's face filled with a fervent pleading. "Katherine, you've done so much for all of us your entire life! Please just let me do this one thing for you. I promise that I can make it work for everyone."

Part of Katherine longed to believe her sister—somehow getting to be with the man she loved—*I love him!*—and *somehow* still saving her family. "Elizabeth, I want to believe . . . but it sounds too good to be true. It feels like a dream."

Elizabeth smiled the biggest she had yet. "You just worry about getting him here, and *I* will arrange the rest."

I don't believe her . . . I can't believe her . . . but Katherine's heart, healed by the tender care of a master physician, was too strong now to be contained.

"I *do* believe you somehow—but what of Mr. Sterling?"

Elizabeth smiled with a glint in her eyes. "I will take care of him. You only need to get Charles here even if you have to drag him back."

Katherine rose from their bed, an anxious desire to run all the way to Limeridge blossoming in her chest. "This is *ridiculous!* He will think me such a fool!"

Elizabeth clapped her hands. "We are *all* fools when we are in love. But you must go! We have barely enough time to fit it all in."

Katherine threw on a jacket over her simple dress and slipped on her shoes. "Distract Father. Tell him that—"

"Do not worry about the details, only go!"

"Still, don't let Father down, I beg of you—it might kill him. And James will be here any day, stall him, please don't tell him, or send any letters to anyone—*anyone,* until I return. I need to formulate a—prepare a—something . . . rash." A light turned on behind Katherine's eyes and she was grabbing her gloves. "Tell Mother that I will not be coming to dinner, or breakfast and likely not the dinner or breakfast thereafter." She rushed toward the open door.

"I love you, Katherine! I will tell them that you needed to visit the Dentons—it is *almost* true." The words followed Katherine out as she gave in to the heady delight of running *toward* the one you love instead away from him.

Katherine slid down a span of the banister like she did in nursery school, then she dashed down the rest of the flight and through the corridor, grabbing the first available fur before leaving the house with an ecstatic *bang* from the slamming door behind her.

"I will take Ebony and sleep in the saddle if I have to. William said she was the fastest horse he had ever encountered." She stopped dead in the cobbled courtyard. "Oh William." She clasped her hands together and looked up at the grey, cloudy skies. "Oh William . . . I was untrue to my heart when I left mourning for you. But I would be untrue to my heart now if I were to ignore my love for Charles. May I be released from the bands of our past love that I had so happily entered with you?"

Katherine stared up at the slate clouds, the same slate as that night so long ago. Then that same cold wind blew strong, forcing her skirts around her and stray hairs to escape their pins. Up above, that vaporous ceiling parted allowing some little light to shine through, warming her face like a touch for just a moment, and then it was gone.

One happy tear cooled her cheek like so many times before. "Thank you, William. May you rest in heaven with all the Holy Angels."

And she took off running.

I wonder if that stable boy has much experience with being a chaperone.

Chapter 19

June 14th

I will have to save this little piece of paper until I can transcribe it into my journal. My heart dares to hope, but my mind screams that it is too late. I might lose silver for only a passing chance at gold . . . but hope—love—is worth the pain!

—Katherine, the road North

Sir Charles Patrick Francis awoke as the carriage stopped before Limeridge Hall in the predawn light. He made sure that the footmen helped his great uncle into his quarters and then he drifted to his own rooms.

My own rooms . . . my mother always said that I would attain higher than my father's station. I only wish that she had lived to see it. Limeridge Hall was large and mostly empty beside the dozens of servants and staff. *It would have been warmer with more family . . . or with someone to share it with.* Charles reclined on his large, down-filled bed and slept the rest of the morning.

Around noon, a footman knocked on the door. "Sir Francis, Lord Harlow is preparing for luncheon, and he requests your presence."

Charles groaned from his four poster, "I did not sleep well in the carriage and was hoping to rest some time longer. When does he 'request' my appearance?"

The servant paused and continued with a guilty voice. "Within the quarter hour, sir."

Charles sighed. "So be it. Please, send my valet. I will need some help getting dressed."

Fifteen minutes later, a washed and dressed Charles with dark bags under his eyes sat at the table in the smaller dining hall with Lord Harlow. Charles stared at his food, disinterested despite its splendor. "Could we not have eaten luncheon at two as we are used to?" Charles asked, rubbing his eyes. "I barely slept the entire way to Limeridge."

Lord Harlow cut a piece of meat before responding. "No. You've said it yourself that I need to eat to regain my strength, and I wasn't going to wait around an extra two hours simply for tradition's sake. You need to learn to sleep in a carriage. Most people find the rhythm soothing."

Charles only nodded and took a slow bite from a roll. The two of them ate in silence for several minutes, having recently learned the other's equal preference for quiet at meals. They had learned much about each other in the short time since Charles arrived and the subsequent decision for him to become his heir. Lord Harlow preferred that Charles do everything he "suggested" while Charles preferred not to, having been a self-made and self-governed man from his late youth. They were finding their way through it steadily, if roughly.

Another round of breads and meats were carried in by servants and served to each of the men as they continued in silence. Lord Harlow looked intently out the window as he chewed until a dark look crossed his brow at something he saw.

"Footman, a word."

The servant stepped forward and bowed, remaining low so that the Lord could whisper in his ear. Lord Harlow was more accustomed to shouting his orders, but his heir had made it a matter of health to maintain greater decorum.

It will be doubly beneficial, for if he were ever to truly be in distress, there would be a differentiation from any mild annoyance. Charles smiled at the thought.

"I appreciate your courtesy in whispering, Uncle . . . but what did you tell him?" The footman's expression had been one of shock before he hurried out of the room through the oaken door behind Charles's chair.

Harlow waved his hand, but his eyes remained angry. "It seems a *farmer* wandered in from the village. I sent the footman to send them off." Lord Harlow muttered something incomprehensible beneath his crackling breath. Then he glared out the window and nodded. Charles looked, but all he could see was the footman exiting the great doors and shooing off an unseen visitor. Charles shook his head and continued eating.

Lord Harlow sat frozen for a moment, his mouth agape with a chunk of meat he had just deposited there, sitting unchewed and forgotten.

Has he gone and had an apoplexy on me?

"Are you quite all right, my lord?"

Harlow closed his mouth, chewed twice, and swallowed, placing his elbow on the table and leaning toward Charles. Being on either end of a great table, the lean did little to close the distance, but Charles placed his fork beside his plate and folded his hands to listen.

"I have many acquaintances and kindred who would be interested in shackling you to one of their heirs with my descending title." He spat at the thought. "Have your feelings changed about that country girl? It wouldn't do for your debut as a lord-to-be with you pining away after some rotten apple."

Charles sat up straight. "My feelings have not and will never change."

Harlow scowled. "That's your youth talking. You will marry a woman, have an heir, and then, only then, will you be free to do as you please. If you have no heir, my blasted cousins will squabble over Limeridge before you've even breathed your last." The door opened and closed quietly behind Charles and Lord Harlow stretched his crooked back straight, suddenly looking the commanding lord he had been decades ago. He wiped his mouth slowly with his napkin and dumped it onto the table.

Charles responded, "If I am not to have my Katherine, what difference will it make that I did not have an heir? What would I be propagating but an unhappy arrangement of bodies and fortunes? I was well enough off with the horses. Why would what happens after my life of solitude be of any material issue to *me*?"

Lord Harlow answered calmly with more ice in his voice than the shadowed corners of the cold castle. "Refusing this duty is the same as refusing to be my heir, for I will *not* have my legacy destroyed by those pompous idiots I am forced to count as relations."

Charles tilted his head but said nothing.

"Perhaps after she has married and provided her *businessman* an heir, you will change your mind." The slightest increase of his brow indicated a question. Charles thought for a moment before speaking.

"Uncle, I chose to accept your offer to be your heir for two reasons—I cannot say the order in which my mind assessed them, but it was for both reasons just the same." Charles raised a finger. "One, so that I might care for my grandmother's sole remaining brother with the authority of more than just my schooling and vocation as a doctor, and," he held up the other finger, "Two, that I might become a lord and win the hand of the woman I love." An audible gasp escaped someone behind Charles, but he continued without glancing back.

"As it is, I am happy to wait upon you and wait upon her for the time when both of you need me. I am at your bidding to do all that is necessary in aiding your health and running the estate and your affairs, but I will never oblige you to marry someone for the sole purpose of 'producing an heir.'"

Harlow crossed his arms, somehow sitting even taller than before. "You have never and *will* never be of the same class as this *Applehill* Miss So-and-so." He gave an instinctual head-only bow as if she were in the room. "Before you were below her, though I daresay not by much. And now you are as high above her as she is the soil and sand beneath her dainty feet. This *cottage* they inhabit is barely 200 years old and as small as one of our outbuildings—"

"My lord, the cottage is well kept and—"

"*Their estate is run into the ground!*" The old lord stood with the strength of his indignation. "You would connect yourself, *and MY title*, with such a scandalous house as this? A woman out of mourning not even a month after the death of her betrothed and flirting with every available fortune within grasp? You would throw away *generations* of noble reputation to condescend to such a lowly match?"

"Yes, my lord, I would—"

"May I remind you that *she* refused *you!* She is connected with that businessman—the only man who has profited as much as you have from my personal tragedy. What makes you so *willing* to spit in my face for a woman such as that!?"

As Charles stood, he pushed hard enough against the great table to shove it an inch towards his great uncle. "*BECAUSE I LOVE HER!*"

Lord Harlow slowly sat back into his seat. Charles had never yelled at him before.

He continued. "I saw her at her lowest. I saw her in the depths of anguish and pain and my heart *longed* to be hers. Perhaps it already was. I know it was foolish of me, but I could not accept that a woman—any woman, let her be young, old, plain or beautiful—I *would* not accept that any daughter of divinity should be laid so low."

"Yes, it was foolish of me but as I strove to serve her in any way I could, even as a lowly commoner, I came to know her. *Every second* I spent with her I loved her more—from her painful beauty to her aching wit. Each moment I fell more deeply in love with her . . . and my situation became more and more, *ever* more wretched."

Charles leaned across the table, his hands placed ahead of his forgotten plate. "I love her, and no matter what she may or may not think of me, I will *never* be free of her. I was bound to her when I was below her station, and I would pull her up to my new station by those same bonds if she would have me." Charles's strength leached away with the hopelessness of his situation, the knowledge that the love of his life would be married to someone else in a matter of days. He sank slowly back into his seat.

Lord Harlow looked over Charles's head with his lips pressed firmly together, sharing the look that Charles had worn not two days previous. Then he slapped the table and spoke. "Well, what do you have to say to all that then, eh? Will you just stand there all day disrupting my *private* luncheon with my nephew?" Lord Harlow crossed his arms and scowled over his nose.

Charles opened his mouth to speak, but a familiar melodious voice responded instead, filling his broken heart with searing hope.

"No, my lord . . . I do not mean to disturb you all day." Miss Katherine le Chevalier stepped forward and curtsied low to the lord and then nearly as low to Charles, as her eyes darted to his face then back to the floor.

"Kath—Miss le Chevalier, what—why—how did you come to be here?" Charles whispered, afraid to wake from this dream.

"Since you left, I have been lost. I drifted through the days like the shadows on a clock face, passing time but leaving no impression . . . " Katherine swallowed and glanced at the stern-faced lord whose mask of wrinkles glared unwaveringly back at her. "I came to say that with an undying admiration . . . and regard . . . I am inclined to tell you—"

What if he hates me for what I said?

Charles stood and crossed the room in two bounds, stopping before her to look deeply into her eyes. He raised his hand, lightly touching Katherine's cheek with a finger. The butterflies within her burst into winged flames like phoenixes, their roaring fires arching from his touch to her very center. Katherine caught her breath and his hand in hers, as he softly whispered with hope in every syllable.

"Do you love me, Katherine?"

Katherine's throat caught on the words that beat frantically within her leaping heart. *Can all that he said before be true? Could he truly still love me after the terrible words I said to him?* Katherine released Charles's hand and took one step back to look him in the eyes. "Sir Charles Francis, I have somehow loved you from our first meeting."

Charles closed the distance once again, pulling her into his encircling arms. Katherine's pain dissolved as she crushed into his chest. All that remained was a deep desire to never leave his arms again. Loving warmth radiated through every limb and digit, through her cheeks and face, tingling in her parted lips. And just as one embrace had changed her heart forever, this embrace filled her with the love she had been bereaved from all that time.

Katherine whispered, "I cannot share how many times I have kissed you in my dreams . . . "

Charles looked down at her and her chin tilted up. They breathed only two hands apart, the natural magnetic forces of lovers' lips pulling all the way down to her lifting heels. *One hand . . .*

Lord Harlow hacked a laugh. "This changes nothing! She is engaged to another man, and I will forbid it—so long as you are my heir." Harlow crossed his arms with a firm expression, immovable as Limeridge itself.

Charles closed his eyes and grimaced, loosening his hold on Katherine but not releasing her from his arms. Katherine's already pink cheeks reddened further, glancing at Lord Harlow.

Katherine's eyes welled up as Charles looked down into her loving face. "Love . . . is worth every cost." Charles turned to his uncle. "I know that your word is law, and once stated you will not go back on it—like you disavowed my grandmother for marrying beneath her, you will have to disinherit me." Charles threw off his overcoat as Harlow's eyes burst alight like angry embers.

Then Charles took Katherine's hand and led her from the dining hall. Harlow fumed in his great chair as they did.

Charles led Katherine quickly to the entry. Katherine spoke as they hurried. "Don't you have to collect your things? I'm sorry to say that I don't expect him to have you back . . . "

Charles laughed, squeezing her hand lightly with an aching familiarity like they had been holding hands forever, *but I never want to stop.*

"Nothing here is mine, most of my belongings are still in my flat in the village. I hadn't a mind to pick them up yet." They left through the front doors and Charles sent a footman to collect his horse. Thom stood with his tan gelding and Ebony, tapping his foot anxiously.

"Ma'am, these footmen are pretty angry . . . "

"Yes, we're leaving now, Thom," Charles said, smiling at his little agent. Then he turned to Katherine. "How can this be? Won't the shame destroy your family?"

She swallowed. "Just as you gave up everything for me, I am willing to do the same . . . and Elizabeth seems to think she can work it all out somehow." *Though that seems less and less possible the longer I am away from her excited expressions.*

"Well, I hope she wasn't planning on the lord's money as part of the solution . . . " Charles cringed at the old house as his horse was led up by a confused looking footman. "Because *that* is not something I can offer any more."

Katherine closed her other hand around Charles's. "We will make it through."

He smiled. "Yes, even if we be penniless paupers." Charles helped Katherine mount her horse then he hopped up into his own.

Katherine smiled at him, sad at seeing him lose such a beautiful manor as Limeridge, *but pleased that he would do so for her.* She opened her lips, feeling more aware of how disheveled she must look after a full night of riding post. "I may have forgotten to mention that Elizabeth's plan *might* involve us being married . . . on the eighteenth."

"Married in only four days?" Charles asked. "Do you think I would be fit to be your husband so soon?" He looked into Katherine's smile with a hunger she had never seen before.

She gulped as something within her echoed back the same desire. "I should say yes."

"You *should* say, or you do?"

Katherine laughed as Charles trotted up beside her to take her hand again, refilling her overflowing heart.

Chapter 20

June 17th

The eve of my wedding day. I see the familiar trees and landmarks from my sweet Ebony's back, catching glimpses of my beloved guiding his great stallion. I do not know how, but something whispers to my heart that as long as I am with my Charles—the king of my heart—all will turn out right.

—Katherine Soon-to-be FRANCIS, the road to Applehill.

The closer the three horses drew toward Applehill, the greater Katherine's disquiet resounded. After the heat of standing before Lord Harlow's ire, and the warmth of being encircled in the strong arms of her beloved doctor, the wintry cold and ominous feelings of the altercation to come felt all the colder. The fear chilled her to the very center. Still, the hope of what was to come shone brightly, casting the fears to the side whenever she imagined her life with Charles.

Her third, and final, betrothed stayed close on his mount, taking turns speaking with her and Thom. Katherine would have enjoyed the leisurely ride much more without a chaperone but how often she imagined Charles pulling her in for a kiss . . . *it's probably best that he is here.* Katherine blushed as she contemplated her impending nuptials in only one day, and one extremely uncomfortable conversation, away. She looked over at Charles's intent face as Thom shared some inconsequential detail about work at the stables and she blushed deeper. Trying not to follow the vague thoughts of what his lips might *really* feel like. *Today's troubles are all I can handle right now . . .* Still, she eyed Charles's strong back and confident seat on his steed with a quickening of her heart.

While she fought with her aching imagination, the horses *finally* turned down the drive to Applehill. With a wintry shiver, all the dreams of wedding silks were replaced once again by the cold and calm face of Mr. James Sterling looking deep into her eyes with the face of her buried first betrothed.

The horses' hooves clicked and clomped over the old cobbles, echoing the skipping and pounding of her racing heart. They made the last turn and slowed as they pulled up in front of the cottage. Katherine and Charles had already agreed that he would hold back at the door to allow Mr. Sterling to save face. Katherine had accepted Charles's petition for him to step in if Mr. Sterling seemed especially enraged, but she had only accepted this because she knew that James would never lash out in anger, and it had been the condition to prevent Charles from stopping by his flat for a sword or pistol.

"It will not come to blows," she had said. "I am the one dishonoring *him*, not the other way around, and we will apologize—grovel, if we have to—as best we can."

Charles wasn't completely convinced that Mr. Sterling would be so reasonable, but he had figured that he could always borrow a weapon from somewhere, so he had yielded.

We are already compromising so well together, Katherine had thought.

The horses snorted as they stopped, sensing the food at the end of their journey. Mr. Sterling exited the cottage. He looked a little nervous, but otherwise his usual brisk self.

He must not know yet.

"Good day, Miss Katherine . . . it is pleasant to see you."

Could I really have lived with such cold civility my whole life?

"Good day, Mr. Sterling . . . likewise." Her core tightened and her voice shook a little as he walked forward and handed her down from her horse onto the step the footman had brought forward. Katherine walked toward the rest of her family coming out of the cottage.

"Elizabeth, it is good to see you. And Mother. And Father . . ." She curtsied to her parents still holding Mr. Sterling's hand. *I must do everything I can not to anger him . . . I do not know what Elizabeth has planned.*

She looked over to where Charles had dismounted from his horse and was directing the grooms to take the animals away. Seeing him gave her the strength to turn back and speak. "I have some news for you all that I think best shared in the drawing room."

Enough proposals and refusals have happened in this courtyard for the next century.

Lord Blakesly looked at Lady Blakesly, his smile at seeing his daughter turning to confusion. Lady Blakesly nodded her look to her husband saying that she didn't know what was going on either. "Just so, let us enter," the lady turned to one of the servants and whispered. She would be requesting tea for the new arrivals and for chairs to be set up in the drawing room where no one would disturb the meeting.

Charles delayed past the last person entering the house, watching the horses be led away, before entering the door that was still held open for him.

"Sir, will you be joining the party in the drawing room?" the footman asked, directing him toward the door that was closing behind Elizabeth's full skirts.

"No, thank you, my good man, I will be invited in shortly, but I should like a chair to sit in nearby."

"I'll see to it, sir."

Inside the drawing room, chairs were already arranged in a semicircle roughly facing the window and each other. Mr. Sterling escorted Katherine to her seat then he waited for Lady Blakesly and Elizabeth to sit before he and Lord Blakesly sat at the same time.

"What would you care to share with us . . . my dear?" Mr. Sterling sounded as awkward with the verbal affection as always. Katherine saw Elizabeth cover her mouth, looking a little pale but still smiling.

I really hope that you know what you were doing, Elizabeth . . . and I hope you didn't just do this to help me at the expense of the rest of the le Chevaliers.

Somehow that thought had not yet crossed Katherine's mind until this moment. *Oh, please let it not be that . . .*

Katherine shook her head to clear her thoughts and replied to Mr. Sterling. "You have been immensely kind and considerate in your time spent here, your proposal, and in the letters you have sent me." Katherine looked at her father who was beginning to look concerned.

"Mr. Sterling, I must call off our engagement."

Lord and Lady Blakesly gasped, then Lady Blakesly whirled her head around at Elizabeth who had not responded as she had. James likewise looked from Katherine biting her lip to Elizabeth's stony expression.

Mr. Sterling did not speak at first. He only released Katherine's hand and sat still, his thoughts obviously running like his mills and factories behind his eyes. Then, in his characteristic calmness, he looked at Katherine again. "May I ask why?"

Katherine swallowed, looking over at Elizabeth who nodded with a smile and then her father who had a mixture of shock, hurt, confusion, and a bleak acceptance to his fate. "I—I do not love you, and I feel that it would not be . . . be worth—or would not be right for us to . . . well, to marry." She had gone over what she would say an infinite number of times, but no preparations could have been sufficient for his cool gaze.

Mr. Sterling's ears turned redder, but his voice remained calm. "We knew that when we signed the marriage contract. My sentiments have not changed. I feel—felt that we would grow to appreciate each other. What has changed so drastically in yours?" He folded his arms, his facade breaking a little, offense showing in the placement of his mouth.

I never imagined kissing those lips.

Katherine's eyes moved up to his own over the marble perfection of his handsome face. There was a lot for a woman to love in Mr. Sterling . . . *but I am not that woman.* "If I must be specific . . . I am in love with someone else."

Lady Blakesly began fanning her pink face, once again looking at Elizabeth with disbelief at her daughter's neutral reactions. "Am I the last to know *everything* in this house?"

"No, Lady le Chevalier . . . it appears that I am." Mr. Sterling removed an invisible hair from his immaculate sleeve. "Who is he? Is it Lord Alcott, or that fop Braxton?"

Katherine swallowed, shifting in her chair. "Neither . . . it is Charles Francis . . . Lord Harlow's new heir." *At least, he was.*

Mr. Sterling stood, his hand to his breast in surprise. "The doctor?" And whether he had been listening, or couldn't wait any longer, Charles chose that moment to enter and bow.

"Mr. Sterling . . . "

"Mr. Francis . . . " Mr. Sterling did not return the bow. "It would seem that you are the one profiting from my misfortune."

"Like you have profited from my uncle's." The men stood as still as tigers thrust into the same cage.

Katherine stood between them with her hands up. "It is my fault that you have been treated this way, and I beg for your forgiveness."

Mr. Sterling nodded curtly. "I give it freely of course. It is not un*common* for one such as I to be cast aside when an *heir* is made evident." He then bowed slightly. "I wish you a happy marriage." He straightened and removed another false speck. "Now I would not want to offend, but I must be going. The papers print by two and I must have my announcement ready. I would not want there to be any confusion about my status, the other lords may want to revoke their contracts."

Katherine's mouth opened but no words came out. Charles maintained his strong stance, though he advanced to stand beside Katherine. Mr. Sterling bowed to Lord and Lady Blakesly who could only look him in the eye briefly before looking away. Katherine looked at Elizabeth whose lips were quivering with something other than fear, something Katherine could not place as she presented her hand for James to kiss. He hesitated but then bent down to kiss it. Just as his lips parted, Elizabeth jumped up from her seat, startling him backward.

"I can't stand it anymore. I must say it now."

"Miss Elizabeth le Chevalier, can you settle yourself for *once?*" Lady Blakesly hissed.

Elizabeth beamed through teary eyes. "That's just it, I *will* settle this, once and for all time. James, I will marry you." Now it was everyone else's turn to gasp.

James took another step back, a faint color rising in his cheeks. "Why—why would I—or we . . . do that?" His calm demeanor was broken by Elizabeth placing her hands lightly on his shoulders and leaning conspiratorially.

"Because I believe that you are quite taken with me . . . and if it is lady-like enough for me to say, I have been taken with you since the moment I first laid eyes on you at my debut ball."

Katherine looked at her sister's glistening eyes.

This is your solution? I don't see how this will solve "everything."

Elizabeth winked, a tear escaping past her wide smile.

Mr. Sterling looked the most out of sorts that he ever had, sweat glistening on his marble temples and color in his usually cold cheeks. "I . . . I am not sure about what you are saying, but I haven't—" Mr. Sterling gulped as Elizabeth wrapped her arms around him and pulled him into her strong embrace. His cheeks and ears went even redder, as red as liveried officers, but he did not push her away. "How . . . we have no agreement, Eliza . . . I need a title if I am to progress in my influence, and this title is tied to the eldest daughter. I do not have the luxury to marry for love alone."

He does love her! I am proven the Leah to her Rachel it seems . . . She smiled in wonder.

Elizabeth squealed and hugged even harder, laying her head on his shoulder. "You do love me! Oh, you do not know how pained my dreams have made me. Loving my sister's betrothed with no *way* to communicate my passions or to stop them in their place!" Elizabeth kissed him quickly on the cheek then backed away with the regal bearing of a princess. She extended her hand and looked away, with the obvious intent of using his hand to sit. He obliged, with eyes only on her.

Lord Blakesly had grown paler by the minute, his wife turning pinker such that they looked like one carried all the blood between the two of them.

Once seated, she patted the chair beside her. "Let me tell you *all* how this will go." She pointed at the chairs across from her and Katherine sat with her hand in Charles's. "This is all very simple. I've thought it through several times, and it will work *perfectly*. Now that we know where everyone stands in their hearts." She paused and looked at James, taking his hand in hers with only a small protest escaping his lips before settling down to listen once again.

"We will have not one but *two* weddings tomorrow. I will marry James, and Katherine will marry her strapping sir stable boy." She winked to show she meant no true disrespect.

James dabbed his temples with a handkerchief. "But Eliza . . . my dear Eliza," the loving words came so much freer when he said them about her. "I've told you already that I cannot agree to this. My aspirations would be dashed—I don't have the luxury to choose love."

"Yes, yes, aspirations, aspirations. When I am your wife, we will speak of these aspirations, and we will plan them properly—I've been studying. But *this* will not dash them. This is the simplest of capers." Elizabeth sat up like a governess teaching letters. "I have been mistaken for the eldest on as many occasions as I have been out and by nearly every person I've met. Thus, we simply *update* the agreement with my name, add an announcement of the dual marriage and the confusion about which sister was meant to inherit the title will go out with the wash!"

Lord Blakesly looked like he was about to have an attack of his nerves while Lady Blakesly simply tapped her lip with her finger. Lord Blakesly spoke, regaining some of his color as his wife's normalized. "But that would mean Katherine giving up her birthright—her very birth order—so willingly?"

"Certainly! She has the love of her life . . . and we will take care of them. They can live with us forever. Oh, say you will, Sister?" Elizabeth's eyes pleaded as her hands pulled Mr. Sterling's enclosed hand to her heart. "I never cared for the title, but this is a way that we can both have the love our hearts have longed for."

James the supplanter like Jacob of old . . . or Elizabeth the supplanter. Katherine took Charles's hand and squeezed it, *and he's the mess of pottage.*

Katherine stood and crossed the short distance to kneel before her sister. "I would be honored to call you my elder sister." Then she kissed her on both cheeks and curtsied like they had been taught as children together.

Elizabeth laughed, then started bawling, hugging a now perpetually startled Mr. Sterling and then releasing him a moment later to hug her now "younger" sister. "I was so afraid that it wouldn't work!"

Lady Blakesly rose, followed by Lord Blakesly, who now looked full of wonder, to encircle the three figures in a rare embrace.

Katherine wiggled her way out as Elizabeth blubbered to her mother about how happy she was. Then she made her way over to a grinning Charles.

"So, it's settled then. I get the love of my life and you get your age miraculously shrunk by two years. Many a lady would envy you," he said. "If they wouldn't envy your financial prospects . . . " He looked down, ashamed to take her from the world she was raised in.

Katherine smiled and extended her hand like her sister had just done. "Charles, *my* Charles, any woman that did not envy me for having you would be *daft.*"

Charles's eyes flashed with a desire that called to Katherine's own. Then he kissed her hand. She cleared her throat and turned to the now seated quartet. "Father, Charles and I would like to take a stroll together. Should I have a man sent to fetch Mr. Banks to arrange everything?"

"Yes, yes. Indeed! We have much to prepare before the morrow!"

Then Charles took her hand and led his new betrothed from the drawing room.

⌒⌒⌒

"This will be our last walk together before we are man and wife," Katherine said over her shoulder as the fading sun fell into the trees. Ever since the crazy events of that morning, they had taken every moment they could spend together, but soon they would have to part until the ceremony.

Charles skipped along, kicking stones like a boy. "I still cannot believe that you love me in return. I had hoped and prayed for so many days and nights. Now we are walking together, *really* walking together and soon we will never have to part!" Katherine allowed him to lead her into a close embrace. The cold of that endless winter swirled around them, but in his arms she felt warm and safe. Deep within her a spark glowed whenever she was near him and when they touched it exploded into light.

Katherine whispered into his chest, "I worry that when I finally kiss you . . . and you press your lips to mine, that I will simply combust, leaving nothing but a pile of smouldering ash."

Charles raised an eyebrow, mirth playing with the desire she saw every time their eyes met now. "I would put you back together again . . . so your heart could burst once more."

"And again, and again, and again." She squeezed harder. Here in the light of the cottage windows they were safe to be close. Katherine wasn't entirely sure she trusted herself alone with him anywhere else.

Soon.

Charles released her from his embrace but kept holding her hands. "I suppose they will be wanting us for cards . . . but I had a thought to visit Ebony one last time, to get her blessing." His eyes gleamed.

Katherine sighed. "You sound almost as business-oriented as Brother James." Elizabeth had coined the pet name for him, saying it sounded "less cold."

"I will try not to be too long on this *errand* but may have a little to do with *Brother James's* business after all." He took her hand and placed it in the crook of his arm, and they walked the now dark, yet still familiar cobbles toward the stables. They took their time, savoring the last quiet they would have before the day of wedding preparations and an afternoon and evening neither could wholly put out of their heads.

Much too soon, the stables loomed with their ancient beams before them. The foul weather meant the lanterns were already lit despite the summer sun staying out later. Charles hesitated a moment before leading Katherine through the large doors. The stable master sat at his desk reviewing a ledger that he placed face down the moment the two entered. Charles nodded to him, with a firm expression, then led Katherine quickly over to Ebony's stall.

It was hard to believe that this horse was considered lame only a few months prior. She whickered and bucked restlessly, giving even the most robust stallions a run for their money in disposition.

I am so happy that Charles was there to stop me. I wonder . . .

Katherine looked at Charles. "Were you afraid that night that I might shoot you?" She stroked Ebony's muzzle as the mare nuzzled her other hand searching for a treat.

Charles grinned. "If I am to be completely honest, I was a little at first, but once you let me come close, I was no longer worried . . . it would not have been the best way to go perhaps, but it certainly would not have been the worst." He laughed.

"You never thought about telling anyone . . . about what you saw?"

He leaned against the old beam. "I could barely believe I had seen it myself . . . seen you. But I would be the greatest of all liars if I said I didn't remember every single instant of that late night meeting."

Katherine's first instinct was to look away, the usual color warming her cheeks, but then she looked right into his eyes, allowing the warmth to spread through her. "I would be the greater liar if I said I didn't either."

Katherine could have felt the intensity of Charles's look even without seeing it glowing in his eyes. She leaned forward with a small smile and whispered in Ebony's ear just loud enough for Charles to hear. "You wouldn't tell on us, would you?" Ebony whickered, making her bridle jingle as she shook her mane. "I didn't think so." And in a single step, Katherine wrapped her arms around Charles and pressed her tingling lips against his. She felt his yearning mirror her own as they breathed together, their lips locking as their arms held each other close.

Katherine pulled back to look at her betrothed with a sheepish grin. "I'm sorry . . . I should have let you kiss me first. I hear men care about traditions like that."

Charles pulled her back in close. "I don't care . . . so long as I get to kiss you second." He kissed her gently on the cheek. "And third," He kissed her on the other cheek, "and fourth . . . " He bent lower to kiss her lips again and suddenly Katherine became *incredibly* aware of the sounds of the stable *and that there were still people there!* And she took a quick step back. She shook her finger even as she struggled to catch her breath.

"That's enough of that. They'll be wondering where we've gotten to."

Charles lightly grasped her hand and pulled her close one last time. "We can leave in just one more moment . . . " He looked over his shoulder and leaned in close so she could feel the warmth of his presence, giving her shivers up and down her back. "I just wanted to say that I look forward to seeing . . . your hair braided again." Then as Katherine's will dissolved into nothing but longing, Charles took a step back and bowed with a playful grin.

"Enough for play, now to 'business.'" Charles turned quickly, stepping out of the stall.

The cool air of an open window played with the heat on Katherine's neck. She blew the stray hairs off of her face. She turned to Ebony who was flicking her ears, recognizing energy in the air. "Why do I want to both strangle him and follow after him?" Ebony shook her head. "You don't know? Well . . . I suppose that this is what it feels like to be a wife." She patted Ebony one last time, then straightened her gown and smoothed those flyaway hairs. Then she proceeded out of the stall with the same poise she had once carried with little else but a borrowed cloak.

Charles stood by the desk, turning through the stable master's ledger. Then the stable master himself rounded the corner.

"What do you think you're doing?! Put that down! You think just because you're some fancy lord now you can walk into another lord's stables and review his books?"

Charles slapped the ledger down on the desk with such a noise that the horses nearby whinnied and reared in fright. "The *lord's* books, are they?"

"Y-yes, the lord's books. You had best be giving them back or else—"

"Or else, what? I learned recently, from a reputable source, that you've been charging two pounds a week to each of the lord's *friends* to stable his horses here. And heaven knows what other fees?"

That is what Thom had been sharing on the ride!

The stable master stood straighter in his indignation. "How dare— Why I *never*—what are you accusing me of?"

Charles leaned in, unafraid. "You heard me plainly. You have been defrauding your lord's acquaintances *and* your lord, absconding monies that rightfully belong to him."

The stable master paled but did not back away. *Two pounds a week! Per horse! That would be a small fortune!* Katherine looked at stall after stall of thoroughbred horses shaking their expensive, and lucrative, heads.

"You have no proof! And who will believe a glorified groom playing at nobility?" The man spat, nearly hitting Charles's shoe.

Charles held up the ledger. "I'm holding it right here. If that is not so, then Mr. Banks will clear your name when I show him." The stable master lunged for the book, but Charles retreated in practiced fencing form. "I know how to avoid a mule, sir." He dodged a punch then stepped over to Katherine.

The stable master grabbed a shovel from off the wall and turned to follow them with a threatening posture. "I'll be wanting my book now."

Charles smiled and lifted his cloak off of his side to reveal a familiar dark steel pistol in his belt. "I felt I might need to borrow this earlier . . . I wouldn't threaten me or my betrothed if I were you."

Fury melted to fear in the stable master's eyes as the shovel fell from his hands. "What are you going to do to me?"

"I will be giving the news of your villainy to my lord promptly—I think the new heir will be pleased with how his rents have appreciated in value." Charles led Katherine carefully toward the door and continued, "If you value your freedom, I suggest that you leave all the gold you owe to the estate on your desk and flee." The two of them paused at the edge of night as Charles looked back to say, "I would hurry if I were you. I am a fast walker."

The stable master tripped over his desk as he scrambled back into the shadows of the ancient stable.

Then Katherine and Charles huddled close as they walked quickly back to the cottage.

Chapter 21

June 18th, Our Wedding Day

I have no words . . . only joy.

—Katherine, Applehill Cottage—a waking dream

❦

The morning dawned on a flurry of activity. The whirlwind preparations left no corner of the house untouched as maids and ladies in waiting scrambled to prepare not one but *two* brides. Mr. and Mrs. Denton arrived early, but Lord Blakesly who had been up since before dawn finalizing paperwork with Mr. Banks and Mr. Stewart, received them graciously.

"Such a beautiful house," Mrs. Denton said. "I am *so* glad that it stays in the family.

"Yes, now that we have learned of the stables' rents, I think we will be in for quite a long time with this old place." Lord Blakesly smiled as his wife turned the corner.

"Thank you, Mary! I hope you will visit as often as you are able." Lady Blakesly was up at least as early as her husband answering final questions from the cook and various villagers brought in to help on this special day. Lady Blakesly embraced her sister and the two of them moved to the dining hall discussing the remaining tasks in rapid-fire familiarity. Mr. Denton smiled and drifted off to review the preparations.

Then a footman ran up. "My lord . . . a carriage just pulled up."

Lord Blakesly frowned. "Yes, I am sure quite a few will pull up, it is a *wedding* today."

The servant bowed but still looked nervous. "The valet said that it is Lord Harlow arriving . . . "

Lord Blakesly blanched. "Let me get Mr. Francis."

Charles stood watching his great uncle descend the carriage step with only a little help from his footman. The old man glared at him.

"Is *this* the welcome I should expect from my only living family?"

Charles's face was impassive though his stomach was roiling. If he had known that his young bride was biting her nails hiding behind the curtains of an upstairs window, he would have taken strength from her, but as it is, he spoke out under his own will. "What are you doing here, Uncle? I will not be swayed from my decision."

The old man scowled. "Yes . . . yes, I see that. You must truly love her to throw everything I have to offer away so easily." He walked a few steps before waving for a cane. "I suppose that means that *I* must sway from mine."

Charles's brows rose, the only sign of the sudden hope within his breast. "Uncle, what do you mean?"

Harlow scowled again. "Will you make me say it twice? You're reinstated . . . despite your choice in partners."

Charles swallowed the harsh words he had been preparing to send the old man away and rushed to give him an arm. "I am humbled by your gracious approval . . . but may I ask why you've decided to bestow this unimagined blessing?"

Lord Harlow watched the scurrying ants of his servants directing the carriage away and a sad smile formed on his wizened face. He blinked a tear that rolled down the deep lines and crevices of his weathered cheek. "My son loved his wife so . . . but she died giving him his son . . . and now that son and his son are gone too." Lord Harlow looked into Charles's eyes. "It is worth a little scandal to have family in the hall once again." He wiped the tears from his eyes with a familiar scowl. "But *don't* make me say it again!"

"Uncle, I am astounded . . . I never would have expected—"

The lord chuckled, his scowl breaking. "Well, if you only ever judge a person by their first impression, you will miss the chance for them to surprise you . . . "

"And isn't it delightful when they can?" Charles wiped his own tears, and he embraced his great uncle. "Thank you for further filling my heart with joy on this most joyful of days."

"Yes, yes, that's all well and good. Now let's get on with it. It's too cold for my old bones to dally on the steps of this little cottage."

Charles smiled. "Yes, my lord, I will send for you promptly," and he led him inside.

A servant directed them to an awaiting table in the music room—where food was being taken while the wedding took up the dining hall. There Lord and Lady Blakesly welcomed their new relation and the families shared a quiet but pleasant breakfast while the final arrangements of the few paltry flowers the villagers could gather from gardens and meadows alike continued to flow into the house.

The friendly silence was only broken by the twittering from Lady Blakesly—a sound unfamiliar even to her husband—upon hearing that Mr. Denton would be taking up the assistant parson position at Limeridge to replace the retiring parson in only a few months.

"So, your old master will need to find himself a new replacement?"

"I think that he might just live forever, and may Providence let it be so." Mr. Denton smiled, his cheeks rosy from his tempered joy.

◦◦◦

As the stream of flowers nearly dried up, the dining hall was set for the beautiful event. Upstairs Katherine and her sister held hands and laughed as their hair was plaited and pinned, giggled as their stays were cinched, and whispered as they descended the stairs together. All the sadness and pain of the past several months dissolved in the ecstasy of knowing they would be with the men they loved forever.

Lord Blakesly waited for them in his officer's uniform with tears in his eyes and a great smile upon his face. Mr. Banks and Mr. Stewart had reviewed the recovered gold and the offending ledgers, and they had learned that the rents were significant. The estate's affairs might not be as rich as diamonds, but they were not the lump of coal they had seemed to be before. With the loss of the stable master, who was being pursued by agents of the law, Mr. Banks had chosen a man who he certified was honest, to take the former's place. That man had named young Thom as his second and with this elevated station, Thom would have enough to ask for his sweetheart's hand . . . when he was a *little* older.

With his house in order, Lord Blakesly could stand proudly next to his new in-laws without the shame of his failing estate hanging over his head.

Lord Blakesly beamed his first unburdened smile in years as he watched his beautiful daughters descend the stairs together. "My two *eldest* daughters . . . you are simply stunning." He lifted both arms with Katherine on the unfamiliar left side as the "younger" sister and Elizabeth holding her head just a little higher as she glided down the hall on the right.

She truly does look the elder . . . Katherine smiled as the three of them entered the small but warm room full of the people they cared for most in the world. At the head of the room a small pulpit stood with Mr. Denton smiling at his nieces down the aisle, the village parson at his side winking at Mr. Charles. Beside them waited James and Charles. They both smiled and Katherine saw with relief that whatever spell had turned James's face into William's was now replaced with that of a happy brother. *Besides the hair, they really don't look that alike.* At least, she would continue to tell herself this. Charles on the other hand looked like the man she wanted to spend the rest of her life with.

Today and always.

Lord Blakesly bowed and handed each daughter to her soon-to-be husband and turned to sit with his wife. Katherine took a moment to look at the familiar faces of house staff, village associates, cousins, and friends. A red-eyed Lord Alcott sat in the back with an especially cheerful Sir Braxton. Galloway and Rodney seemed to have passed on the opportunity to witness Elizabeth's wedding. Lord Harlow sat beside Lord Blakesly in the front row and another stern-looking man sat beside him, likely Mr. Sterling, Sr.

Charles lifted his hand to lightly touch Katherine's chin, sending waves of delight down her neck and into her shoulders. "Are you ready, my love?" he asked.

Katherine smiled like the summer sun they had still yet to see. "Oh yes, please!" And the dearly beloved couples held hands, ready to make vows through life and forever.

Epilogue

I must admit that all the talk about the sun winking out had me troubled be-times, but now that the solstice is past and the sun is still in the sky, we are left to live our happy lives together.

Elizabeth and James are unbelievably precious. Her animation has rubbed off on him—a little—and his kindness is never more evident than when they speak together. It is nearly impossible for me to imagine what life would have been like any other way. Even their prospects are blooming as horses do not care about how wrinkled an apple is, and they are now up to two nearly full stables!

Some days I still awake with shadows of the darkness that beset me, but every pain, sorrow, and fear is consumed in my love for Charles and in his love for me. When he holds me in his arms, I can barely remember my name, let alone something as inconsequential as heartbreak or even the end of the world—though I am jubilant that the world is still here.

I am Mrs. Francis! My husband at this very moment is lying in bed with his sweet eyes tenderly closed. I must rejoin him in a moment, but the need to record these overwhelming feelings of love compelled me to relinquish our warm sheets and stand shivering by the vanity to scrawl quickly and simply:

I did love again.

And it is absolutely wonderful.

—Katherine Francis, Limeridge Hall

P. S. Although Lord Harlow is continually complaining that he won't live to meet his grand-heir . . . I think he might be in for a pleasant surprise!

Acknowledgments

This has been an amazing experience. Thank you to everyone involved in the production, promotion, and printing. I look forward to the next project.

Cheers,
Jack Chatelain

I want to thank everyone who helped this "dark horse" come to light. I would be truly ungrateful if I didn't name some of you, so here we go:

Thank you to my parents and siblings who read to me when I was young, edited my papers through high school, and continue to cheer me on and support me even now. This is evidenced by my mother, Bonita Jackson, beta-reading this work and helping fix anachronisms.

Thank you to my wife and children for lending me to this work. Writing is incredibly time-intensive and family often bears the opportunity cost. I love you forever.

Thank you to the heroic beta-readers who helped turn a first draft into an emotionally fulfilling adventure; namely Bonita Jackson, Robbie Lepp, Bryan Samuelsen, Aubrey Jackson, Jillian Fritz Christensen, and the members of the *Pensive Scribblers* writing group: Gina Bacalski, Sandra St. James, Gurcharan Sakizzie, and Meaghan Shamo.

Thank you to our illustrious editing and production team: Angela Johnson who signed us, Rachel Hathcock who performed the substantive edit, Valene Wood who performed the final edit, Heather Holm who finalized and polished the text for publication, Courtney Proby's beautiful cover design, and all the amazing professionals at Cedar Fort Publishing for bringing this adventure to you.

Last but not least, thank YOU, dear reader. All of this was for you (especially if you are the type to stick around and read the acknowledgements!).

Sincerely,
    Scott T. E. Jackson